PRAISE FOR
THE FURROWS

"The furrows of grief, in Namwali Serpell's telling, are a sur-real and hypnotic fantasy. This book reads like a ghost story, a murder mystery, a thriller, a redemptive love story that never loses its knife edge of danger. . . . A daring and master-ful novel about how we respond to the mystery of death."

—KIRAN DESAI, author of
The Inheritance of Loss

"Namwali Serpell's deep unity of imagery and voice is at the employ of a wild talent for narrative pivot and surprise; what seems at first a meditation on family trauma unfolds through the urgency of an amnesiac puzzle-thriller, then a violently compelling love story. The final pages take flight with vision-ary intensity. *The Furrows* is a genuine tour de force."

—JONATHAN LETHEM,
author of *Motherless Brooklyn*

"In Namwali Serpell's hands, grief is a kind of possession. *The Furrows* is a piercing, sharply written novel about the conjur-ing power of loss."

—RAVEN LEILANI, author of *Luster*

"Grief is dogged company. It shapeshifts and proliferates, hi-jacking thoughts and ravaging sleep. But Namwali Serpell's riveting prose urges me to believe that sometimes the true work of grief is to rupture us so thoroughly, we become capable of telling—and living—another story."

—TRACY K. SMITH, author of *Life on Mars*

"*The Furrows* is a triumph, a book that succeeds brilliantly in reconfiguring and retuning itself in pursuit of its essential subject. In this novel of grief, time flows, stretches, collapses, bends, stutters, and echoes, responsive, as it must be, to loss. Namwali Serpell narrates with an acute awareness of what resists and eludes conventional narration, producing a story that is wonderfully unpredictable, arresting, haunting."

—JAMEL BRINKLEY, author of *A Lucky Man*

"What makes *The Furrows* so thrilling is its ability to constantly surprise and keep us on the edge of our seats. But its real brilliance rests in Namwali Serpell's audacious refusal to allow the complicated layers of guilt and grief to remain unexplored. In this spectacular and genre-bending book, she has permanently shifted the ground beneath us, and where we stand by the end is in a new place where mourning and longing and sensuality not only exist at once, but transform into something revelatory, and perhaps even healing."

—MAAZA MENGISTE, author of *The Shadow King*

"Namwali Serpell's gift soars. . . . She takes pain and loss and cooks up a storm. Currents of grief, guilt, and greed are unpicked with ruthless precision. *The Furrows* establishes her as a literary powerhouse."

—JENNIFER NANSUBUGA MAKUMBI, author of *Kintu*

"A stunning and highly original novel exploring the shadow-life of grief. In Serpell's hands, longing becomes a story of uncanny repetition, and the logic of dreams feels intensely, compellingly real."

—ISABELLA HAMMAD, author of *The Parisian*

"Who could have imagined that a novel about loss and long grieving could be so soaring, so sexy, so luminously beautiful and poetic, such a rich and shimmeringly scored piece for three voices?"

—NEEL MUKHERJEE, author of *The Lives of Others*

"A deeply felt novel that deserves to be read. So eloquent and assured that I easily fell into this sweeping, gut-wrenching tale of loss, grief, and identity."

—NICOLE DENNIS-BENN, award-winning author of *Patsy* and *Here Comes the Sun*

"Beautifully written . . . It blew me away."

—ZOË WICOMB, author of *You Can't Get Lost in Cape Town*

"One of the world's most exciting contemporary novelists . . . I'm eagerly anticipating this new work from her."

—*Literary Hub*

"Lyrical, daring, assured . . . [an] intricate, genre-bending novel . . . Serpell disrupts our expectations, over and over [and] blurs the line between our dreams and our waking lives."

—*Oprah Daily*

ALSO BY NAMWALI SERPELL

Stranger Faces (2020)
The Old Drift (2019)
Seven Modes of Uncertainty (2014)

THE
FURROWS
AN ELEGY

THE
FURROWS

AN ELEGY

A Novel

≈≈≈

Namwali Serpell

HOGARTH
London / New York

Published in the United States by Hogarth, an imprint of the Random House Publishing Group, a division of Penguin Random House LLC, New York.

HOGARTH is a trademark of the Random House Group Limited, and the H colophon is a trademark of Penguin Random House LLC.

Portions of this work were originally published as "Take It" in *Freeman's: The California Issue* (Fall 2019); and "Will Williams" in *Disorder: Amazon Original Stories* (June 2019).

LIBRARY OF CONGRESS CATALOGING-IN-PUBLICATION DATA
Names: Serpell, Namwali, 1980– author.
Title: The furrows: an elegy / Namwali Serpell.
Description: First Edition. | London; New York: Hogarth, [2022]
Identifiers: LCCN 2021059855 (print) | LCCN 2021059856 (ebook) |
ISBN 9780593448915 (hardcover) | ISBN 9780593448922 (ebook)
Subjects: GSAFD: Mystery fiction.
Classification: LCC PR9405.9.S37 F87 2022 (print) |
LCC PR9405.9.S37 (ebook) | DDC 813.6—dc23
LC record available at https://lccn.loc.gov/2021059855
LC ebook record available at https://lccn.loc.gov/2021059856

Printed in the United States of America on acid-free paper

randomhousebooks.com

2 4 6 8 9 7 5 3 1

First Edition

Book design by Victoria Wong

For Chisha

. . . people do not die for us immediately, but remain bathed in a sort of aura of life which bears no relation to true immortality but through which they continue to occupy our thoughts in the same way as when they were alive. It is as though they were travelling abroad.

—Marcel Proust, *In Search of Lost Time: The Fugitive* (1925), trans. C. K. Scott Moncrieff and Terence Kilmartin

I

≈≈≈

1

≈≈≈

I don't want to tell you what happened. I want to tell you how it felt. When I was twelve, my little brother drowned. He was seven. I was with him. I swam him to shore. His arms were wrapped around my neck from behind, his chest on my back, his knees pummeling my thighs. At first, his small heavy head was on my shoulder, and he breathed in my ear, the occasional snort when water came in. His head bounced. My shoulder ached. His hands were knotted at my collarbone and I held them there with my hand, both so that he wouldn't let go and so that he wouldn't choke me. With my other hand, I pushed the water away.

We had gone to the beach for the day, just the two of us, alone together. This was allowed. This was our whole summer. Our family lived in Baltimore, or in the suburbs really, a place called Pikesville. When June came and set us free from school, and set my father free from his job teaching chemical engineering at Catonsville Community College—my mother was a painter, so she was always free—we would drive three hours down to Delaware, to a town near Bethany Beach, where every year we rented the same narrow gray house with a skew porch out front.

Every morning, after breakfast and cartoons, my brother and I would leave our father to edit his articles and our mother to dab at her paintings. Wayne and I would change into our still-damp swimsuits and I would pack us Capri Suns and Lunchables from the fridge. We would walk along the roads, cutting through a gap between the fancier houses to reach the beach. My mother had told us that the gap was called No Man's Land, which Wayne misheard and took to mean it belonged to a man named Norman. We'd sneak quietly through Norman's Land, then tromp over the boardwalk, our flipflops knocking against it, and find our favorite spot on the shore, which was marked by clumps of sea grass.

Wayne was a nutty brown, a scrawny creature, a good kid. He played so hard, as if play were work. I was too old to play, so I watched him play, and helped sometimes. That day, I buried him for fun's sake. We dug a shallow trench with cupped hands, like dogs, like gardeners. The topsand was cane sugar, the undersand brown sugar. When the trench was big enough, he tumbled into it and I packed the sand onto his body, patpatting it over his hands and over his bony knees. Under the fluorescent sun, he lay still as a magician's assistant.

He asked me to cover his head with our straw hat and I said, "No, you'll suffocate!" He flinched, as if to grab for it himself, then remembered that his hand was buried. Too late: the mound of sand over it had sprouted a crack. He glanced at it, at me. I patpatted the sand back flat. After a moment he said it again, he mouthed, Cover. My. Head. I touched my sandy finger to his sandy cheek. "Close your eyes, Wayne," I said, and placed the straw hat over his squinching face.

I had stolen that hat from a fruit vendor before Wayne was born, when he was still in the womb. Our mother, pregnant and craving, was buying a pear at a stand at a farmers' market. The hat was rolling at the fruit vendor's feet like tumbleweed. It beckoned me and so I picked it up and put it behind my back, switching it quickly to my front when we turned to leave. My mother didn't notice until a block later. She twisted my earlobe till it stung and hissed, "It's too late to give it back now, you little twit!"

Although our family had owned the straw hat for many years now, it was still too big for either of us kids to wear. We used it for carrying things instead, its leather chinstrap serving as a handle. We had used it today to bring lunch and a towel. Now it swallowed his head completely.

"You're a dead Mexican," I giggled.

"Olé!" he muffled from under the hat.

"I mean cowboy," I said.

"Ahoy!"

"That's a sailor."

There was a pause. "Yeehaw!" he said.

I didn't answer. I didn't laugh. I walked away from his buried body, staggered off into the sand pockets toward the greenish sea, bored but deeply satisfied that he would be surprised to find me gone when he lifted that dumb hat off his face. My turn to trick him for once.

My toes were already wet by the time he realized I was gone. He leapt up and tossed the hat and gangled his way toward me. Yelling pellmell, splummeshing past me into the water. I watched his bronze back vanish, then retreated and sat beside the empty trench with my arms around my knees. There was no one else around. It was bright and hot, the end of summer. Then the clouds came and lowered. The wind rose. The waves rose.

Dear Wayne. You swam into the furrows. At first, you didn't know it because you were under the surface and you faced down as you swam, staring at the vault of the sea below. Then you felt the sky darken above you, a shadow passing, and when you came up to breathe, you were suddenly inside them, the great grooves in the water, the furrows. On either side of you, those whirring sheets of water, the foam along their edges sharpening like teeth. On either side of you, the furrows chewing, cleaving deeper. They ate you up. You were alone out there and the world took you back in, reclaimed you into its endless folding.

≈

He was joyful and swimming and then he wasn't. I ran in. I swam to him. I reached him and we grappled some until he managed to get on my back and wrap his arms around my neck. I held his knuckles in my hand. I turned and swam us to shore. He dragged me back. Halfway to the beach, his small heavy head began to beat against my shoulder in an unreasonable way. That was the word I thought: *unreasonable.* A word our father would say. I knew to hold my breath and dive through the waves like our mother had taught us. But what about Wayne? Did he remember to dive, to hold his breath? There was no breath in me to ask or remind him.

The wind whipped. I clutched his knuckles like a junk of bones in one hand, pushed the water away with the other. We rocked, his knees bumping the back of me, his head knocking my shoulder in that unreasonable way. It made no sound, but they found bruises later. I felt him soften and something inside him came into me then—*ssth, ssth, ssth*—came into me in little waves. More and more ripples until it was done and my insides felt full up—his body swept clean of him, mine filled to bursting. I swam like this, doubled, an emptied sack on my back, my fingers raw with clutching.

I woke up on the beach alone, on my back, sputtering, my throat raw. I turned my head and puked, mostly lacy water. Puking didn't hurt; it was a comfort. Water sucked at my feet, intermittent, insistent. I was confused about exactly how naked I was; my swimsuit was tangled in the crevices of my body. There was seaweed stringing my arms, and the grit of sand and salt disturbed my sense of my skin, its limits, where it began and ended. Exhaustion crowded me, from the top of my head all the way down my back. Pain, the throbbing in my head and my shoulder, made me rise onto my elbows and look around. Everything was blurry until I cleared the coves of my eyes.

I couldn't figure out where I was. There were black stones studding the shore, a trail of them leading to a bristling cluster of grass. Just past that, maybe twenty yards away, I caught a glimpse of a dark form flung on the sand. It was bent, obscenely bent. The sea tugged at it. I stared at it. Was it my brother? His arm? His leg? All of him? It could've been a tree limb. Panic beat inside, for me, for him, for me, for how far apart we were. I watched the bent thing being dragged into the water. I watched it disappear into the sea's frothing mouths; I saw it bobble up once and then go. I didn't move, or couldn't.

I woke up on the beach alone and figured out that I had blacked out again. I was shaking fiercely. I turned to look out at where I had seen my brother but there was nothing but smooth sand now, and those stones dot-dot-dotting over it. I tried to get up but I couldn't. I curled slowly onto my side, grit grinding grit all over me. Rain came and went, waves came and went, shouting hoarsely at one another.

I don't know how much time passed but when I opened my eyes, there was a head blocking the gray sky above me: a bizarre alien head, too big. I recognized the shape of our straw hat. Was this man wearing it? For some reason, I thought that if he had found our hat, then my brother, whose body I'd seen rolling in the surf, must truly be dead.

"Where's Wayne?" I asked the man.

The man turned and pointed to where I'd seen that bent form. Then he shook his alien head and yelled into the wind, which ate the words right out of his mouth. He leaned closer. He was white, in his forties or fifties, wearing a skyblue canvas windbreaker. I remember seeing his lips form the word "home" and how he mimed gestures of politeness—"Can I touch you?" expressed with a pat, a questioning look—before he lifted me up. I remember the steady leverage under my shoulders and knees, then a heavy tottering momentum over the sand, the rain pattering my face, the wind galling my ears.

The man put me in the backseat of a car. My eyes opened briefly when he asked where I lived and I saw the light embedded in the roof, a square. The storm was loud, then quiet—he had shut the door. He drove to the address I'd given. I knew we'd arrived because of the cold and the noise that came in when the car door opened.

Time stuttered again and my father came in through the front door, snapping an umbrella shut with a burst of rain spray. He saw me sitting alone at the bottom of the stairs, wet and sandy, trembling in my swimsuit, my shoulders draped with a stranger's windbreaker.

"Hey, baby. Rough out there. You get caught in it?" He smiled and frowned at the same time. "Where's Wayne?"

≈

Later, he said I told him what had happened. It must have been incoherent, inconsistent, perhaps self-contradictory. I have since pieced together, for example, that in the early days, I didn't always mention the bent thing I saw being pulled into the water, and what I said about the windbreaker man varied enough with each telling to rouse suspicion. I don't even remember that first telling.

The next thing I remember after the stairs is being in the bathtub, hot water around me, the air above me feverish with steam. Goosebumps came and went. There were muffled shouts or loud whispers beyond the bathroom door, which shook whenever another body entered the house downstairs. The blow-dryer lay on the floor next to the tub, its shape like a head with the longest pout imaginable, its mouth kissing toward the blue windbreaker and my swimsuit, which was still wet and gritty and looked like something strangled. There was sand everywhere, eddies and sprays of it patterning the grayish tiles.

They left me in that bathroom for hours, it felt like, though I'm pretty sure now that it was actually less than half an hour. I watched the steam percolate the air, watched and watched and didn't notice the exact moment it disappeared. The water drowsed over me.

Then there was a boy made of sand standing beside me. I was a dreamy kid, I still have vivid dreams, but I had never seen such a thing. I vaguely suspected that I'd slipped into some kind of hallucination from the exhaustion. The boy was empty. I mean that the sand he was made of was so grainy, so patchy, I could see right through it. He didn't speak. He grinned and his cheeks crumbled. I wanted to fling my hand at his head. I wanted to make that grin bigger, emptier. I wanted to grab the blow-dryer and smash it into him and turn him into clumps on the floor. I wanted it to be over and done.

I felt something knocking around in me, like I was a sack now, too, or the sand beneath which I'd buried Wayne on the beach. This was a new feeling, this inner stretch in every direction, the beginning of a yawn that never ended. I inhaled deeply, held my breath, slid down under the water, and lay still. The sloshing bathwater popped roundly into one ear, then the other. Quiet down here. Hollow. The boy made of sand crumbled up into the air and hovered like a shadow over the water. Sand fell off him, plopped into the water, and sank toward me, threatening to muddy me.

I shut my eyes and began to count. I pictured the alarm clock in my bedroom, its screen a black rectangle across which spindly green limbs formed segmented numbers. 2 switched its leg from left to right to become 3, a dance at the knees. 5 grew another leg to make 6. Then 8 lost a leg to make 9. I could hear my heart thudding to the count. 13. 14. 28. 31. The numbers sped up, flashing behind my eyes. 53-62-86-91—I startled up out of the water and gasped. I blinked around, heaving. The boy was gone. Someone was banging on the door. That was the thudding sound, not my heart.

2

≈≈≈

"You okay, Cee?"

It was my father. Through the bathroom door, I could hear the pit of worry in his voice. He would not come in. For several months now, he had not come uninvited into any bathroom or bedroom when I was in there. He must have been knocking for some time. I launched myself out of the tub, skidded on the floor, legs shaky. A headrush fell over me like a hood made of black static.

"Coming," I said, gripping the sink.

"Okay," he said, quieter. "I need you to talk to some people, tell them what happened." My father's footsteps receded.

I wrapped a thin towel around my body, and then combed my wet hair, clutching it at the root and starting at the ends, wincing as the knots caught. I pulled it back into a ponytail that would expand into a curly poof as it dried. The mirror was still steamed up and I remember noticing a handprint there, edging and texturing the steam. It was smaller than mine, clearly Wayne's. I wiped my hand straight through it to see myself. My face was different in the smeared reflection but I didn't linger to see how.

My eyes stung, my lungs felt loose, my limbs sore but

somehow light. The feeling in my arms reminded me of a trick Wayne had taught me, part of a series that included pressing your closed eyelids then letting go to make an explosion of stars appear, and karate-chopping your bicep in just the right spot to make a bump in the muscle surface. For the floating-arms trick, Wayne would make me stand in an open doorway, firmly pressing the backs of my hands against the jambs on either side for a full minute. He would stand before me, solemnly counting backward, with Mississippis between the seconds to slow them down. When he reached zero, he'd step backward and I'd step forward. Our eyes would meet and our smiles would dawn, and as if wings had sprouted at my wrists, my arms would rise on their own. That was how they felt now.

I pulled on shorts and a T-shirt, both dirty, plucked from the laundry basket. This, I felt, would surely be allowed. No doubt. Special circumstances. The corners of my mouth began to twitch unbearably. No matter what, I thought, I had been *brave*. And just thinking the word *brave* made my chest expand. The feeling grew inside me like a giant soap bubble, colors sliding on its surface as it spun. *Brave*. I think I imagined—laughable now—that there would be comfort and admiration and a kind of awe awaiting me.

My father was standing awkwardly at the bottom of the stairs. My damp feet made brief silhouettes on the wood as I descended. The sound of crying in the kitchen grew louder. My mother. Had my father been crying, too? I didn't ask, but when I reached him I took the opportunity—special circumstances—to hug him, to fell my full weight against him the way one fells a tree. I crushed my nose into his sternum, smelling first the tang of fried food in his sweater, then the environmental detergent my mother used, and finally my father's specific smell: Dial soap, coconut oil, aftershave. I looked up at him from within the grip of his arms and saw where his two-day bristle had crept into the old scar under his chin. He seemed taken aback by the hug but he recovered and carefully separated our bodies.

He left his hand on my back as he guided me into the living room. For a moment, I imagined there would be flashing things inside: badges, guns, cameras. Sitting there instead, in an armchair by the sofa, dressed in a suit like this was a party or a wedding, was Grandma Lu. Her hair was hotcomb smooth, barely ruffled by the summer storm still tantrumming outside the windows. She always wore her hair pressed, the back curving into a high bun, the bangs curving over her forehead like a doll's. As always, she cast a judgmental eye over my messy hair. She might have been judging my mother's inability to tame it, but I felt the blame because I was old enough to do it myself and besides, Grandma Lu did not like me.

It seemed to me that Grandma Lu was largely reconciled to my mother. Long before we grandchildren were born, Grandma Lu had made peace with the artsy white woman who had married her shy, brittle son. Over the years, they had learned that they could talk to each other if they stuck to simple things, like pie crusts and popular movies. They shared recipes for desserts that Grandma Lu was far better at making; they shared a fondness for movies with happy endings and a lot of heart. I sometimes overheard them giggling about the indiscretions and charms of certain movie stars. That was what Grandma Lu talked to my mother about. Grandma Lu talked to my father about nothing; it didn't matter what they talked about; he was her son.

Grandma Lu talked instead to her grandson. Wayne apparently looked exactly like our father had as a child, just lighter. "More sand than mud," Grandma Lu would smirk. Lighter in the other sense, too: Wayne always seemed less burdened by the world. I remember that when Wayne was maybe four or five, Grandma Lu had shown him a picture of our father at the same age. You could tell it was an old picture because the whites were yellow, the blacks were brown, and the boy was barefoot. Wayne had asked boldly, "Where am *I*?" and "Why wasn't *I* there?" and "Where are his friends?" A real charmer. Grandma Lu had especially loved how, when Wayne had heard her answers, he'd handed that old picture of our father back to her and said, "Grandma Lu? *I* would have played with him." Grandma Lu *loved* Wayne.

But Grandma Lu did not even like me. And I, now wedged sideways into the corner of the couch, one leg hitched, one leg stretched out, felt accused. My father had left me with her in the living room, with a promise to return shortly. She and I sat for a few minutes, in a silence that was both a relief and an agony. I looked at her once, a flinching glance, and caught a glimpse of her mole, a black raisin under her jawbone. Normally it nested somewhere in the folds spreading down her neck, but it liked to travel. I knew this was an illusion, like one of my brother's magic tricks; I knew I hadn't pinpointed the mole's exact location because Grandma Lu's skin was hard to read in the shadowed room. Yet I sometimes imagined that the mole had a personality, an independent life, a will to crawl away from the light.

I didn't understand why she wasn't asking me about what had happened. And how had she gotten here already? It was always like this. Maybe it's because my parents never bothered to keep me abreast of family plans, but it seemed to me that Grandma Lu always just showed up, was always suddenly there. As a child, I often wanted her to *do* something, something grandmotherly like knitting or reading, or even ungrand-motherly like slowly, stolidly biting her fingernails. But she just liked to sit there, be there. Whenever anyone nudged her to action of any kind—"Would you like to come to dinner, Lu?" or "Would you like the paper, Lu?"—she'd sigh, "I'm fine," which implied that the person offering had in fact bothered her while also neglecting to ask her how she was doing. This retort invariably flustered people.

I hated it. I hated Grandma Lu. I was more twelve years old when I was with her than when I was with anyone else. I got salty. I didn't know how to impress her. The precocity I'd honed for other adults disappeared into a swell of indignation. And today, in this desperate waiting time, my hatred had a new edge to it, like the fringe of fire on a burning sheet of paper. It was early evening. The living room was growing dim but neither of us was going to move to turn on a lamp. Both my feet were still up on the couch. Grandma Lu thought this was rude—"primitive" she'd called it once. I pedaled one foot furiously.

A car crunched into the driveway, its headlights flashing in the window, then fanning over the dark room as it slowed. One beam of light windmilled away and the other shuddered to a stop, spotlighting one side of Grandma Lu's face.

"They coming for you," Grandma Lu said.

I didn't know what to make of this and shrugged miserably. Her face was the color of iron under that cool spotlight.

"Ungodly." She could have been speaking about the storm, the unexpected guests, me.

I heaved a sigh and crossed my ankles. The wind pursed its lips and whistled. Grandma Lu leaned forward and seethed at me.

"What you do with that boy, Cassandra?"

My mouth opened, but not to reply.

"I'm speaking to you, child. Where'd you put that boy?"

She leaned farther forward and reached for me. Then the spotlight on the wall went out and we heard the double *click-slam* of two people getting out of a car. Grandma Lu sucked her teeth, shook her head, and sank back into her armchair. Mrs. Genoise, our sometime summer neighbor, a childless divorcée in her forties, opened the door into the living room.

"Oh!" she exclaimed. "It's so dark in here."

She strode over to the side table and turned on the lamp with the shade like a tennis skirt. The light woke up the room so you could see the orange vase choking on dry sea grass, the record player vanquished by dust, the flowerpattern crawling over the Country Style furniture, and my mother's canvases sitting on the floor, propped against the walls. Every summer, this living room became a temporary gallery of her unframed and often unfinished paintings, all of black women—dignified pietàs and breastfeeding Marys with blunt dun skin, their noses always too aquiline, their lips too pillowy.

"Why, hello there, Ms. Louise and Miss Cassandra." Mrs. Genoise looked back and forth between me and Grandma Lu, as if getting ready to lecture us for sitting in the dark at a time like this. Instead, she rubbed her hands together with a papery sound and asked, "Should we see about fixin' up some dinner?"

Grandma Lu said, "Hmb." She turned her head, linking her hands in her lap.

I scooched off the couch and went to stand dutifully next to Mrs. Genoise, who flashed her teeth at me and rubbed my shoulder. She turned to speak to Grandma Lu, then thought better and tucked her lips into her mouth, nodded goodbye, and steered me out of the living room, into the musty, window-less hallway.

≈

Our summer rental was an old house: floors more creak than wood, no right angles to be found, and separate rooms for every purpose. This hallway ran next to the staircase that led to the upper floor, and it connected the living room, the dining room (which we never used), and the kitchen, the door of which was closed. Behind it were the sounds of an event. Standing like intruders in the hall, Mrs. Genoise and I heard the door from the backyard into the kitchen open and shut, the *flip-flep* of the screen door. People were coming in: more voices, murmurous, individual words like jetsam in the general noise. I heard the word "dead" or "dredge," and my insides inflated and ballooned up my body again.

"I want my mother," I said. I did not, in fact, want my mother; I wanted to know what the people in the kitchen were saying. The house was beginning to feel appropriately heavy, like something had happened. I moved toward the kitchen door but Mrs. Genoise—I had underestimated her—restrained me.

"No, Cee," she said quietly. "If you don't want to sit with your grandma, then we can wait right here. Or we can go on upstairs. But they're not ready for you in there yet."

"I feel dizzy," I said, frowning. "I want to sit down."

Shadows flitted in the gap under the kitchen door. Suddenly, Mrs. Genoise was leaning over me, her face very close to mine.

"Listen to me, Cee." Her voice hissed thinly like water from a leak in the garden hose. "If you know where your brother is . . . I need you to tell me. Where's Wayne?"

I shook my head, confused. "I already told Dad—" I stopped. There was a boy made of sand behind her in a dark corner of the hallway. The next thing I knew, I was convulsing and it was because Mrs. Genoise had me by the shoulders and was shaking me as she whisper-yelled, "Where is he? Where's Wayne? Where's Wayne?"

I felt a different hand on my back, a steady one. If I concentrate, I can still feel the impress of his palm there—its caution, its care, its fear. The shaking stopped. My father was glaring at Mrs. Genoise over my head. She lowered her eyes. When she made to speak, I interrupted: "Where's Mom?"

"Let's go in here." He guided me a few steps away from Mrs. Genoise, who just stood there, trying to swallow her lips again. He knuckled my chin to turn my face up to him.

"You have to tell them exactly what you told me, baby. Tell it straight, okay?"

I didn't understand why he would say that to me. But before I could ask, my father had ushered me into the dining room. A white policewoman sat at the long wooden table. I found myself suppressing an impulse to call Wayne to come and see. I was cowed by this woman, the authority she represented. My father seemed to feel the same way. He leaned against the wall, his crossed arms binding himself, his eyes down.

The policewoman introduced herself—I don't recall her name—then said, "You must be Cee. Why don't you sit here so we can talk? It's okay, we just need to ask you a few questions."

I dragged out the highbacked dining chair across from her and sat. The windows rattled in the storm. Out there, thunder bellowed, clouds churned, lightning clattered, and the sky theatrically wrung itself of rain. I wouldn't have described it in those words then but that's how I remember it—the original storm, the only storm of my life, the truest one. It would stall the helicopters for days.

The policewoman opened a pad. I turned my hands over on

my thighs. My fingertips were still wrinkled, from the bath of course, but for a moment I imagined it was from the sea. How strange that skin should grow crannied when it's too wet, while the ground gets that way when it's too dry, ruts carving into them as the sun bakes the water away.

"Okay, Cee." She looked up, her pen poised like a beak ready to scratch for worms. "Can you tell me what happened?"

So, I told her what happened. How Wayne and I played together, how we always did this, how every day we did this, it was allowed. How I buried him in the sand and how he ran ahead of me into the water and how I stayed on the shore and watched. How the wind picked up and the waves got big and how fast it all was. How I saw him disappear into the great grooves in the water and so I swam out until he could wrap his arms around me from behind and how I swam us to shore. I told her about waking up alone and the stranger who found me. I confirmed that the front door to our summer house was always unlocked. I confirmed that I hadn't seen the stranger before that day, and that I did not know where or when he'd gone, but that he was not there when my father had come home. I confirmed that the straw hat was still missing. When it was all done, the policewoman asked if I needed a Kleenex; no, I didn't need a Kleenex. She asked if I was cold; no, I wasn't cold.

Then the policewoman asked me this: "Cee, do you know where your brother is?"

I blinked. I had just told her what happened. Was this woman, in the navy-and-gold uniform that made her look like a poorly wrapped gift, asking me about *heaven*?

"I don't . . . Did you find him? On the beach?"

The policewoman looked past me, over my shoulder. I

glanced there, too, but my father said nothing. His arms were still crossed and his watch—the silver Seiko with a chain strap— sat right under his heart. His glasses were rainbow smudged. When I turned back, the policewoman was staring at her pad. I concentrated. Something was rearranging in my mind and all of a sudden, what I knew had happened to my brother came undone. My father had asked it, Grandma Lu had asked it, Mrs. Genoise had asked it. But only now that the woman in uniform had asked me a version of "Where's Wayne?" did I feel the implication of this question thrill through me: my brother was somewhere to be found.

I stood up. "Is he in the kitchen?" I asked.

The policewoman looked up, her lips parted. Why did I ask this? Maybe because whenever we came back from swimming at the beach, my brother and I would always run up the outside steps to the back door into the kitchen and straight to the fridge. We would sit and drink our Dr Peppers at the kitchen table, but our mother wouldn't let us go anywhere else in the house until we had gone back outside and blasted all the sand off our bodies with the garden hose. Wayne's hand was too small to hold the trigger on the nozzle, so I would do myself first, quickly, efficiently, lingering only on the nape of my neck because I'd get a rash there if I didn't. Then I would hose Wayne down. I was long past enjoying this process but he had recently begun to grasp its pleasures, shrieking as he dodged and directed different parts of his body toward the spray I aimed at him: his wobbling elbow, his STOP!!! hand, his hula-ing butt, his contracted face bursting with gulping hiccups of laughter. Around us, light would fall. The sound of the crickets would swell to a ringing in our ears. The puddles we'd made would bronze, grassblade tips stubbling their surface. The outdoor security light would spitz and thunk to life. Under its greenish-white glow, we'd wipe our feet dry on the steps and slump our way inside, just escaping the bugs, just in time for dinner.

I wondered now if they'd washed him off—laid him in the grass, aimed, and squeezed the thick trigger. Would a spray that strong leave dents in him? Or would it only make him clean, awaken him, unbend the obscene thing I'd seen?

"Is he in the kitchen?" I asked and stood up.

I could almost see him, stretched out on the table there, his head where our father's plate should be. The policewoman looked annoyed, like she thought I was playing games. She smoothed her pad shut but said nothing as I hastened toward my father, pushed past him to open the dining room door, ran unimpeded across the narrow hallway, and flung open the kitchen door.

I scanned the room. A policeman, I remember he looked very young and pale, was standing at the back door as if guarding it. A frying pan sat empty on the counter. It smelled of warm copper, old French fries. The linoleum kitchen table was bare but for a crumpled Kleenex, so crisp in its folds it looked like origami. My mother was sitting at the table, her hands flat on its surface. The rest of her shook clumsily, her thin brown hair—was it already graying then?—hanging over her face, quivering. She was wearing one of my father's suitjackets, but no shoes or socks. The combination made her look homeless.

Mrs. Genoise was sitting next to her, stroking her back in a circle, which made me feel nauseated. Someone behind me— my father or the policewoman—must have communicated something to Mrs. Genoise, because she nodded and whispered into my mother's curtained ear. My mother raised her head and turned it toward me but she did not look at me. Her eyes, wet with tears, seemed to look right through me, at my father maybe. The fridge cleared its throat and hummed.

"Where's Wayne?" I choked out, like a catch had released.

My mother looked at me now, really looked at me, and with her face still runneled with tears, she opened her mouth and she laughed, once, like a shout.

3

≈≈≈

Here's the thing: It isn't just that what has been done can be undone. It's also that an undoing can reconstitute. Dead matter can gather itself together. The knitting of hair or bramble or sand breathes life into the inanimate. These bunches, these groupings, these tangles of nothing that turn into something—sandcastles, tumbleweed, dustbunnies—have always disgusted me. Why should lifeless particles join like this into discrete forms? What do they want from us? To my mind, they are needy creatures, grotesquely dependent.

I first realized this at Dr. Rothman's. Two years after my little brother died, but left us no body to confirm the fact and mourn, my mother told me I was going to the doctor's. I prepared myself for the rituals of the pediatrician's office: my knees tensed for the rubber hammer, that miracle of reflex; my nostrils anticipated an antiseptic tang, my tongue the compensatory lollipop. But as soon as we arrived—"a new doctor," my father muttered as he parked—and we got out of the car, it was clear to me that this was no clinic.

It was a small bungalow. Dead leaves lay in thick mats of neglect on the porch. A withered baby bouncer sat bright and terrible by the door. My father knocked, and a man opened it.

Humid air from inside the house puffed out and I caught the bitter scent of lavender. The doctor wore a cardigan—a pattern of triangles and mesas in orange and blue and white—and trousers that had given up at the ankles. At first, I thought he was wearing two pairs of glasses but then I saw that his lenses were just unusually thick.

"Hello there," the man said profoundly, as if I were news. "I'm Dr. Rothman."

"Hello," I mumbled, the dance of a cat's tail behind him distracting me. I turned to my father but he was already hurrying down the porch steps with a backhanded wave. He often passed me over to others like this nowadays. I still couldn't tell whether he was afraid of me or for me. I followed Dr. Rothman inside.

The glass of the ceiling light in the hall was foggy, a trapped sun making itself sweat. The paint on the walls was blistered. The hardwood floor was muddy and smeared, the planks of wood somehow dirtier than tree bark. And there was all of this dead matter, gathering as if in commiseration or desperation, dust competing with a thin mess of cat hair, everything wilting under the damp that ruled the place like a law. It was a house turned animal, regurgitating itself. It was the opposite of what I expected of a doctor's office. It was bad for my allergies and for my adolescent acne, both painfully persistent. After every session with Dr. Rothman, I would look in the mirror and find that another rash of pimples had sprung up, quick as mushrooms after the rain.

I disliked Dr. Rothman. I despised his sallow eyes behind those thick lenses and his fishlips with their soggy questions. He was the first of the "new doctors," the parade of serious men and women who would ask me an endless roll of questions because my brother died in my care. When I first learned about catechism at St. Anthony's, I would feel a faint sense of recognition. Dr. Rothman, my first questioner, my first reader, did not take notes as the others would. He was older—in his sixties—and often yawned if I spoke for too long. I grew accustomed to how he repressed his yawns, tensing and inflating his jowls, making a concertina of his neck.

His questions were always about the living Wayne, about the years before he died. For a long time, I thought the man was stupid—my little brother had barely lived before he'd died—until I realized that there might have been a method in making Wayne present, or a mercy. Because at home, the world was tilted now and Wayne's absence in our lives had become the drain toward which everything ran.

"Tell me again about the drawings," Dr. Rothman would ask. "What did he draw?"

"People."

"And did you teach him that? How to draw people?"

"Well, I tried to teach him how to draw the eyes. He never colored in the dark part."

"The dark part?"

"The circle in the middle, you know, the um."

"The inner circle or the outer circle?"

I shrugged. "The outer one?"

"That's called the iris. But are irises always supposed to be dark, Cee?"

This seemed like a trick question but Dr. Rothman's head was bobbling seriously.

"Well, I guess my mom's eyes are gray. And yours are . . ."

I leaned forward as if to see and I smiled, trying to charm him the way Wayne would have. Dr. Rothman didn't smile back. But he did take off his glasses to show me his eyes, those sea creatures living inside the double-paned tank of his lenses.

"Blue," I said.

He put his glasses back on. "I know you have brown eyes," he said. "And your father does, too. But do you think that maybe Wayne was drawing your mother's *gray* eyes?"

"No." I shook my head. "He wasn't drawing just my mom. It was, like, a group."

"A family?"

"Maybe."

"So maybe he made all the irises gray to look like your mother's eyes."

"Right, but no, I mean whatever. Wayne didn't draw them at all."

"Eyes?"

"Irises."

≈

Despite his concern for my mother's eyes, that they be fully represented in my consciousness so as to integrate my "mixed ethnic identity," as he put it, my mother thought Dr. Rothman was a bad man. She didn't like that he brought up race so much. "Why does it matter?" When I came home from one session bearing a yellow paperback with the sanserif title *You Are Perfect,* she shook her head and said, "That man is corrupt in his heart." Then again, if my mother was to be believed, there was a lot of corruption lurking in people's hearts, especially after Wayne died.

By this time, I no longer trusted anything she said. Because although years had passed, my mother maintained that Wayne hadn't died, that he was still missing. She thought we would find him if we just did the right things. She'd say that, literally: "We just have to do the right things." It was not easy to trust a woman who had spent the week of the initial search for Wayne's body lying face-up on the sofa, blasting Nina Simone. The weather had stayed stormy, which made the search nearly impossible, and sometimes, when she wasn't weeping to "Ne Me Quitte Pas," she would sit and stare at the window and say, "The sky is weeping, too." I felt I was seeing her truly for the first time—not only the way we all come to see our parents as fallible humans, but also the particularities of her whiteness, the way she seemed to seek expression of her feelings only through black art.

When we got back to Baltimore, everyone said it was important for my mother to keep busy. She took to wearing her silk Chinese bathrobe every day, and in the mornings she would sweep royally around the kitchen, umbilically attached to the telephone by its long curly cord, as she made the daily round of calls to keep the search going, her skin flushed pink, the fuzz on her cheeks visible with sweat. Sometimes she kept busy by cleaning, a hurricane of mopping and scrubbing, or by exercising in the den downstairs in front of the TV. Sometimes I joined her, doing tick-tocks or cartwheels on the thinly carpeted floor while she huffed through aerobics, her robe jerking and wafting and getting in the way. Sometimes I sat and watched daytime TV with her after and, every once in a while, went over to the couch and removed the floppy Ziploc from her swollen eyes, then went up to the kitchen to pour out the water and refill the bag with ice cubes. I'll never forget that blue smell of melted ice, the faint sparkle of pain in my Achilles tendons and my young-girl nipples, the curbed bedlam of sitcom laughter.

I told Dr. Rothman none of this at the time. It would take years for these memories to cohere, to take form and take on life, to become things that needed attention.

"So, your brother liked to draw a group of people. What kind of people? Tall? Short?"

"Tall. They leaned sideways. But I don't think that was on purpose."

"Oh?"

"Wayne just didn't know how to do lines straight because he was lefthanded. My grandma said that was bad luck but my dad got mad and said that she was stuck in the past."

Dr. Rothman didn't reply to that and he didn't yawn, not even in the disguised way. His silence was irritating, a tangle of stalks growing and poking me. I kept talking to squash them.

"Wayne always got in trouble for drawing on the walls. It didn't wash out. I told him he would get in trouble." I shrugged.

"I see," Dr. Rothman said. "And did he get in trouble? Did you tell your mother about the drawings on the walls?"

"Yeah, but it didn't matter. Wayne was sneaky. He just drew them behind the furniture instead."

I could tell that the condescension in my voice was distasteful to Dr. Rothman. I knew how utterly abominable I was as a teenager—that was half my excruciation. I sat back in my chair, disliking him, my throat choked with wanting him not to dislike me, with wanting him to believe me.

≈

The story they pulled from me a thousand, a million times went like this: "I felt him go and he was gone."

"No," my mother said. "Why wouldn't that man have tried to save Wayne, too? Why wouldn't he have brought him home to me?"

"Wayne was already dead by then," I said.

"No," my mother said. "Why didn't that man wait with you at the house until help came?"

"I told him to leave!" I said.

I didn't remember this, but I knew the man had gone

because I remembered sitting alone inside, my trembling thighs. I remembered my father coming in the front door, asking me questions, bustling me upstairs and into the bath. I remembered soaking in the tub. The crumbly boy.

"No," my mother said. She didn't believe me. "It doesn't make sense."

She had other hypotheses. Maybe I was lying about the windbreaker man or had imagined him. Maybe I was the one who had selfishly—or fearfully—left Wayne behind. Maybe the windbreaker man did exist and he had kidnapped Wayne. Maybe a seven-year-old boy was of more interest to a middle-aged man than a twelve-year-old girl. No matter what maybe, the one thing she clung to, my mother's one firm belief, was that Wayne was out there somewhere, waiting to be found. And without his corpse, no one could convince her otherwise.

So, in our family, there was a story, there was this lore, but it split in two where Wayne had left it. It split, then circled around the empty space where he should have been, and joined back together at the point when I walked into the house without him. The lore was a loop at the end of a rope, a lasso endlessly tossed, catching nothing.

Me, every time: "I felt him die. I know he's dead."

My mother, every time: "Where is he? What really happened that day?"

My father, one time, when he'd finally had enough: "Why does it matter? Either way, the boy's gone."

He didn't otherwise intervene in the impasse between me and my mother, which came to dictate our lives. I know now that she was beside herself with grief, that she had slipped into some other groove, some other reality. But I felt betrayed. I will be honest with you. I cried more for my mother's betrayal than I ever cried for my brother's death. It wasn't clear if guilt or hope was prompting her theories, her hypotheses, which varied depending on the time of day, on the day of the month, on moods that orbited a moon of her own. Though her inconsistency was precisely her weakness, the fact that she refused my account embittered me. It occurred to me more than once that I could take it back and make something else up. No one knew what had really happened. And people make things up all the time.

But I *was* consistent—if not about what happened, then about how it felt. What they pulled from me a thousand, a million times, therapist after therapist, doctor after doctor, catechism after catechism, got worn down to a certain smoothness. No matter the details, it ended the same way: "I felt him die. He was dead." You have to understand: I didn't *want* to believe this. My mind, in fact, seemed to refuse it. How many times did I undo it? How many times did I dream, with relief, that my brother was alive, then wake to the crisis of him dead?

≈

One night, I came upstairs to go to sleep and saw a gap of light under the door of my bedroom. It was Wayne's old bedroom; I had insisted on taking it over. I opened the door. My parents were inside, sitting next to each other on my bed, hunched over. My mother was weeping; my father looked guilty and a bit bored. Beside them, my dresser was pulled out at an angle, baring the lighter space on the wall that it usually protected from dust. And there, inside the wall's tan line, I saw a sketch of three stick figures, two tall, one short. When had Wayne drawn them? The figures listed to the right, their oval faces smiling and punched with their round, blank eyes.

"I'm starting a foundation," my mother announced the next day when I came down for breakfast. "I'm calling it Vigil." She looked up from dozens of yellow Post-its, spread in a methodical, fluttering puzzle over the table. I stiffened but said nothing as I poured myself a bowl of Frosted Flakes.

"We have to take the clues seriously," she muttered. "The signs. We have to investigate."

My father ignored it, the entire thing. When he used one of those Post-its as a coaster for his coffee, my mother just sniffed.

"The police have investigated *so* many times," I whined to Dr. Rothman that week. "They did a search, they dredged the shore, we put up the flyers. It was on the local news for weeks. They went to every single house in town." I shook my head. "I gave my report, like, a thousand times."

But Dr. Rothman wanted none of this aftermath. He wanted only stories about a living, breathing Wayne. He asked about my brother doggedly, as if to keep us on track, to keep us focused until we reached the interesting or the useful things. Only then would the good doctor spring to partial life, his brow twitching. But as repulsive as I found him, I felt relieved whenever we talked about Wayne's drawings, as if I were finally giving him something worth his while. And Dr. Rothman gave me some things, too, I will admit. He put some concepts in my hands, containers for the murk of feelings in my home. He put the pen in my hand. He taught me to get it all out, write the dreams down, write letters to Wayne. He taught me about versions of things. He taught me that grief doesn't choose its timing well: you never know when it'll grip your neck.

For instance, the way Wayne had cried when he couldn't find his stuffed kangaroo was not so different from the sound our mother made when I found it in the car a year or so after he died. I had dropped a Pez canister and was hunting for it under the driver's seat in front of me when my hand landed on the kangaroo. It was covered in dustbunnies, like it was being devoured by a horde of them. The car was still moving. My parents were chatting absently. I shoved the stuffed animal into view, into the space between the front seats, and my mother gasped. Wayne had given the kangaroo a name corresponding to no language, to no one else's notion of a name. None of us—not I, not my father, not my mother—could remember that strange name now. As my father drove us home, my mother sat weeping in the passenger seat, smoothing the kangaroo's long ears, slipping a finger into its pouch.

Shortly after the kangaroo reappeared, my mother kept herself busy by throwing out all of the toys in the house. I ran to my father, crying. Not because I still played with any of the toys she was tossing and not because they reminded me of Wayne, but because she had not distinguished between his toys—black, white, red, wands, cards, string—and mine, a fuzzy rainbow clutter of dolls and various arts and crafts.

"Why is she doing this?" I moaned to my father.

"She just needs to." His voice was tight, distracted. He was sitting in front of the desktop computer in the study. His hands on the keys were ashy at the knuckles.

"You don't care," I sobbed, standing next to him. "Why aren't you stopping her?"

The tears on my cheeks felt ticklish and comforting. One eye was crying more than the other. I was too old for this and we both knew it. But my father didn't scold me. He rolled the chair back from the oak desk and pulled me onto his knee. He ruffled my curls and kissed the top of my head, his lips saying, "Shh." I was too old for this, too. I leaned back and rested my head on his shoulder and let my crying wash through me, staring blankly at the screen as he typed in search terms. I wish I'd paid more attention then to what he was searching for.

≈

Over the months, we found more and more of Wayne's drawings, those bundles of thin lines on the walls. Behind the couch in the den. Under a windowsill next to the upstairs toilet. Inside the door of a high-up kitchen cabinet we never used. Behind the curtains on either side of the living room windows. They were always in pencil, the same three stick figures, sometimes in a series. More like clones than a family. My mother spoke of haunting, but more often of signs.

"He's trying to tell us something," she'd whisper from inside a cage of her fingers. "We have to find him. We have to investigate."

"These are old drawings, Char," my father maintained. He had taken to painting over each one the moment we found it. He was as adamant about painting over them as my mother had been about throwing out Wayne's toys. But he didn't ever paint over the first one they'd found, behind my dresser. I didn't let him. It felt important to the balance of the situation that it stay there. I made sure I was always too busy in my bedroom whenever he came in the open door with a paint can and brush, a shower of dried paint like a far-off galaxy on his ratty old Marley T-shirt.

"I don't like the smell of the paint." I'd wrinkle my nose. Or: "I'm doing my homework." I'd shake my head. Or: "Do you have to do it right now?" I'd look up from a jigsaw puzzle, its mainland flush against the wall he wanted to paint, unfinished islands around me. He left it.

At night, I would investigate the drawing on my own, carefully moving the dresser, lifting it so its scrape on the floor would not betray me. I pictured Wayne's hand crudely fisted around the pencil, his bottom lip pouting, his tongue peeking out with focus. I hovered my finger over the lines so as not to smudge them. I redrew the figures behind my closed eyes as I tried to sleep. I compared the drawing to the others. I compared it to how that day I had looked in the steamed-up mirror and seen that splotch of clarity in the middle of the fog, a handprint too small to be mine, how I had wiped my hand straight through it.

The day I caught my mother drawing on the walls, I felt a thrill of confirmation. I had come into the study to fetch a pair of scissors and found my mother, on her knees under the oak desk, facing the wall. Her head was tilted so her hair was hanging to one side. I watched her draw a long leg down from a rectangular torso on the wall. Her shoulder bumped the desk leg and she said, "Ow" and giggled to herself. I listened and watched. She began to hum the itsy-bitsy spider song, which she'd recently decided had been Wayne's favorite. I tiptoed away, my heart thumping triumphantly.

I found my father in the kitchen, bent over a nearly empty fridge, its platinum light making the new white in his beard glint. A packet of frozen pork chops sat on the counter. His lips were parted when he turned and looked at me. He seemed dazed. I told him in a heated fluid rush what I had seen my mother doing in the study. "There's no time," I said as I turned to the door, we had to catch her before she finished. My father straightened up but he didn't budge. The fridge light cast flat ovals on his cheekbones.

After a moment, he began to scold me. He had noticed that I was no longer much of a truthteller, he said. He had noticed in fact that I was always telling tales, like it was some kind of a joking matter, he said. My eyes flooded with wet fury. My ears got hot. He was punishing me, it seemed, for what I had said about my mother. But even as I burned and melted, not saying a word, I knew that my father would not outright call me a "liar." That word and its variants were considered cusses on his side of the family. Like many children forced to work around the constraints of taboo, my brother and I had always circled "lie" and "liar," snuck up on them.

"Don't be *sssly*!"

"You're the *ffflyer*!"

And so that day, my father called my news that my mother was drawing pictures behind the furniture and pretending they were Wayne's any and every word other than "lies" that would still warrant a thorough telling-off. He went through as many synonyms as needed—stories, tales, fibs, nonsense, foolishness—to let all the time in the world pass us by, to let my mother finish her drawing and crawl out from under the desk undisturbed.

4

≈≈≈

I'm alone at a bistro. It feels subdued outside; there isn't much light coming through the window to my left. Early spring is gnawing at the clouds, revealing little chunks of yellow and blue here and there, but not enough to dispel the gloom. It's too cold to sit outside on the patio and the wind has just blown everything—white paper mats, red cloth napkins—to clutter. I watch as a waitress dashes out to clean up the mess, her face fraught with futility.

I'm waiting for a younger cousin on my dad's side, a girl named Lauren. I flew in last night to meet with a new Vigil donor; Lauren is visiting colleges around here. Lauren is at a truly awful stage of life. On the verge of her twenties, she's too smart and not pretty enough. You're supposed to be pretty if you're mixed race—some sort of averaging out of the stronger features of each side—but sometimes you just come out looking jumbled. I feel a twinge of pity for her and rehearse a lighthearted greeting, but my irritation soon swamps my fondness.

Why does my mother insist on such niceties, even though my father has severed himself from us completely? I know that women are the ones who knot and mend the ties that bind a family, but with my mother it always feels cynical, like she does it for the foundation. The last time I'd seen Lauren was at a Vigil fundraising event in Philly that I had organized. Lauren had spent the whole night nodding with wide eyes at everything I said, her pressed hair wafting, and every now and then exclaiming things like "Oh, wow! We're exactly the same person, but, like, ten years apart!" I had found this horrifying, certainly more grating than flattering.

I check my watch. Lauren is now thirteen minutes late, late enough for me to suspect that she might not come but not yet late enough for me to leave. I send her a text and turn back to my book to distract myself. This is the first obvious thing he says to me.

"Reading?"

I look up. "Mmhm."

"Right, obviously." He grins. "My bad."

He hasn't even taken off his jacket and he's already talking to me, choosing the awkwardness of conversation over the clear choice for two strangers alone together in a restaurant: toothless smiles, blissful distance. He's already chosen another awkwardness by sitting at the round table next to mine instead of one of the other empty ones in the place. He's that sort of sociable person, the bane of airplanes and trains. But it's not surprising that he would be so presumptuous. He's so attractive, he can assume the kindness of strangers.

"What you reading?"

Primed by my impatience for Lauren's arrival, I long to snap at him or ignore him. But his voice is pleasant—gravelly and warm, like he's a contented bear—and there's an etiquette to these things, given that we're both black. I tell him the title.

"Huh. Never was much of a reader myself." He chuckles and opens his napkin with a flourish. I almost expect him to tuck it into his collar like a bib. "Can't concentrate, you know?"

I smile vaguely and nod, allowing my gaze to return to the page, as though I'm so compelled by the story that I simply cannot . . .

"You live around here?"

My stomach tenses. "No."

"It's hella cold here! I just flew in from Oakland. It's in the eighties out there right now."

"I'm sure," I say without looking up.

"You like the heat?"

I resign myself to it. "No, not really," I say and place the novel down beside my plate. It lies there, thickly splayed, a subtle rebuke.

"Oh, my bad, I didn't mean to interrupt your reading." He sounds sincere but he's still looking at me expectantly. I consider picking up the novel again, calling his bluff.

"No, no, it's fine. It's hard to follow anyway." I smile.

"Yeah, never could get into reading, you know?" He tucks his head in, pshawing himself.

He seems the slightest bit shy now that I've focused my attention on him. He's absurdly easy on the eyes, classically handsome, tall, fit. His close-cropped hair is edged at the temples. The skin on his face is clear, darker than mine, the shade of brown that mine will be come summer. He has barely visible but permanent-looking creases in his cheeks. This makes it hard to judge his age, not only because smiling seems to be the default state of his face, but also because when he's smiling, he gets a quickmoving light in his eyes that turns him young. It reminds me of how sunshine twists and scurries underwater.

As we inch into small talk, I find myself wondering what I look like to him. I never know if men see me as slim or regular-sized or perhaps even, from the warped perspective of white culture, fat. It seems to change with their age, their expectations, the clothes I wear. It's relative even to myself. You glance in the mirror each day, and some days it isn't you but a goblin glaring back. And how do you know if it's the image that's changed or your vision? I try to reassure myself. Nothing is real anyway. It's all just electrical signals in the mind. That's why it feels odd to run into someone you had an unexpected sex dream about. The sharpness of the memory, the remainder of lust, the paranoid need to keep it secret: all just signals, each as strong as your awareness that it never actually happened. Different kinds of desire can seem interchangeable, I think, like how the familiarity of this man feels a bit like the intimacy of having dream-fucked a friend.

The glass window next to us shudders. We've been chatting for a while now. He's taken every opportunity, I've noticed, to move in on my space, in increments. Making an animated point, he'll angle his chair toward me as if to communicate better. When I reply, he'll lean in as if he can't hear and then nudge his chair forward. It's almost sexual, the way he moves out of the orbit of his table and into the orbit of mine, using his hips to shift his chair across the faux-marble floor. He's practically sitting at my table now. We're playing the game, lounging together in a web of old lines like a worn-out hammock.

"Well I don't know, they have a lot going for them, the rain's probably gonna come and ruin the holiday for us, don't you hate that? It's not like I don't know it, I just can't *do* it that well, and I don't understand why they gotta remind you all the time, I sure do miss that home cooking, well mothers are like that, you know? Are they, I wouldn't have guessed that at all, I always said school spirit's a waste of time, you feel like you'll never belong, that wasn't the first time or the last to be honest, at any rate, she's mostly a good manager, she's got the chops to keep things running smoothly, Philly, for real? I'm not sure what the policy is on that, the spices are like *my god*, there's no way to get there unless you go all the way around, sometimes I wonder how people that age manage in a world like this, hm, what *is* it about? Some people have this sense of entitlement, three or four times, maybe? *Privilege* feels like the wrong word, we just kept watching it over and over, like, there's no way this is happening again, yeah but what can you do? You gotta live, right? You do what you gotta do, ain't it hard just to live?"

A thudding snarl of helicopters comes across the sky and it does not pass, it stays. The plate-glass window beside us shudders again. We glance at it.

"Is that the . . ." I have to raise my voice to be heard.

"The second time? Yeah."

We laugh. He's now undeniably at my table, the appetizers we've ordered soggy with neglect. I take a sip from my water glass. The *slink-clink* of the ice cubes is barely audible under the staccato of the choppers. It's embarrassing and pleasant to realize that we've been talking about nothing—something I usually despise—for so long that we've lost track of time. The air between us is brimming with vibration, as if our lips, the way they brush as we speak, are making a snare beat beneath the words. It's always a surprise, isn't it? The possibility of sex. A breach of the borders of body. This scenario would seem less real only if we were outside, the sun shining down, my shoes higher and pointier, his business-casual more business, a hotel room in our future.

He covers a burp with his smooth brown hand. It feels so much like I've met him before. But he's got rougher edges than I do. By comparison, my voice sounds bougie to me, even a little Valleygirl. I look away, out the glass window. The name of the bistro arcs in reverse across it in gold letters rimmed with red. There's no one outside, the street is bare, a side street near the common. There's a creamcolored building across from us, baroque balcony rails curling inward. It's an old neighborhood, a place with time packed in, tightly looped cycles of wealth begetting wealth. The helicopters are disconcerting in such an old place. I wonder after Lauren and check to see if she's replied to my text. She hasn't and it's been almost an hour. I gesture to excuse myself and turn to one side and try to call but it goes straight to voicemail.

When I hang up, he's talking to the waitress, who wears her hair pulled back tightly. She nods and smiles eagerly at his dessert order. I'm immediately drawn toward him, which amuses me, the sudden current of jealousy I feel about this woman who is only doing her job. He turns to me.

"C?" he says.

I look into his eyes and the light there twists. And I know. It's Wayne.

The world dilates and the window beside us shatters. Broken glass flies at us, and even as I'm ducking under the table and his hand—larger than it had looked grasping a salad fork—is on the back of my head to keep me down! down! he's yelling, and even as everything is flashing, the bistro's ambient light snuffed, the emergency light swinging across the room with the regular sweep of a lighthouse beacon, and even as the helicopter blades continue thudding at the same rate as my heart and I can feel the entire left side of my body prickling, even as all this is happening, as my knee grinds into the litter of broken glass and my ankle buckles and my shoulder hits the table leg, I'm thinking about what it was like to be in the car in the worst Baltimore winters. How the windshield wipers on our Buick had scraped across the ice while the de-icer whirred and sprayed that blue foamy liquid, how the ice had crackled and broken up and crumbled to frost. Why on earth is this what I'm thinking? The chill I feel, maybe, the ice water that must have spilled into my lap when it all exploded, the sense that the world's structures have collapsed so that before and after may as well be the same thing.

The sound of sirens is piercing without the window to muffle it. I'm on my knees under the round table. As I try to unwind my ankle from beneath me, I look at the empty space where the window had been, at the vague light outside. It's like they say; it's like a movie. Everything's moving too slowly. I see people running down the cobbled street. A darkhaired woman in a gray suit with a peach shirt drops her purse by accident and crouches gracefully to pick it up again. Two men hurtle toward her and one almost trips over her stooped form, leaping away just in time. Another woman, older, Indian or Latina, hobbles by as fast as she can, holding the hem of her navy dress. She loses a shoe. Another man picks it up but unable to stop and give it back to her, he tosses it and keeps running. Why are they running? It could be a riot or a bomb or . . .

There's an ellipsis of low blows to the earth. I come out of my haze and fling my leg at the chair blocking my way out from under the table but only manage to knock my shin against it. Deeper inside the restaurant, the waitress, my brief nemesis, is screaming, and there's a crackling, ripping sound that I can't locate, followed by what seems to be its echo, a faint boom. I look around in a panic, searching for the man, and for a second all I can see is steam fanning up before me with a steady hiss. Then his face appears through the fog, widow's peak first. My whole body floods with electric life. I move toward him, toward survival. He's pulling on my arm, extricating me from under the table—he wants us to move farther into the restaurant, away from the window, to safety—and now he's on his feet and reaching his left arm down to me. I grasp it and our arms pull long and taut between us like a single braided rope, and as I rise the purest, cleanest knowing again surges up in me.

"It's you," I whisper as the faux-marble floor beneath us cracks open as easily as an eggshell.

5

≈≈≈

Dear Wayne. You were moving along a groove, the one carved into the world for you. The morning was golden. The roads were as gray and smooth as the skin of sea-born creatures. At the crossroads, you were blindsided. You were as if blind and an immense force came at you from one side. As you stepped forward unaware, it came and knocked you out of your furrow and into another, plowed you up and over, put you in another place, elsewhere, where. I don't want to tell you what happened. I want to tell you how it felt.

≈

When I was twelve, my little brother got hit by a car. He was seven. We were crossing a road together, just the two of us. This was allowed. This was our every weekday. We would walk together from our house in Pikesville to school. St. Anthony's was only eight blocks away, the lower, middle, and upper schools adjacent. We lived in a part of the county where roads are named for the trees long ago planted along them. Elm Hollow, Deep Willow, Cedar. There was barely any traffic but for slow-passing cars driven by neighbors we knew, neighbors who waved through the windshield, lifting their thermoses to their smiles. It was safe to walk to school, alone together, holding hands.

Wayne loved school. He was fawn brown, a gangly kid, the heat of growing still burning up all his fat. He did his homework with the perseverance of someone licking a scoop of ice cream before it melts. But I was in that spell—too old, not old enough—when it was embarrassing to embrace my love of learning. And mornings are rough on me, always have been, always will be. Everything wakes up too quickly around me and my body struggles to catch up. Wayne was fine though, happy even, to be alive in the waking day.

It was spring, warm and bright, the air choked with flowers and furry seeds. We walked quietly along the sidewalk, under the trees, through dappled, applegreen light. Wayne paused, still holding my hand as he leaned over to pluck a spindly stalk with his other hand. He raised it to his nose to sniff it, then held it to the light and spun it between his fingers to helicopter it, all to show me how miserably boring I was in the mornings.

He tried again: "You see that squirrel?"

"No."

"Right there, Cee!"

I ignored him. He was always trying to trick me with vanishing things.

"Gone now anyway," he mumbled. He was sliding the stalk up his sleeve, practicing. I glanced at the top of his brown head, at the loose heartshape of his widow's peak.

"I dreamed about Grandma Lu last night," he said.

"Mmhm."

"She was riding on a dinosaur 'cause Mom broke the car down again."

I chuckled and sighed and let go of his hand. I hated to hear him claim our grandmother's love, even if it was only in a dream. Anyhow, we didn't have to always hold hands. In the winter, our wool gloves squeaked against each other. In the summer, Wayne's palms were sticky with breakfast. Today, I simply felt more dear to myself than anyone else. I was morning-tender and I wanted to protect myself from Grandma Lu's blatant preference for Wayne. So, I dropped his hand and walked ahead, just a couple of steps, my stride gaining length as we began to cross the road. Wayne called my name, in a question. Sometimes he accidentally called me "Mom," but that day he said my name.

I turned my head. He was crouched down, picking up his fallen weed stalk. This softened me. So, though I kept moving toward the other curb, I extended my hand back for him to grab, like I was a relay runner about to take off, awaiting the baton. Wayne grinned and sprang from his crouch and jog-stepped to catch up, his hand reaching for mine. As our fingertips touched, I glimpsed a dark moving form, a whirring mass. Sunlight hit glass and spun inside it. Wayne flew sideways, his fingertips slipping from mine like sand. The engine growled, the brakes yelped.

Somehow after those sounds, I heard the impact, the thud of the car ramming into my brother, the sound of my brother as he hit the road, of my backpack as it slid off my shoulders. More thuds came as the car veered up and over the curb and onto the sidewalk in front of me. I ran around it, my thigh skimming its side—it was warm and throbbing like skin—my hand pushing off the back window to speed me on my way. It still took forever to get to him. He had flown so far.

When I reached him, he was on the ground in an obscene position, his legs scissored under him. I knelt beside him so fast I found bruises on my knees later. His lips and eyes were open but unspeaking, unseeing. Blood was inching out beneath his head. I laid my hand on his chest and felt his heart slamming up at my palm. Behind me I heard a car door open, and the flat slaps of someone running in shoes not built for running.

At first, I didn't understand what this white man was shouting. He was wearing a blue windbreaker, a yellow button-down under it, and brown pants. All his clothes were too tight. As he squatted by Wayne's body, gaps flared between the buttons of his shirt and I saw a rip in his crotch seam. Finally, the man's words punctured the swell of refusal in my ears. He was telling me not to touch Wayne. I obediently lifted my hand away from his chest.

"Shit," the man said through gritted teeth. "We gotta get help."

I looked around. Apart from his silver sedan and the four stop signs standing guard, there was no one around, nothing resembling help. The man wiped his hand across his forehead.

"Fuck," he said, near tears. "I was just . . . I was just turning the radio up."

I looked down. Wayne's face was already swelling. His arm twitched once, twice.

The man rose to standing. "We gotta get an ambulance." He walked toward a house set back from the road, tall and white with a green door. He cupped his hands to his mouth, shouting across the lawn at windows blanked out by sunlight.

"Hello! Help!" He ran up to the house. "Somebody call an ambulance!"

He banged on the green door with his fist. The sun glared on the back of my neck. The man gave up and tried the house next door. Why was no one home? Why were there no other cars? The man's sedan was still settling, buzzing and ticking in its angled perch up on the curb. Steam issued from its hood with a hiss. Wayne's backpack was somehow under it. The man was returning now, cursing, looking around wildly.

"We live here," I managed to say. "Down the road."

"What's that? You do? Is anybody home?" The man knelt heavily on the other side of Wayne. He exhaled to steel himself, then bent over to hover his ear above my brother's open mouth. The man winced at what he heard or didn't hear. "Your mom?"

I nodded. My father had left for work but my mother might not yet be at her studio. The man glanced back at the sedan, then looked at me.

"All right, listen, I don't think it's drivable. I'll wait here with him—you go and get your mom. Tell her to call 911."

I shook my head. I wasn't leaving my brother. I didn't even have to say it.

The man sighed. "Okay, let's carry him home, and call from there."

I nodded even though this contravened his earlier instruction not to touch Wayne. The man seemed to realize this, too, because he took a deep breath before maneuvering his hand under Wayne's head. Blood flashed red on the cuff of the man's windbreaker, then darkened as it seeped in. He grimaced as he put his arm under Wayne's knees, gathering his legs like a bundle.

"All right, here we go."

There was a terrible sound when Wayne's head unstuck from the road. The man stood heavily, staggering a little.

"It's close?"

I nodded, staring. Wayne's head hung back over the man's forearm. The side of Wayne's face was raw and pink like cat food. His mouth was still open but did not appear to be the source of the wet popping sounds coming from him. His eyes seemed to widen—but that might have been the light, the angle—before they closed.

I was trembling. I pointed the way home and we rushed down the road in that direction. I walked quickly, gingerly, though my arms were empty—I'd left our backpacks where they'd fallen. There was no traffic, no other cars around. The light through which we moved glowed green from the watchful trees. I desperately needed the bathroom. The man swung his head from left to right in a kind of trance. He was huffing. Sweat flowed down his face, soaking the collar of his yellow shirt and blue jacket. I thought about his sweat mixing with Wayne's blood and how awful that would be. The man saw me looking.

"He's not heavy." He licked his upper lip. "Just awkward to carry. How far?"

"Down there." I pointed again.

That's when Wayne's head began rolling around in a strange way, an unreasonable way, my father would have said. Wayne's eyes were thin white slits between purpling lids. His face was puffed up, blurring his features, and the pink crannies in his cheek began to fill with darker blood. He looked like he was shaking but that might have been the man's staggered lope. Still feeling the taboo on touching Wayne, I reached out and instead grasped his white sneaker, which had a splotch on it the color of Grandma Lu's favorite nail polish.

I squeezed, the leather gave. And, as if through the perforations on top of his sneaker, I felt Wayne *ssth*-ing into me. Something left him, filling each of my fingers like straws, those five currents merging in my palm and shooting up my wrist into my forearm, picking up momentum as they navigated the corners of my elbow and armpit and finally flooded my chest. Wayne's limbs jerked as wide as they could in the cage of the man's arms—the man flinched but kept walking—then subsided, swept clean. My insides felt filled to bursting.

I let go of my brother's shoe and ran, dashing up the driveway to the front door of our home. I glanced behind me once. The man was crossing the front yard, coming toward the house with Wayne's body in his arms. I took my keys out of my pocket and unlocked the door. Leaving it open, I raced inside the house, climbing the stairs two, three at a time, heading for the bathroom I shared with Wayne. I sat down so fast, I almost slid off the toilet seat, wrangling my jeans and underwear down just in time.

As I released my bladder, I panted with the effort of having run up the stairs. Wayne's cargo shorts from yesterday were on the tile floor, seams flagrantly exposed, his underwear still locked loosely inside them, the soil of his boy body smeared faintly there. The blow-dryer was layabouting on the floor, too, its head with the longest pout imaginable, its cord curling out of the socket like a pig's tail or one of my own locks. I listened for people downstairs, for the man to come in, for my mother to scream, my father to shout "Help!" into the phone, but the sound of my pee splummeshing down was too loud.

I felt it knock up inside me then, a vaulting, heaving thing. My back arced forward with the motion of a dolphin. No time to wipe. In one motion, I turned and knelt, then puked into the toilet, blinking tears from the force of it. I stared down at the lacy mess of Frosted Flakes. Pee dribbled down my leg. Another bout of vomit flung out of me, neon yellow in the toilet bowl. I coughed and waited. One more jerk but nothing came up. I blew my nose into some tissue. I cleaned myself up, changed my underwear, and pulled my jeans back on.

When I went downstairs, there was no one home. Where was my mother? Where was Wayne? I walked into the kitchen, sunlight angling across the counters. I glanced at the microwave. Still morning. 8:42 became 8:43, the two's leg shifting from left to right to become three, a little dance at the knees. The front door was still open and it moaned as a brief wind blew. I closed it and went to the kitchen to pour myself a glass of water.

I sat at the kitchen table and sipped, feeling sorry for myself. Maybe they had all left for the hospital. My father driving fast but controlled. My mother in the back, crying and whispering to Wayne, laid out, his head on her lap, his dead face bleeding into her dress. The man in the passenger seat, sweating, explaining, not wearing his seat belt. I could still feel the scratch of acid at the back of my tongue from puking. I wasn't hungry. My insides felt full up.

The phone rang, a solid stream of beeps like a robot rolling its *r*'s. I jumped to my feet and snatched the receiver from its cradle so fast that it fell. It hit the floor and spun on its back, its cord looping. As I picked it up, I heard my mother's voice blurting sharply from it.

"Cee? Is that you? The school called. You guys didn't sign in today?"

"What?" I put the receiver to my ear.

"You'd better have an explanation for this when I get home, Cee."

"Mom, where are you?"

"Where's your brother? Let me talk to him . . ."

"What?" I looked at the mooncolored numbers on the microwave: 3:16. I blinked. Amazed, I moved into the living room, where I could see through the front window. A shadowy lump sat in the middle of the gilded grass. I peered at the blueish crumple. It was the man's windbreaker. My mother was still barking in my ear.

". . . I said, where's your brother?"

"I—" Through the window, the afternoon sky looked dull and bright at once, like the chapel window at St. Anthony's, aglow with ancient color.

"Where's Wayne, Cee? Where's Wayne?"

6

≈≈≈

My walk home from St. Anthony's upper school often took me past dandelions, and some days, I would think about the time my mother first taught me about *dent-de-lion*. As I recall it, we were sitting in our backyard, itchy legs in the grass, tingling faces in the breeze. Wayne was sitting a few feet away, peering at something on the ground. I must have been about eight years old then, Wayne just out of diapers. My mother pointed at a yellow flower.

"Dandelion. *Dent-de-lion.* The teeth of the lion. It's the leaves they're talking about. You see? You can eat them, you know." She showed me. I shook my head and made a face. She laughed and pointed from the yellow flower to a furry white globe next to it. "The sun becomes the moon," she said, humming with the song of it. She wrangled the stem, plucked the moon. "And the moon becomes the stars." She blew, sending the seeds in a galactic shower. She laughed. I laughed. Wayne crouched over his mystery. The day squatted lazy above. The air was eerie with the insects and the fizzing pylons. Grass always marred my mother's legs, green stains nestling into red marks where the blades bit into her pale skin. Those marks, like the wrinkles in her face, always made skin itself seem like a stretchy fabric one might wrap and unwrap with ease.

I was thinking about this the day my father decided to leave us. I was sixteen, walking home from school alone. My backpack was creaking and sweaty against one side of my back. My father had told me to wear it on both shoulders to protect my spine—there had been PTA meetings about this—but we upperschoolers knew the diagonal sling conveyed a necessary nonchalance. The backpack rocked against my shoulder and yellow eyes winked from neglected lawns and I remembered my mother's lesson about entropy among the weeds, the dusty bitterness of the plant's serrated leaves. *We use our teeth on lion's teeth.*

Only when I got home from school and found the kitchen clean and sunlit and my mother missing did I realize what day it was. How uncanny that I had been bringing to mind bits of green stuck in our teeth and Wayne's small back across the yard. I stalled going down into the den, where, I knew, my mother was awaiting us. I toasted a slice of white bread and slathered cream cheese over it, then leaned against the counter to eat it. My father came into the kitchen and we traded nods. He plucked a ginger beer from the fridge, twisted it open, took a swig, put it on the counter. There was a shared sense of preparing to endure.

We both disdained this family ritual. I don't know what he thought exactly, but personally, I prided myself on my own memories of my brother, which I kept present to myself willfully, sliding them along as if on an abacus before falling asleep each night. A trip to the mall to buy a birthday card for Mom. Trotting barefoot over the road to catch the ice-cream truck, wincing and giggling. Raking leaves, tossing snowballs, splashing in puddles.

My father picked up his bottle from the counter with resolve.

We made our way downstairs together like we were in the dark, I descending before him, he with a hand on my shoulder. In the den, the TV was frozen in a zigzaggy blur that looked like it should have made a tearing sound. The air was thick with the spooks of microwaved food, TV static, stirred-up carpet dust. There were bowls of peanuts and Chex Mix on the coffee table. My mother was sitting in the middle of the couch, gripping the remote control like the railing on the edge of a cliff.

My father and I sat on either side of her—we didn't have a choice. My father rebelliously chugged his ginger beer. I slipped off my shoes and pulled my knees to my chest, resting my chin in the chink between them. My mother aimed the remote at the TV and the zigzag calmed to clarity, like wind dying down on the surface of water.

On the screen, Wayne was dressed in diaper-plump cargo shorts and a blue polo shirt. He ran around in a circle. The picture nodded up and down. It was a bright day, the image receding into a white blur whenever the camera tilted up too far.

The couch's joints cracked as the three of us leaned forward. We always watched these videos as if something were going to happen, as if this were an actual story, with events and a climax. It was possible. We owned hours and hours of these home videos and hadn't yet seen them all. Whenever Wayne's birthday came around, my mother carefully chose from stacks of labeled, dated camcorder tapes, then went to the art studio at Catonsville to transfer them to video.

Last year, I had spied on her process. I'd sat at the top of the staircase to the den, trying not to knock down any of the framed family portraits that descended the wall alongside the stairs. I had peered through the railing at my mother sitting crosslegged on the carpet, staring fixedly at the camcorder cradled in her arms. From my perch, I hadn't been able to see the screen, only my mother's face and the camcorder tapes, small black rectangles, congregating on the carpet around her. I remember thinking that there were enough of them to build a transformer the size of Wayne's body when he'd died.

That was the Wayne I saw when I counted my abacus beads of memories: the seven-year-old's silhouette, limbs grown just out of his control. Not this sturdy toddler trotting through brightness. Except that today, oddly enough, I had happened to remember him around this age, a toddler in our backyard. But this wasn't Pikesville.

"Where is this, anyway?"

My mother's silence chastised me for not knowing.

"California," my father finally said.

"Grandma Rose's?" I asked, leaning back to ask him behind my mother's hunched form.

"Yeah," he said. "You and me must have stayed here on that visit, I'm thinking."

The tightness in the air meant that this had been one of the bad times, one of those times my mother had up and left, dragging one of us kids with her. My mother began to cry quietly, her brow gathering its pleats.

On the TV, Wayne was doing a dance, stomping his foot and turning around, his eyes downcast. He spun in a circle and kicked and mewed through the fluttering wind. Thin streaks flew across the screen, spiraled, vanished—my mother's hair blowing into the frame.

"Whatcha doin' there, Wayne?" the camera asked in a high-pitched singsong. There in California, baby Wayne called out a reply to her. It wasn't a word but the camera said, "Oh, of course!" Wayne walked around, looking at the ground. He kicked, trying to fling something off his foot. What *was* he doing? An ambulance siren went past in the background of the video and the camera veered instinctively. Fingers propellered into view: my mother waving at something. The camera zoomed in on Wayne, then jerkily zoomed out again. He was sitting on the sidewalk now, smacking his palms on a dark splotch in front of him.

"You got it now, Wayne? You caught your shadow?"

He grinned up at us. The video cut.

It resumed under dimmer light, evening or morning, a time of day that thins the sun. The camera was careening around a house that I now recognized as Grandma Rose's. I had visited her home in San Francisco many times but seeing it on-screen was like being sure you know a song on the radio but getting the lyrics wrong when you try to sing along. Wayne sat on a rug, his joints webbed in a striped onesie, his fingers and cheeks strung with saliva. There was a stark white animal skull on the wall above him, a Joshua Tree souvenir from which, Grandma Rose swore, a horde of red ants had once poured.

The camera panned across a framed black-and-white film poster—*La Jetée*—and through a doorway, where it landed on an uncooked chicken, sallow and majestic, freckled with pepper, then bounced to Grandma Rose. Her happy, tired face filled the screen, her voice conversational, silver bracelets chiming as she reached up to smooth the gray wisps off her brow.

The camera settled with a clunk onto the counter, still running. The world fell into order. Grandma Rose was stirring something on the stove, her hip cocked. She wore a black turtleneck, black cigarette pants, a white belt—almost parodically French, even though she had lived in the States for over twenty years by then. My mother, surprisingly chubby in daisy pajamas—post-pregnancy weight, I realize now—crossed the camera's still eye, her ponytail twitching on her back, Wayne on her hip. She sat on a stool and pulled him onto her lap. All you could see was her leg, his arm, and their very different profiles.

I glanced at my mother leaning forward on the couch beside me. She had abandoned her crying the way a child does, sheer distraction cutting it short so fast that her cheeks were still wet with tears. My father caught my eye behind her back and shrugged. The Annual Wayne Video was usually a babybook page on-screen: scenes of him waving or eating or playing or doing magic tricks with that recessed focus in his eyes as he made things come and go. One time, there had been news footage from his last day and my mother had done a voiceover narrating all the "leads" in the "case" that still needed to be pursued. And another time, there had been a theme my father and I couldn't guess, and my mother's face had congealed into a disappointment that lasted for days.

But in this video montage, Wayne seemed almost incidental. As if to affirm this impression, my mother now pointed the remote at the TV and raised the volume on the conversation in that California kitchen. Grandma Rose was demurring.

"It's not a problem. You stay here as long as you need to, chérie."

"He says it's the last—"

"Of course he says that, chérie. But we don't even know how many times."

Grandma Rose cast a look over her shoulder, an eyebrow raised, and turned back to the stove, steam scrolling up behind her. The look and the move were beautiful. I have lost hours of my life to gazing at the one family portrait where Grandma Rose appears, which hung toward the bottom of the wall along the den staircase. She looks like a Hollywood starlet, the rest of us like Muppets.

My father spoke up in the den. "Char?" he said. "What's going on?"

I looked at my mother, who was ignoring us both with an intensity that seemed to have a tremor of laughter in it, the way heat ripples the air. The very fact that we didn't know what was coming was precisely her point. She was the only one in this family who ever paid attention to anything. She was the one who had arranged the family portraits along the stairs, alternating the white relatives and the black ones—Locketts then Williamses then Locketts. She was the one who had recorded these videos, and now compiled them into an elegy every year. My father and I watched her, frightened by how much we owed her.

On the screen, she began speaking one long sentence, making a confession that stopped Grandma Rose's stirring arm and turned her by degrees until her pretty face, riven with age and concern, took up the background of the shot. There had been an affair, years before, with another man, and my mother was considering telling my father, to take revenge on him for his own misdeeds. The sound went in and out, but the words were clear enough. As they took on weight and meaning, my father gripped the arm of the couch with one hand, then gripped my mother's arm with the other, then finally let go of both and stood and went upstairs.

I was only sixteen, too young to hear this broken, grown-up talk—it was the first I'd ever heard of these liaisons, as Grandma Rose was referring to them—but I stayed, I watched, I saw it through. I thought about what it would be like to tell my latest therapist, about how this would shift the weight of trustworthiness in our balance sheet. It almost felt as if there would be a scene at the end of the tape revealing the face of this other man my mother was talking about. But there was only Grandma Rose on the screen shaking her head profoundly, then a narrowing to black—my mother here in the den had turned off the TV. She looked at me blankly, as if only now realizing that I was there and that I had heard everything. But the worry in her face soon dissolved. She picked up the barely touched snacks and marched up the stairs at a clip, the bowls rattling like maracas, the family portraits on the wall stirring beside her. I heard a door upstairs shut.

I knew my parents would start fighting and waited to hear their raised voices. But then they didn't, which was worse. The murmur above intimated something different from the disappearing quick of their usual arguments. I switched the TV back on. All afternoon, all evening, I lay on the couch, wrapped inside a quilt of sitcoms, the same commercials stitching them together.

≈

A convenience store in Brooklyn—or a notion of Brooklyn pastiched from iconic scenes and broad stereotypes. The bell on the glass door chimes, the linoleum is scratched and bruised, the aisles are crowded with brightly colored boxes, brand names crying out, familiar and illegible. The counter is a window, so compressed by the shelves of goods around it, there's barely a gap through which to exchange words, glances, banter, and barter. At first, no one is there to sell the packet of gum, with its tongue-pink packaging. Then a head pops up from below— what was he looking for?—like he's a jack-in-the-box.

"How can I help you, Cee?"

My name is out of his mouth before I recognize that it's him. It's Wayne. He grins wide, flaunting a gap in his teeth. He is seven years old. His chin barely reaches above the counter.

"You're alive?"

He tilts his head and salutes me. "Been here in Brooklyn the whole time."

"But you died."

"How've you been, Cee?" He's a man now, my father's height, his voice gravelly. He reaches through the gap toward me over the counter, his hand grips my throat, and I'm

alone, nap drool wetting the weave of the shambly couch in the den. The television *tch*-ing quietly, blinking at a human pace. A phone number scrolling under a white woman gesturing and gibbering wildly, seeming at once ecstatic and afraid. I touched my hand to my collarbone, felt a quick joy—he's in Brooklyn!—then a grip of pain. No, he isn't.

Aching behind the bridge of my nose, I made my way up the den stairs, pausing at the portrait at the top, a charcoal sketch of "Wayne, age nine." Everyone said it was good that my mother was working on her art again, even if Wayne had become her only subject, endless reproductions of photos and camcorder freeze-frames. But I found this one grotesque. That title. Wayne had died when he was seven. This hypothetical portrait, this unfamiliar face, was another way his death had skewed us all apart, the way a missing tooth grows gaps between the others. Our memories of him now conflicted in dire ways. My mother had hung this bad, wrong portrait, had even used it for Vigil publicity materials. I glared at the prophesied face, already outdated, then made my way up to my bedroom.

I skipped brushing my teeth. I skipped pajamas. I turned off the light and crept fully clothed under the covers. After a few minutes, there was a knock at my bedroom door. "Come in," I said. My father came in and closed the door. My bed wheezed as he sat down, his hip crushing my toe. We readjusted, trading sorries. He hadn't tucked me in for ages. I knew he was there not because I needed him but because he needed to be away from my mother. We followed a silent script in which he reassured me and we were both reassured. But when he put his hand on my covered foot as preface to parting, all of a sudden, I did need him.

"How did you and Mom meet?" I asked.

My father didn't say anything. My mother had told me and Wayne this story a thousand, a million times, sometimes revealing new details, inserting jokes and reflections, but sticking to the same plot. I knew that plot by heart. It had been a bedtime favorite as long as I could recall, all the way back to the days when we still called her Mama. My question to my father had been prompted in part by habit: my sleepiness, the extra weight grounding my bed, its shifting warmth. He had never told us this story himself and I felt foolish for asking about it tonight, of all nights. But then, as if a latch that hadn't been properly closed had clicked open, he spoke.

"Well," he said. "We were on the same flight."

I exhaled and bundled down. It was the same story. His words a bit different. "I was headed out to finish up at school. She was going home for the summer holiday. Soon as I sat next to her, I noticed she was pretty. But—this might be hard for you to understand—you couldn't just *notice* a pretty white girl back then."

"Oh," I said. "You mean like—?"

"Yes, it was really like that. I mean, there were white girls at school. It was the seventies. Things had changed, were changing. But we were all still separated out, you know—no signs or anything, people just keeping to themselves. Airplanes were complicated. You never knew who was gonna sit next to you.

But she was friendly to me. Which made it worse in a way, you know?"

This part of the story wasn't familiar. My mother hadn't said any of this. I nodded so he'd go on.

"I'd only flown a couple of times before. I was straight-up terrified." He chuckled. "Your mother was a real regular. I wouldn't have been surprised if she knew the pilot personally. She just rattled on and on. You know how she gets." We laughed but it died quickly. "Anyhow, she could tell how scared I was. And she talked me through it. Helped me out with my seat belt. They got all tangled up, our seat belts. That made me even more nervous but she just rattled on through it. The other folks around us looked pretty peevish. But once we took off, the engines drowned us out and they turned away and I relaxed a bit. I remember—I remember her hair smelled like cigarettes and perfume. I know it now: Red Door. She was dressed like a hippie, but still proper. Light blue dress. Sandals." He paused. "She had real gold on her fingers and in her ears. My granddaddy taught me how to tell, the difference in the shine. Anyhow, most times, I'd have begged for a piece of quiet. But you know, it helped, all that chatter, distracted me from thinking about this metal can getting tossed across the sky. She told me near about anything that came to mind, seemed like."

I knew what was coming next and I smiled for the comfort of it.

"Why was I so nervous? she asked me. Church, mostly. So, we talked about her end-of-days and my end-of-days. She asked me what I would do if it was the end-of-days now. Maybe not the best thing to bring up on a flight. But again somehow, it helped. I said—I think I said, 'I'd think of my mama.' She laughed. So I said, 'Okay, I'd say a prayer.' She laughed even harder. Then she said this thing. Crazy as all get-out to say to a stranger she just met. She said, 'If I were about to die, I'd find the closest man around . . .'"

I silently mouthed the next words along with him.

"'And I would plant one on him.'"

His laugh rocked him on my bed, which clucked agreeably.

"That was some crazy talk to say to a stranger, especially a brother. Anyhow, then we hit some rocky air. Man, I got hit with the nerves, real bad. I was huffing—my asthma was worse back then—and your mom, this—she was just a young woman, she said, 'All right, it's gonna be all right.' I didn't believe her but then she reached over and—and she held my hand."

I frowned and sat up. "C'mon, Dad. You can say it. Mom already *told* us the real story."

"What real story?" Behind the smile in his voice, he sounded surprised, put out even.

"How the turbulence got worse and the plane was all *teeter-tottery*"—my mother's words were coming out of me now, I didn't have any other language for it—"and you were so scared that she leaned over and planted a kiss on you, smack-dab on the mouth."

My father was quiet. I couldn't quite see his face. Something creaked. A footstep in the hall, the birch outside my window.

"You thought it was end-of-days," I explained patiently. "Right? You thought—"

"Yes, we did. We surely did," he finally said, his voice punched raw.

"But it wasn't—" I pressed on, my eyes straining to make out his in the dark. "It wasn't the end," I said, finishing the story the way my mother always had. "It was the beginning."

After a moment, I heard a tiny snap, a gentle knock— I didn't know it then but my father had left his Seiko watch on my bedside table. He kissed my forehead. We traded good nights. He shut the door behind himself. I lay in the dark, counting my beads, sliding them along the abacus of my mind, thinking of the gaps between people and between memories, how everything we do is a leap across them. Time began to slip forward, fast, faster, then at a furious speed, propelling me through the night until my eyelids flipped open to a stopped dawn with no color at all.

7

≈≈≈

After my father left for good, my mother and I began to speak a new language. It was the same old English, except we somehow needed more words to work around all the ones we couldn't say. It reminded me of this skit from a comedy show we'd all loved when I was a kid, something Grandma Rose had taped from the BBC. Two priests sitting on a bench, unable to recall a particular name. *You know. Whatshisname. Walks on water.*

I couldn't even say all the words to Dr. Jacinta. She was my new doctor, a bespectacled Argentinean whose concern for me brimmed visibly in her eyes. I didn't feel all that fucked up. But Dr. Jacinta seemed always on the verge of tears, her voice suffused with maternal concern as I recapitulated my week as a senior at St. Ant's: the boys, the cutters, the SATs, the humiliation of being the last person at my school to fill-in-the-blank. It was all crushingly boring even to me, that much worse because everyone knew that everyone in the world, in the history of mankind, had gone through this. "It's called a phase for a reason," I said. This made my mother laugh but seemed only to disconcert Dr. Jacinta.

That poor woman, with her pink spectacles and her slight lisp and her crusted makeup. She had fully taken on board my belief that my brother was dead, not missing, and even though that was probably for therapeutic reasons and not trust ones, this made me like her more. This also meant that she absorbed each word of our sessions like a blow to her very soul. Whenever the door to her office closed behind me, I would make my way back into my thickets of hormones and feelings and Dr. Jacinta would put her head on her desk and weep for the sorrow of being a teenage girl.

Or so I imagined. All I knew for sure was that she worried about me. Maybe it was the lingerie I wore as clothing. Or the shade of lipstick (Uterus, I think it was called). Or the knee-high thrift-store boots I had dyed pitchblack, more and more of the friendly brown leather peeping out every time it rained.

It was probably the cutters. None of the cutters was in my AP classes. I saw them only at lunch and after school. There was a hollow behind the library where we'd sprawl and talk and smoke and sometimes, in a ripe intimacy, cut our skin together.

"I don't think what we do is *that* crazy," I expostulated to Caleb, jabbing the air with half a Camel Light while keeping one eye on J. He was doing that gorgeous idiotic thing he always did: letting his hair tumble over his eye and blinking until his lashes were tangled in it. Liz, the new girl, was next to him. Liz was exquisite, androgynous. Her blue-black hair was somewhere between manga and a bowlcut. It quivered now with her mechanical giggle, a sure sign that she was high. Caleb was likely stoned, too, but he always seemed to think that he was listening to me and that what I was saying was related to whatever he was thinking, whether it was Y2K or his favorite movie, *Blade*.

"I know, yeah, right, right?" he said, nodding.

"People do this sort of thing all the time for, like, political reasons." I took a drag. "Hunger strikers. Martyrs."

"Right, right." Caleb's nodding took on a hiphop rhythm.

"Hello?" I raised my eyebrow.

He caught my eye and laughed. "Nah, nah, I'm totally with you, Cee. Cutting is totally political. Vampires, too. They're like this underground, like, force. Or conspiracy."

Val scooted over to us. She started whispering to me about Liz and J. I didn't want to hear about it, so I rolled up my sleeve and showed off a set of sketchy cuts. They fit perfectly in the grooves of my inner elbow. *Ooh,* Caleb and Val cooed. Disguising the cuts this way, hiding them in the nooks and cracks of our bodies, was what distinguished us from the dumb Goth kids you always read about. It had been my idea.

Liz's jaw had jutted in a skeptical circle when I'd first suggested it. "No way."

I'd rolled my eyes and said, "Well, *I* don't wanna look like a fucking zebra, do you?"

Liz, whose forearms were already as laddered as torn stockings when she'd arrived at our school, had glared at me. But the others had laughed. It was devious, I know: a half-black, half-white girl joking about zebras. I often did this—called myself an Oreo or a halfrican or a mulatta or a lightskinned, just to get it out of the way, to take control over a difference that could be wielded to hurt me. I didn't feel tortured about it. It was kind of a power move.

In the end, J had jumped in, his tongue rapid, his eyes blank: "I think it would be cool to hide it. We could do our scalps. Or between the toes. Or at the knuckles. Or behind the ears."

"Exactly," I'd said, feeling a rush of warmth to my stomach, even though J hadn't been looking at me when he'd said it, but at something he was shredding into the knot of his crossed legs.

I will never forget this moment, like I'll always remember the one time I made him laugh so hard that he teared up, his lashes thickening even more. I can never exactly recall the joke I'd thought up, though—some pun about a spoon-and-egg race—and J was stoned and no one else found it that funny. But still. I kicked myself later for taking the precaution—a protective measure I use to this day—of saying that someone else had told me the joke. Watching J take pleasure in a joke I'd conjured had been ruined by not being able to claim it as my own.

≈

I remember these moments so well because they were my evidence that I was meant to cut with J and then fuck him. I had somehow bullied Dr. Jacinta into accepting this destiny.

"You, like, cut *each other*. It's incredibly hot."

I said this matter-of-factly, in total ignorance. I had never even heard of people doing this. I had made it up out of thin air, like the joke that worked.

"Also?" I paused for suspense. "I also really want to draw a picture *in* his skin. Like a tattoo. He's part Korean. His skin would make such a beautiful canvas, you know?"

Dr. Jacinta's chin flinched as if she were throwing up in her mouth a little. Then she sniffed and slid her thin fingers under her glasses to dab at the dampness. It occurred to me for the first time that my therapist might just have allergies. She changed the topic, asked about my latest dream. Wayne and I had been picking mushrooms together at the base of a huge tree. He'd started running around like a hellion, stomping the mushrooms to smithereens, disintegrating the flesh of their gills over the ground. (That struck Dr. Jacinta, that they looked like flesh to me.) I pulled out my dream notebook and read the rest to her:

> *"Wait, Wayne," I say. I kneel, putting my hands on your shoulders. "You're dead."*
>
> *"No, I'm not!" you scoff. You are still young. Your skin is smooth and brown. The whites of your eyes are spotless.*
>
> *"Yes, you are! You're dead," I say.*
>
> *"No I'm not!" you insist. "Pinch me!" You stick out your arm so I can clip my index finger and thumb around your skin.*
>
> *"Oh," I say.*
>
> *"See?" you say.*

I looked up from my notebook. Dr. Jacinta nodded and explained to me again that these dreams weren't just dreams. They were a symptom of what she called "ambiguous loss," which is when there is a death but no body. Like the visions of the crumbling boy I'd had when it happened, she said, this was a structure of "melancholia" or "bad mourning": a rhythm of loss and replacement that would endlessly repeat until I accepted Wayne's death. I didn't know how to "accept death," though. I still don't and I don't really care to. Death is quite literally unacceptable, unreasonable, unimaginable. Imagining death would presuppose a consciousness that death itself would negate. Dr. Jacinta nodded when I said all of this but seemed irritated by my philosophizing. She changed the topic again.

"Have you spoken to your father recently?"

"Nope. He's still in Savannah. Seeing this lawyer woman. I think she's Vietnamese or something? Also? I've decided that my mom can go fuck herself with this name thing."

≈

Over the years, my mother had become more shrill with her grievances. And now she had a new cause to latch on to. Her mother, my grandmother Rose, was dying. She was only in her sixties, but as long as I could remember, Grandma Rose had had cancer. "It is almost my familiar," she would say with a sad smirk. She had lost both breasts to it early on, which, in her ebullient way, she had taken as an occasion to get fake tits two bra sizes bigger. Every time I visited her, I would forget to pack for how cold it gets in Northern California and I would end up borrowing one of her sweaters and we would laugh together at the loose pouches over my chest that Grandma Rose's silicone bulbs had stretched into it.

Now the cancer was back and spreading. Whenever I came home from school or from Dr. Jacinta's, my mother would be sitting at the kitchen table, waiting for me to make yet another call to San Francisco. I resented this. Grandma Rose would pick up the phone all cheery and snarky, sounding like the grandmother I knew and loved for all of five minutes before disappearing into a quietness bred of pain, drugs, fatigue. Lately, my mother had been trying to get me on board with a name change on Grandma Rose's behalf. My mother wanted me to change my last name from my father's surname, Williams, to her maiden name, Lockett, which would otherwise soon be lost, as she was Grandma Rose's only child.

"It's the least you can do, Cassie," my mother said. "We don't even have to change it officially. You could just start using it. We could tell your teachers. Your friends."

"But I like the name Williams. Lockett? Ugh. It's so . . . symbolic."

"You'd think you could do this one thing to honor your grandmother's line."

"Grandma Rose doesn't even want me to! It's not even her real name. It's her ex-husband's name. I never even met him!" I was pacing the kitchen, clearing plates and washing mugs and wiping counters. I often cleaned while we argued. It contained things.

"It's my maiden name." My mother crossed her arms, a parody of indignation.

"You take it then!"

"You know perfectly well why I can't take it."

"Why not?"

"He has to be able to find us."

For a moment, I thought she meant my father and was stung with guilt. But then I realized this was absurd—of course my father knew how to find us. He'd moved to Savannah, not Mars. No. My mother meant Wayne. Rage rose in me and I picked up and threw the nearest thing, a dishtowel that made a disappointing *poof* against the counter. This was the oldest of my mother's missions: to be ready, always, for her dead boy's return. To be vigilant. I had quit trying to convince her that this was impossible years ago. I knew my role; I knew by now to lie. I calmed myself, as Dr. Jacinta advised, by counting to ten, then sat at the table next to my mother. She was crying.

"Don't worry, Mom. He'll find us." The words were like gutterwash in my mouth.

It's like swimming. You stroke and kick to get to the outermost edge of the wave. You feel the momentum: go on go on go on. But always, something tugs you back into the scooped water, the furrows, those relentless grooves. This is the incomplete, repeated shape of it: sail into the brim of life, sink back into the cave of death, again and again.

≈

Around then, I began to insist on both Williams and C., which I used to avoid the awkwardness of not knowing whether the second syllable of Cassandra should rhyme with *sang* (the white pronunciation) or with *song* (the black one). I also began to practice my signature. Now, as an adult, scratching random lines at the bottom of rent checks and credit card receipts, I often marvel at how much rehearsal I put into this obsolescent skill. But if required to sign something more important—a will, a legal document—I know my fingers have the blood of that movement coursing through them, that body knowledge: how to sign "C. Williams" into legitimacy. At seventeen, that last year of high school, my signature became my standard doodle, littering envelopes, books, folders. I once even cut it in miniature— with a safety pin and a mirror—into the back of my knee.

J saw it. I was lying on my belly in the hollow, pretending to read Proust while the other cutters lazed and joshed around me. A cool finger ran across the scab-puckered skin under my hem. I looked back and saw J kneeling beside my splotchy thrift-store boots. He glanced at our friends, licked his finger, and ran his finger again across the signature I'd etched. A transitive kiss. He winked slowly and I saw a new cut above his eyelid. I winked back the only way I knew how, by closing both eyes and opening one. He stood and strode off, the sunlight hugging to him, a perfect fit.

A couple of days later, the phone rang. I picked it up in the kitchen.

"Cee?"

"Yeah?"

The expectant silence was an empty corridor. I felt a chill and a warmth all at once. It was J.

"Oh! Um, hi!"

"Um, hi!" He echoed me, mocking me but in a kind way. He'd never called me on the phone before. "So, remember how we were talking the other day?"

My blink in reply to his wink. Did that count? There had been another encounter. I had bumped into him in the hall, and my chewing gum had dropped from my mouth onto the toe of his Doc Marten. We'd both stared at it for a second before I'd bent sheepishly to pluck it off. In my hurry to make it disappear, I had made it worse—by popping it back into my mouth. "Oops!" I'd blurted and raced off to gym class, trailing disgrace like exhaust fumes.

"Um, yeah, I remember?" I said cautiously.

"I really liked what you said."

I smiled and picked up a pen and signed the back of the Yellow Pages on the counter. I thought I could hear him smiling back through the phone.

"I liked what you said, too," I said. I signed the Yellow Pages again. The silence clicked wider, like someone had cracked a window in the corridor.

"Mom?!" I asked, aghast. She had picked up the receiver in the living room.

"Hello? Oh, sorry!" she said. "I need to make some Vigil calls, Cassie. Hi Val!"

J laughed.

"Whoops! That's not Val!" my mother said.

"Mom!" I cried.

J hung up.

"Ugh!" I said, curling my fist around the pen and stabbing the phonebook with it.

"What?" my mother said knowingly.

She and I berated each other over the phone, our voices

echoing in real time from the adjoining rooms. This was our way—a normal quarrel darkening quickly with everything between us. Eventually, the whining dialtone broke up into a plaintive beeping. But we gave up shouting only when the lady came on the line and politely advised us to please hang up and try again.

≈

Dear Wayne. We're in the mall, in the food court. The skylight above is murky. The seated customers stare at us, slack-jawed, limp-handed, their food lumped on red trays. We're on a stage of some kind. You're in a suit and a top hat, a dapper seven-year-old. I'm in a cardboard box, my head popping out one side, my legs out the other. This feels normal, allowed, a magic show. You make an announcement to the audience, secretly pinching my thigh so I know that you're here and you know that I'm here. There's clapping. You lean over my face and whisper in my ear. "Ready?"

I nod. "Wait. When did you come back?"

"I never left!"

Relief washes up my spine, from my tailbone to the top of my head.

"Wait," I say. "Is this a—?" I look up at you. You're pointing a gun toward the skylight. It's black and heavy and too big for your small brown hand.

"Don't worry, Cee," you say without looking at me. "It's just roses and

my heart, beating hard. A pure, absent moment, a gap in the weave, solace: He's alive. Then loss, sharp and smooth, piercing through, pulling a thread of rage behind it: He's dead. One second, then another, each stitching me back into time, into a before and an after and no folds. The dreams all had different tones and intervals, but the same beats, like a knockknock joke. Or a backward knockknock joke: first the punchline ("I'm back!") and then variations on the hook ("Who's back?") and finally, that knockknocking against the inside of my ribs.

I tried to ease myself back to sleep but then a real knock came to my bedroom door.

"Come in," I slurred.

My mother stepped into the room, clutching a big book with both her hands: it was the phonebook, my doodles like inky lesions on the cover. She was going on and on, *How could you, how dare you, do you think it's funny . . .*

"What are you talking about?" I wormed myself out of bed, walked over, and lugged the phonebook from my mother's hands into the cradle of my own forearm. I looked down at it. "I don't get it." My eyes and voice were still furry with sleep. "It's the phonebook?"

"Why would you do this, Cassie?"

"Mom, it's a doodle. It's my signature. I know it's not Lockett, but—"

"It's-not-your-name, goddammit."

I stared at it, seeing nothing but my own handwriting. My mother grabbed the phonebook out of my hands again, and it flexed in a thick curve, its pages clinging like layers of skin. She held it up, and took one step back, two, and there it was, *whatshisname, walks on water,* the word we no longer said to each other: *Wayne Wayne Wayne,* it said, enormous across the cover in witchy letters. I gasped. She slammed the book on the floor and walked out. I had a moment of suspicion—I remembered those plagiarized stick figures she had drawn behind the furniture after Wayne died—but there was no denying my handwriting or his name. I had absolutely no memory of writing it. I still don't. I suppose I must have scrawled it there while deep in the heady distraction of a boy on the phone.

≈

He called only once more, months later.

"Cee?"

"Hey."

We breathed in the staticky stillness. I worked a kink out of the spiraled cord.

"I wanna rape you."

He said it as if it weren't the first time he'd said it or thought it, like it was rehearsed. Pleasure imploded in the base of my belly. I was so shocked by the feeling that I hung up. But it was a scene I began to rehearse whenever I touched myself.

It would be many years more before I realized that it had been Caleb who had called me, Caleb who had wanted me, who had wanted to "rape" me. Goofy, stoner Caleb. All that time I had thought my secret phone admirer was J, who continued to flirt with me unrepentantly even as he managed to get Liz knocked up by the end of senior year. They had a shotgun wedding that summer. I went, of course. I drank with them and toasted them and hated them and never spoke to those people again. Over time, I knew, all of them would sour inside their flawless skin, like waxed fruit at the supermarket.

≈

Dear Wayne. Your foot's in a cast, like the time you got it stuck in the spokes of your bicycle wheel and twisted your ankle. An accident, you explain as we walk along the sidewalk at dawn. You're on crutches, swinging beside me with the rhythm of a veldt animal.

"Wait." I glance down at your heartshaped hairline. "You're dead, aren't you?"

"Everybody *thought* I was dead," you correct me pedantically. "I was just away, on a trip."

"A trip?"

"Yeah!" you say. "This is our reunion."

"Wait." I turn to you.

"What?"

"This is another dream, isn't it?"

"No!" You shake your head, a sitcom kid, all exasperation. "I'm alive! Obviously." You prop yourself on one crutch and stick your arm at me, give me a look. "Pinch me."

I know you want me to feel your flesh, its teeming, living thickness. But I won't. Not this time. You shrug and give a laugh, quick and reticulated as a cat's purr. You swing on ahead of me into the gaping light. Over your shoulder, you call out once, a mockingbird.

"You're nuts!" you say.

And I believe you.

8

≈≈≈

I'm on a tour of a studio lot, a perk from a potential Vigil donor. I've been in meetings with her people for a week and it's the day before I'm about to leave. The lot is mostly empty. I try to imagine the people who are usually here: directors, extras, stars. This is part of the point, I suppose: to look around and picture busy, beautiful faces shifting in and out of focus in front of these caramelized facades. I wonder how it would feel to work here, or even live here. There's a movie where they did that—real people living inside a giant illusion—but I can't remember its name. I see in my mind only Jim Carrey's big white teeth, blank and expectant as the squares on *Wheel of Fortune*.

The people in this tour group don't cohere, which is probably normal. There's an older white guy with four strands of hair he's combed over his pate. There are two middle-aged white women, who are sisterly in the way of sisters who live in the same town and have maintained their family culture; they wear clothing of the same genre: canvas shoes, tan slacks, flowery impressionist blurs on their blouses. There's a family—Chicano or Salvadoran—a husband, wife, young boy, and younger girl, all with a stifled, harassed air. There's another white guy, this one in his mid-twenties, in a business suit too hot for the weather. He wears glasses that darken into sunglasses whenever he comes out of the shade and asks endless questions in an authoritative tone. The guide, a portly Asian woman whose backward walk is pleasingly graceful and has an impressive command of our names, has to repeat the man's queries in a shout so her answers will make sense to everyone else. There's me. And there's the man dressed in dark blue jeans, a pastel button-down shirt, and a black and orange baseball cap. He would seem corporate, a businessman on vacation, if it weren't for his shoes, brilliant white hightops. His grin is wide and prolific. He's beautiful— a category beyond handsome—and this makes me feel both susceptible and suspicious.

He sidles up to me when the tour stops in front of the fake ice-cream parlor. Under the hilly sound of the guide's voice—up and down, up and down—he makes a joke about cherries. I conjure two alternative lives for myself. In one, his comment offends me enough that I tell him to fuck off. In the other, I flirt back until we achieve a delicious camaraderie. Instead, in this life, I smile stiffly and turn away. I always picture these forking paths of transgression but I can never rise to the occasion of slipping into one. My deviance is too buried, too inwardly directed.

By the time we get to the Ferris wheel, which is fully functioning but out of service, my demurrals have allowed a pattern to emerge between me and this man. He makes rough jokes. I smile and turn away. He's teenagery in his teasing, not standoffish or drywitted the way I'd expect. It's frustratingly unclear, actually, whether he's coming on to me or not, an ambiguity that titillates me more than I want to admit.

The tour group shuffles into a Western set, a saloon. It is nothing like the slick-surfaced bar I went to last night, which had lamps that cast light upward and fountains that dribbled over stones in the background. But the set is still somehow reminiscent of a dating scene. I imagine people dressed to the nines standing at the long mahogany bar. They hold a drink in one hand and gesture with the other, as if weighing possibilities, equating pleasures.

This fake saloon, the guide says with a rote peppiness, has appeared not only in several Westerns (old and new), but also in two dance films from the eighties and an indie movie in which the characters visit a new bar retrofitted to look like an old bar. The younger white guy smiles at his phone. I feel unnerved by the desultory staleness of the place, the sawdust like talc under our feet. The tall, beautiful man leans in toward me to make another joke—I catch the word "lasso"—and I move out of earshot. I'm more skittish here, perhaps because of the aura of awkward mating rituals. He again steps toward me, sawdust wafting, and again I shift.

Too far. He doesn't walk away but he cuts off the seeking energy he's been sending toward me. I hadn't meant to end the dance quite yet. As soon as it's gone, I miss it, long for it even. I push the feeling aside—this man has me too off-kilter for a stranger—and press forward as if fascinated by the funfacts tumbling out of our guide, as if amused by the widely held difficulty of bursting through swinging doors.

When the tour moves on to the hangar-like structure of the soundstage and the guide begins to hold forth on its uses, history, peculiarities, I head to the ladies' room I glimpsed next to the saloon, more for the brief peace of solitude than out of any pressing need. I take my time, reapply my lipstick, linger on my face in the murky mirror, trying to see what the man would have seen, trying to see the trace of my yearning. I leave the bathroom, then the building, and inhale the air outside deeply— I always hold my breath in public restrooms.

Across the faux-cobbled street, a marquee curves toward me. It's a movie theater set or maybe a large screening room. It's garish and I wonder how I didn't notice it before. Warmth emanates distantly from it, the goggle-eyed bulbs around its edges lit up despite the sun. The marquee sign reads THE GRIFTERS, the E's reversed for some kind of noir effect, and beneath, TRUE ROMANCE. The empty glass-paned ticket booth looks like a tiny lighthouse. I walk toward it, my footsteps muffled by flat red carpet. I look up at the rash of bulbs embedded in the overhang. Some of them are out and for a moment, I seek an inverse constellation, but there's no discernible pattern. I peer through scratched plexiglass at the old, lurid posters, the curves of the movie star bodies, the movie star fonts. I assume the theater is locked: the guide has been expertly unlocking doors all afternoon with a bulky set of keys.

So I'm surprised when one of the doors opens, and even more surprised that I pushed at it in the first place. The lobby is dark but for the faint glow of an electric sign: a red-and-white-striped box with an orgasmic spray of popcorn. There's another booth-like object in here, also glass-paned from the waist up, but harboring a mass grave of stuffed animals and a dangling silver claw that looks like it should be swinging. I remember this game from bowling alleys. I search my purse for change for too long before it occurs to me that the machine's fake, a prop, and will likely just swallow my money.

I step into the theater itself, the door with its porthole window rocking closed behind me. It smells musty and sweet, like buttery dust. Blinking at the darkness as if to dispel it, I walk down the easy slope. As my eyes adjust, I can make out a mechanical mess on the floor, right beneath the screen. It's film equipment: rivets and spools and ladders, objects I can decipher as microphones and lamps. The screen itself is blank, framed on either side by plush curtains. I turn to look up into the darkness behind me and see that the projection booth is alive with light. Maybe there's someone here. Maybe there's a screening. Maybe that's why I decide to sit down.

I find the spot I always want and never get because I never buy tickets in time: right in the middle of the theater. The wooden chairs are in rows of about a dozen. They have no arms, and their seats are flipped up like they're hugging their knees. I use my ass to push one open and sit. The sound of the hinge creaking and the seat clunking flat is loud in the dark. The screen seems to ripple. The theater is just big enough to give the impression of an audience. A camera could pan around a couple dozen extras crunching snacks, gazing at the screen instead of the movie stars! right there! pretending, in all their beauty, to watch a movie, which is, of course, a movie of themselves in a theater watching a movie . . .

I lean back and close my eyes. There's a cinematic sense of anticipation but maybe everyone feels this way nowadays. Life seems both monotonous and constantly interrupted, a punctuated heartmonitor line of events, with maybe some befores and afters on either side of the peaks. Time doesn't creep like a worm or fly like an arrow anymore. It erupts. It turns over. Shocks. Revolutions. Cycles. On TV, online, in the prosthetic minds we carry in our hands. It's as if something immense or catastrophic is always on the cusp of happening. Everything feels asymptotically dramatic, on the verge, as if only a disaster could undo that universal first disaster: being born at all. We are all heroes of cataclysm now.

I think of something Caleb, my secret admirer from St. Ant's, my aspiring rapist, once said. He had confessed that he often walked around wanting to punch people in the face.

"You fantasize about starting shit?"

"No, it's like—I'm a hero. I save people. I stop someone from hurting someone else. It's always like some fucked-up situation, and I just walk up and knock someone out."

"Dude. You're such a dude."

"Girls don't wanna be a hero?"

Well. I often imagine violence, yes. But it's a knife sliding steadily into the back of my neck or the dead center of my forehead, or dragging under the tender swell of my breast. Does that make me a hero, of a kind? The name Hero comes from a woman, as I learned in a women's rights class. She was a priestess who threw herself into the sea when her son drowned. Or was it her lover? Either way, *hero* should be a mourning word. I think of my mother, hero to thousands of women, mourning for her loss, suffering for theirs.

"Hey."

My eyes snap open and I freeze. Am I imagining it? It feels like when you hear a voice call your name right when you're about to fall asleep . . .

"I didn't mean to—"

"Who's there?" My voice sounds cowed.

"I'm right behind you."

I turn. The beautiful man from the tour is sitting there. I stand up, my purse strap already on my shoulder. He tilts his head and crosses his arms.

"I'm not trying to bother you." His voice says he doesn't mean it.

"Listen," I say, "this is a little creepy, you following me in here like this."

"Actually, I was here first. Seems like you're the one following me."

"Yeah, okay, whatever." I roll my eyes. "Why don't I leave you to it then?" I sidle my way down the narrow row, my knees bumping the chairs in my haste, knockknocking on the wood as if for good luck.

"Wait."

"What?" I turn to him.

"C, right?"

He smiles and I know. It's Wayne.

Everything buckles: my knees under me, the seats beside me, the floor beneath us, the air in my lungs, all of it breaks up and out. There's a trundling sound of staccato blows, then a high-pitched squeal. The projection booth shatters tinnily above us and I'm on my hands and knees, searching for purchase, for solid ground across which to crawl. An alarm barks rhythmically and I hear the man calling for me in the pauses between blasts. I feel a touch. It's his hand groping along my body to find my arm, which he grabs, pulling me to my feet. We're in the main aisle now, his face in mine, he's yelling: "We have to get out of here!" His mouth is so close, I can smell his breath: almond, berry, a darker earthy scent.

A boom slams the air and we hear the groaning thunderousness again, trailed by creaking, cracking noises. He pulls me along, the ground is unsteady beneath us, the earth's center has melted, everything shifts and we stagger. The edge of a seat bites into my side. My foot catches something metal and I stumble, twisting my body at the last second to avoid tumbling headfirst. My purse slips from my shoulder. I curse and let go of his hand to reach for it and when I turn back, he's gone. There's a scrim of smoke ahead of me in the aisle and he has disappeared into it. I taste blood in my mouth and a heavy, broken thing crashes down and lands in the aisle in front of me—the smooth stomach and crosshatched tail of a mermaid statue. I look up to see where it fell from. A baroque chandelier is swinging with abandon.

I understand that I can see more than I should be able to—it's too bright for this space—at the exact moment that I feel the heat and smell the smoke. I scramble to my feet. The theater is coming into focus, blooming in the light of the flames. There are frescoes on the walls. The curtains are pink felt. There are unusable balconies above, from which delicate burning trash drifts down now, like autumn leaves. I hear a shout. The man is standing by a neon E X I T sign, spectral in the smoke. His hands are cupped around his mouth but I can't make out a word.

The rows of seats to my side erupt upward in an arc, giving off a sound like a bowling ball hitting pins. That's when he runs back to me, his arms outstretched as if in a parody or a dream. It's him. I know it. The knowledge spins through me like the gyred light in a marble held up to the sun. Swaying, I turn my head and look back down to the front of the theater, where the screen is flapping and twisting as flames clamor up its edges. He reaches me and grabs my hand. The fire begins to roll toward us, rising in a towering wheel that swiftly surmounts the intervening space, closing in as we run.

9

≈≈≈

My little brother died when I was twelve. He was seven. We were at the park, just the two of us. This was allowed. This was every Sunday. In the late afternoon, before dinner, the two of us would walk alone together to the park a few blocks from our house in Pikesville. It was a paltry park—a rusty playground and a sandpit surrounded by messy green, one end edged by a grove of pine trees—but it served its purpose. Wayne and I would throw a Frisbee around or kick a soccer ball between us as evening grew its shadows on the unkempt grass.

One time, we flew a kite, a flashy silky thing shaped like a fish that Grandma Lu had given Wayne for his birthday. It took a while to get the hang of it but we had a good hour watching it shimmy in the breeze before it got stuck in a tree. Wayne and I circled, gawping up at it for a while, then shrugged and left it for the birds. When we got home, our mother was livid. She stomped around, raging about how much it had cost and how I was older and should have known better. I was certainly old enough to know the real reason that our mother was mad. Without fail, Grandma Lu would ask about it—a special gift for her special boy—on her next visit. And our mother would have to answer.

This Sunday was different because of the carousel. Our mother had read about it in the local weekly paper, *The Bee's Wax*.

"Well, would you look at that," she said at breakfast. "There's a carousel at the park this week. It's on its way to the state fair in Annapolis. They had it in New Jersey for repairs and I guess they figured they'd make some money hiring it out on its way back."

"Is it broken?" Wayne's eyes widened.

"No, honeybaby, not anymore. They fixed it."

"Is it fast?" Wayne's eyes narrowed.

"For you it is," I mumbled.

Wayne was quiet but his body buzzed. My father smiled.

"Why don't you two go check it out this afternoon?"

I sighed. The park was beginning to lose interest for me. Wayne was the ideal playground age: still young enough to enjoy the swingsets and slides, just old enough to feel a new authority over the other kids. These days, he released his energy with the steady concentration of something battery-operated. He would stalk the perimeter of the equipment, command and advise the smaller kids, find a king's peace seated alone in the sandpit. I would leave him there and take melancholy strolls next to the woods. If it was early fall, the season beginning to singe the trees, I might hunt for a perfect leaf.

I had a vague idea that this Sunday would be like that but when we got to the park that afternoon, it was less empty than we'd ever seen it. The carousel had drawn a crowd. Enterprising vendors had set up stalls for those summery foods that all seem to have an essential ingredient of air: cotton candy, soda, beer, popcorn. Mothers herded their toddlers and fathers stood in clusters, chomping at the nothing-food. The kids were in a frenzy at the mere prospect of riding a carousel. There was already a line for it, impatient children snaking around the adults' legs or stomping alongside.

I looked on in despair. No one my age was here—it was all grown-ups or babies. I lamented, not for the first time, our mother's tendency to delegate to me the duty of taking care of Wayne. He was tugging at my hand now, leaning toward the spectacle. Past the crowd, we could make out the peaked roof of the carousel, chains of bulbs lining its edges and stripes. If you squinted, the strings of light seemed to form a giant dewy spiderweb over it. We heard delighted screaming, a tinny song that sounded French to my quasi-educated ears, and a booming voice calling us to *come-one-come-all* in a circusy accent.

Wayne, canny as always, made a proposal. I would stand in the line and he would play on the monkeybars until I got to the front. To sweeten the deal, he gave me his allowance. I used our combined money to buy some cotton candy, a sticky pink afro bursting from a paper cone speckled with tiny images of Spider-Man. I plucked tufts off with my fingers. Wayne plucked tufts off with his mouth. When we were done, he carefully folded the cone and put it in his pocket, then headed off to the playground.

The sun was settling down. I waited in line, my lips tight with sugar. It felt as if I were on hold on the telephone, my mind unaware that it was unaware. I remember a slight undercurrent of desire running through me, but it could have been thirst or exhaustion or being twelve. The man in front of me began calling for his daughter, turning haltingly. The girl's rhyming name, Elaine, made me wonder after Wayne.

I rocked up onto my tiptoes to search among the bobbing bodies at the playground for his green T-shirt. There he was, his solid round skull stippled with his close shave. We hadn't brushed the naps curling at the nape today. Our mother always forgot that kind of thing. His brown bronzed by the end of summer, Wayne was a creature for my watching, for my keep. He turned and looked at me and a piece of his face crumbled off like sand.

I stumbled forward, my back arcing like a wave had knocked me from behind. I stepped out of the line to look closer. Not Wayne. Another boy—and not made of sand. It must have been a trick of the light, which was filtering through the pines, making slow sunset strobes over the grass. Little Elaine—dirty-blond, splotchy-pink—was now squirming in her father's arms. I went back to scanning the undercrowd for Wayne.

"Shit," I muttered.

"D'you just curse?" Wayne was at my side, grinning and sandy. "I'm gonna tell Mom."

"Where'd you go?" I squatted in front of him to line up our eyes. "Where were you?"

"Right here. Jeez, look around much?" He shook his head as if with disbelief.

I grabbed his wrist to pull him toward me. We resumed my place in line. After a while, my grasp loosened and slipped from his wrist to his hand as we inched forward in unison. As we got closer, we saw that the carousel was elevated on a wooden platform that backed onto the grove at the edge of the park. Metal barriers had been set up to form a U-shaped fence around it. Inside it, the parents of the kids on the ride hovered in a loose circumference, gazing up at the carousel with slack smiles. It was pretty fast. The brightly colored horses lifted and fell with a smooth piston motion. They looked edible, candycoated with elaborate braids and stirrups. The younger kids gripped the thick poles lanced through the horses' backs; the older kids were more cavalier—no hands, or just one.

When we reached the front of the line, we saw the man running the show. He was inside the enclosure, bent over to adjust levers sticking out of a black box bound by its own cords. The back of his orange shirt was a map of sweat. The carousel slowed, then came to a stop. The parents inside the fence climbed onto the platform to claim their kids, then filed out through a gap in the fence. The man moved a barrier to open another gap beside this exit and I saw that the front of his shirt read BARKER. His face was more tired than his shout.

"Come one, come all! World's best carousel! Taller than the monkey, shorter than the giraffe! Next in line, step up to the sign! Between the monkey and the giraffe, folks!"

Wayne held my hand as he stood before the goofy, faded sign. The barker nodded and let us into the fenced enclosure. We climbed onto the wooden platform and moved to the inner ring of horses. I lifted Wayne awkwardly—"You're so *heavy* now," I groaned—until he was high up enough to straddle a purple horse with a mane of gold. Wayne giggled, giddy, sliding his butt from side to side to feel out the traction of the saddle. I got down from the platform and stood with the parents inside the fence, shaking my head at his anticipatory glee. His head hung back as he laughed, his hands glued to the pole.

The carousel began to turn. The horses rose and fell, rose and fell, in alternation. The carousel turned faster and soon my eyes were whirring madly as I tried to keep up with its spin. I forced my vision to go out of focus to see if its motion came anywhere near the true gallop of horses. It didn't. I felt happy and bored. There was no reason to count how many times Wayne's purple horse plunged up into view, how many times he waved his small hand at me, how many times I waved back with a smile. The sun was sending up its last rays, but the air was still soft and curved with warmth. Some of the bulbs strung over the carousel gave off more light than others: brighter and lesser moons. The French-ish song went up and down and round and round. Wayne whisked past, his neon-green shirt a flash, his waving hand a blur. I needed to pee. I crossed my legs at the thigh and hit my wrist against my hipbone to distract my bladder. I saw the wind stir the tops of the trees.

"Stand clear! Riders, rein in your horses! Whoa, whoa!" The barker reached under the platform and manipulated the levers in the black box. The carousel began to slow.

"Cee!" Wayne was waving, shouting for my attention as he passed. I waved back as he came around. The shape of him grew starker with each slower spin, as if my vision were holding him tighter. Once, twice, he came clear, then clearer. And then he was gone. Just gone, like a light switched off.

I stared intently as his high-stepping horse came past again, blank, riderless. I stepped toward the platform, still tracking it. "Oh god oh god oh god," I was saying but incredulity tweaked the corners of my lips.

≈

Dear Wayne. I don't want to tell you what happened. I want to tell you how it felt. You were safe in your circle, that lofting, sliding canter carrying you round. You couldn't have seen what was coming. The trees at the edge of the park shadowed your progress. The sun was chastened by the coming night, the moon beckoned by the bulbs above. Regal on your bridled beast, you couldn't have known that your joyful circle would spin fast and wide, that you'd be flung, sent out of life, as if hooks had caught you under the arms and snatched you.

≈

The carousel stopped with Wayne's empty horse on the far side. Parents climbed onto the platform to help their kids disembark, safe and sound. I joined them and strung my way through the tangle of creatures, human and horse, on the platform. I couldn't see Wayne anywhere. I hopped down off the platform and began tracking the inside perimeter of the fence to where the carousel backed onto the woods.

"Miss! You can't go back there!" the barker called out, his voice nasal and highpitched, no circusy boom now.

I walked quickly over to him, panic ricocheting through me. "My brother's gone. He's not on his horse."

The barker grinned. "Oh, I'm sure he just got down on his own. They do that sometimes. What's he look like?"

"He's got a green shirt on."

The barker stared at me blankly, then said, "Okay, gimme a minute. Stay right here."

He moved the barriers to close the gaps in the fence and announced that the carousel was closed for the evening. The music stopped; the lights went out. The people in line *aw*-ed and *boo*-ed and drifted in listless clumps, then gave up and dispersed. The barker bustled about, shutting things down and packing them up.

Then night had fallen and I was alone beside the carousel. A hot vibration filled my ears. How much time had passed? When had it gotten so dark? Where was Wayne? Where was the barker? He seemed to have forgotten about me. I climbed up onto the platform again. In the dark, the carousel was like a beached spaceship, shadowy and buzzing and ticking. My eyes were burning dry—I willed myself not to blink lest I miss something—as I peered into that jumble of poles and limbs, my hand moving from horse to horse. They were slippery to the touch, still warm as if from the recently departed riders. I pushed past their flanks, their striding, rearing legs, their long heads, their round eyes, their black nostrils. They snickered—no, whimpered. I turned my head toward the sound and saw a glimpse of green.

Most of his body was under the carousel but his shoulder was visible, wedged between a tree and the platform. I couldn't fathom how he could have fallen and gotten stuck there. "I'm coming!" I cried as I scrambled off the platform and crouched to peer into the gap beneath it. It was so dark but I could make out the dull glow of his green shirt. I flung myself to the ground—so hard I bruised myself—but I couldn't squeeze under the platform. I lay out on my belly and reached forward until my fingertips brushed something hard and wet—his arm or leg, broken. I flinched reflexively. The whimpering stopped.

Knowledge rushed up in me then, *ssth*-ing into me, and I felt a flurry at the base of my throat. I stretched my arm deeper under the platform, straining it at the shoulder until I could wrap my fingers around the hard wet thing—it was his forearm— and pull. Wayne shifted, in a bad way, a dead-weight way, and suddenly, the barker was next to me, wriggling his arms under the platform, shouting commands at me as we tugged Wayne out together until he was between our kneeling bodies.

It was dark there in the shadow of the woods, but I could smell my brother—his blood and his cotton-candy sweetness and the soil we had overturned when we dragged him—and I could see his green shirt, wrenched above his belly, and I could see, too, that he was all wrong, the angles of him. I felt my bladder give way, droplets of urine seeping into my underwear. The barker put a hand on Wayne's chest, then hovered it over his mouth. He shook his head. "Nothing," he said. "You'd better go and fetch the barker."

I stood up dizzily, blinking at the man I had thought *was* the barker, seeing now that he was shorter, and wearing not that sweaty orange shirt with its helpful label but a skyblue windbreaker. I turned and ran, the pumping of my muscles a relief after the cramp of crouching to pull Wayne free. It took me a minute—or longer, even a minute was too long—to find the real barker. "Mister!" I shouted. "My brother!" He was a few yards past the carousel, coming out of a port-a-potty—the sight of it made my bladder swell again—sucking on a cigarette. He saw my face and broke into a heavy jog, his label jiggling on his chest. He followed me as I turned and ran back to the windbreaker man and my dead brother.

But they weren't there. There was just the shallowest trench in the ground, the groove we'd made when we'd pulled Wayne's body through the dirt. I felt feverish as I crept in a hunched circle around it in disbelief. Just as the barker reached me, I saw something just inside the woods: blue or gray, rippling with sharp folds—the stranger's windbreaker. It looked grimy but newly so—recently dropped. I ignored the barker panting with questions beside me, and used a branch to lift it up. Under it was our Spider-Man cotton-candy cone, rimmed with something dark. I dropped the branch and raced into the woods, calling my brother's name.

10

≈≈≈

My father told me much later how he hunted that man down, the man with the skyblue windbreaker. It was the summer before I went to college. My mother and I had a horrendous fight and she forced me to go visit my father and his new family in Georgia. *Horrendous, forced*—these are exaggerations. My generalized fury as a teenager often stretched reality, and then that's how I remembered it, so it stayed stuck in its distorted, hyperbolic form. The fight with my mother had been trivial in fact, banal. I had gotten my nose pierced—a small silver ring in one nostril—without asking her permission.

I had gone alone to the mall, no one to help choose the ring, no one to hold my hand through it. Only me for the cool of the alcohol, the clamp of the piercing, the cluttered store glowing from the euphoric excruciation, the pain swimming in adrenaline. I had the shakes afterward, my pulse visible. The guy who worked at the store made me stay until the blood had stopped bubbling from the hole and swallowing the ring. I remember that his eyes were silver and that, as he watched me bleed, they held a mixture of something less than patience and more than curiosity.

Waiting for the blood to coagulate made me late to the Vigil session that day. My mother's foundation had been around for a few years but it was still a janky affair. This was before she received the inheritance from Grandma Rose that would change her tax bracket. Back then, the group met weekly at the neighborhood rec center across from the mall. During my summers, I helped host the bereft mothers. They were mostly white, all middle-class enough to afford to keep looking for their kids. My job was to give out doughnuts and coffee, cookies and lemonade, greetings and pity. I can still remember the roll call of loss, the litany: Jeanie (Jake, nine years old, three years ago); Zee (Jane, eight years old, six months ago); Toni (Billie, seventeen years old, seven years ago); Jen (Rob, fifteen years old, five years ago). The Vigil Aunties, I called them.

The day of my piercing, I burst out of the placid light of the mall into cloudy weather, and ran across the parking lot to the rec center, mumbling an apology and tugging at the hem of my miniskirt as I entered the dull drear of that room. Voices lowered; eyebrows lifted. The skirt had seemed adorable in front of the mirror that morning—just the thing for a day of solitary ritual adornment—but it felt obscene in front of these women. It wasn't explicit, their judgment, but it wasn't unfounded, either.

I had gotten over my insular adolescent crushes and now relished being noticed, having realized that my legs made up for my chest, that the inward incline of my knees was fashionable, that my ambiguous shade of brown was desirable. And now I'd pierced my nose, moving further into the aura of being seen. The eyes of older men like the jewelry store guy still intimidated me but I was starting to enjoy even that edge, to flirt with it.

I don't know if it was because I was late or because my mother was wrecked as ever from her endless seas of insomnia and grief. I'm sure the nose ring tipped her over. (Her permissiveness had the arbitrary rules of the white middle class: tattoos were cool, piercings trashy; bras were oppressive, mini-skirts slutty.) She and I turned on each other in front of the shocked Vigil Aunties. I don't remember all that we said, or how we got from fashion to Wayne and whether or not he was dead. I remember only the echoing hiss of the word *disrespect* and her final pronouncement:

"Don't you see?" she shouted. "If he's still alive, it means *you* didn't kill him!"

The room fell silent, as if this electric sparring had shorted everything. I stared at the carpet. My nose was throbbing on the outside, buzzing on the inside. I had always believed I was the one taking care of my mother, placating her by muting the inevitable question: "Where were *you* that day, Mom?" But on that stormy summer day that smelled of metal—the blood, the ring, the lightning in the air—I wondered if, all this time, my mother had thought that she was the one saving me, not from guilt, but from the blame that she secretly held under her tongue, and that, if uttered, would cast me out completely, put me in a place where she could no longer love me. The world is never what you think it is. It can turn over and expose itself to be the exact opposite.

My mother and I didn't fight in the car on the way home, nor once we arrived. But after a few days, she told me she had bought me a plane ticket to visit my father. This was a first. My father had quietly married a Vietnamese-American lawyer, Linda, whom he had met while applying for a waste-absorption patent. Her daughter from her previous marriage, Josephina, was a couple of years younger than me and lived with them in Georgia. I'd seen pictures of them—the courthouse wedding, tacky holiday cards—but we hadn't met in person. We were all in unspoken agreement that there was no need to, that it would breach some etiquette, some sacred line between old and new.

Or so I'd thought. Did my mother send me to Savannah as a punishment? Maybe she knew what my father was going to tell me. Maybe in the clang and bash of that fight at the rec center, she'd remembered that my father had always claimed that he believed me. Maybe she wanted me to know that he hadn't, not completely.

≈

I slept uneasily on the flight. Plane sleep always feels to me like a form of restless thinking. The thoughts are like links in a chain, then the chains start pulling you by the wrists as you stagger along, picking up speed until you start to jog, race, careen and this is how turbulence becomes the bumpiness of a road that I'm rattling along in a giant vehicle, massive firs on either side casting occasional shadows within (my dream making sense of people passing down the aisle), my mind skimming the surface of sleep like a wake in water, lightly enough that it churns up real events into surreal dreams.

In this one, you're sitting across the aisle, smirking, seven years old, and the shadows become tendrils that swarm up our legs, biting us, itching us, they're glass noodles, they're the worms you use for bait (my dream accounting for my father's Vietnamese-born wife and his offer to take us fishing), the tendrils are gray and translucent and they range in size from the tiny smeared line of a bug you've slapped dead to as thick and as long as an arm, and I don't know how to stop the shadows from swarming you, though you don't seem too bothered by them, you let them curlicue around your fingers, your arms, your legs like living-dead vines, so I decide to trick them, I take a tiny chunk of flesh from my nose piercing and place it in a bowl, Grandma Lu's silver mixing one, and the shadow worms promptly gather inside it and form a tangled lump, like when you turn a pot of old spaghetti upside down, and the lump licks slickly with movement, the shadow worms weaving and unweaving and growing even longer and thicker, and I realize the chunk of flesh has been seeded, the worms are hatching from it, my flesh is their origin point and I'm

sick to my stomach, breathing fast, the smell of the plane air like rotting lilies, my piercing gripped with scab from the dryness. Time to slow down, interpret my dream leisurely, shape it like a story. I'd had plenty of practice with this by that point in my life of the mind, so to speak. My latest therapist, Dr. Weil, had recently introduced me to a theory called "life span integration." The premise is that you make a story out of your life. You plot it to give yourself a sense of continuity. In the therapy, you zoom in on moments of trauma—where the line broke or knotted or looped—and undo them, give yourself a before and an after. You try to convince yourself that you did in fact survive, that life kept on keeping on even after everything seemed to fall apart.

The funny thing about it, though, is that you don't reconstruct your life as it actually happened; that would take too long. Instead, you design a fiction. First, Dr. Weil made me write a list: a single memory for each year of my life. Then, in session, I would close my eyes and conjure a vision of my deepest trauma: the moment I lost Wayne. I'd paint the scene in all its detail, immerse myself in all the feelings. Then I'd pause that scene, enter it as my current self, at eighteen, and rescue my twelve-year-old self from the situation. C and Cee would go off somewhere together, a safe place. And as Dr. Weil read out my list of memories to me, I'd convey to young me all of the events that had happened to us before and after the trauma so as to stitch our timeline back together. I chose to project them up on an imaginary screen in an outdoor movie theater, though I'd never been to one.

As usual, I submitted to this therapy while concealing my contempt for it. Pausing time? Two selves? And at the very end, I had to hug my younger self, let her "melt" into me, which seemed both unholy and redundant. What a metaphor! What a story! I did it, of course. I conjured as instructed. But each time I entered the past in my mind, I made the trauma into a drama. I burst up from the ground like an earthquake. I rained down from the sky above. I ran in and whisked off an astonished Cee, carrying her under my arm.

Eventually, I stopped seeing Dr. Weil. She threw me off by switching therapeutic modes, delving deeply into psycho-analytic structures of desire to explain what she called my "obsession" with Wayne. When she mentioned that Freud had connected sexual fetishes to unresolved mourning, I balked and canceled several appointments in a row. One day—I was in a particularly intense vortex, squatting half-naked on the kitchen floor—the phone rang and I gulped back my sobs and an-swered. It was Dr. Weil asking for my mother, something about a bill, an insurance claim. I hung up. When my mother eventu-ally got hold of the situation, I told her I wanted to stop seeing Dr. Weil. We fought about it, about the cost of changing thera-pists again, and now that I think about it, this was what laid the groundwork for that poisonous fight to bloom at the rec center.

≈

I hated that my mother had forced me to go to Savannah. It was a trap to make me do something I already wanted to do while she took credit for it. But being with my father felt crushingly good. It had been a long time but even the irritations were comfy. He had elected on a trip to the beach with me, his wife, and his stepdaughter—a family outing. Only on the way there, the four of us silent in the car as Britney Spears hiccuped and groaned through the speakers, did it seem to occur to him that this was not the brightest idea.

When we arrived, we suffered through that grim routine—man cursing as he searches for parking—until my father found a spot in a strip mall across the road from the shore. That's when it became clear that neither Linda nor Josephina was interested in the beach, not at all, not even in a "sit under an umbrella and drink cocktails" kind of way. As soon as he pulled up the brake, the mother and daughter hopped out and waltzed off together arm in arm, with barely a word to either of us. Though my father looked surprised, he soon brushed it off. He didn't seem to know where they were going or why they'd gone, but that was apparently not unusual for this new family.

I watched them walk away. They had been polite but distant with me so far. Neither was as I'd imagined, though I had seen pictures before and even spoken to them each on the phone for a few strained minutes at a time. Linda wore Birkenstocks, khaki knee-length shorts, and a stretchy white headband to hold her hair back. Absurdly, I had assumed she would be wearing a suit or business casual, probably because I associated her primarily with her job as a lawyer. Josephina wore Birkenstocks, too, and a lot of jewelry—not the pricey, glittery stuff, but that carefully considered morass of metal and leather and string that signifies "Bohemian" for girls too sheltered to have shopped at street stands or flea markets. Josephina had no doubt bought her Bohemia from a store at the mall—sorting through a throng of fake silver chiming in the AC breeze—a store much like the one that I had just visited to get my nose pierced.

My father and I took the beach things out of the trunk, coordinating the balance of their respective weight with our respective strength. I noticed that, as always, he started across the road without warning, without making sure it was safe for me. I decided not to play wounded and hustled after him. We set up on the beach. We had a couple of rusty beach chairs strung with ancient spiderwebs, striped towels in a basket, and a cooler packed with soda (which everybody here called Coke) and Wonder-bread sandwiches that would cling to our mouth roofs like barnacles. My father had put on weight, but only in his belly, which was round and brown, adorned with a few gray hairs. If it could have spoken, it would have spoken in chuckles. We lay back and covered our eyes with sunglasses.

It was hot but the sky was overcast in a nonchalant way—nothing too foreboding, just a tad gloomy. The sea stretched before us, just one blue, the wind casting ripples to our right. The sand was the same color as my skin, and where the water was wetting it, almost the same texture, too. I pulled my knees up and used my fingernails to unstitch the black thread-ends of ingrown hairs. My father bit at his lips, tugging dry slivers from them with his teeth. Both of us would sting later when we went into the water. But this was habit, comfort, this shedding and grooming without judgment. Everything was still. You could hear the uneven breath of the waves coming in and the cozy rush of cars driving by on the road behind us.

"How's your mother's business going?"

"It's not a business."

"I know," he said. "You know what I mean."

A coil of tension tightened under my breastbone. The organization for missing children that my mother had started in our kitchen had taken over our life, but had also centered it, given it stability. Vigil had come to feel like a younger sibling that I was both neglected for and made to babysit, like a new baby brother or a substitute for Wayne. That's the thing about the bad math of this family: you can shift the numbers but there's always something missing, something to carry. I'd been an unofficial and unpaid employee of Vigil for years—my mother grooming me to work for the foundation, I recognize now—but I was about to go to college. This meant that real money was going to enter the economy of our relationship, which had long trucked in the tender of resentment. The question of Vigil's "business" had become forever inseparable from questions of tuition, loans, work-study, even my major—and, implicitly, my future career.

"Vigil's fine, I think. It's good."

"Good." My father nodded with a frown-smile.

The clouds were low. A pelican swooped before us and began to circle. It was close enough that I could see its wide fringed span, the hook of its neck. It was mesmerizing to watch it flap desultory wings, waft expertly around, lift to a calculated height unknowable but to the bird, then plummet into the water. That moment of freefall—or the moment right before, when it decided to drop—made me feel a kind of envy.

I glanced over to see if my father was watching, too, but his eyes were hidden behind his shades, his hand smug on his belly. He was basking. What more could a man want? He wanted nothing; he wanted for nothing. Upon losing a beloved, some people become wanderers or seekers—the body catches the panicked roaming of the mind, sends them off. But after my father moved to Georgia, he settled in. He found work at an industrial chemistry lab and seemed to harbor no ambitions beyond earning his retirement. Linda, my mother, and I—probably Josephina, too—we all loved him, we craved the crook of his finger beckoning us. It seemed that what he felt for his new family was not love, but a tolerant fondness, and perhaps gratitude. I had no idea what he felt for me and my mother, after all this time. Watching him now, I was in awe of his un-botheredness. He had left us in the pit of death and gone on to conquer life. He had left behind our terrible itching urgency.

My itching had become literal lately. Apart from in-grown hairs, I was plagued with bouts of eczema, allergic reactions to wool and, worst of all, to metal—this was what finally made me stop cutting. My week-old nose piercing was not healing well, either. The skin around the ring was taut and hot, puckered like a tiny mouth. It bothered me that my mother might have been right about it being a bad idea.

"I mean, the whole thing is a lie," I said.

My father turned to me. "What do you mean, lie?"

It was a sign of how long we'd been apart that I had forgotten that *lie* wasn't a word I was allowed to use. I had only once heard it said in front of Grandma Lu, when I was ten or so. We had gone to her house in downtown Baltimore for Thanksgiving. We were all crowded around the table in a kitchen furnished in reddish wood and chrome fittings, except for my mother, who had begged off because of a migraine and slumped upstairs after dinner. The adult voices got loud and loose. Some debate or another started to spark and flare and Uncle Eddie pointed a finger at our father and said straight out:

"You a damn lie."

Just like that, no punctuation, the same emphasis on each word like a drumbeat. Wayne gasped. But Grandma Lu's lips only twisted to the side, with a kind of neutrality between disapproval and amusement, as she glanced up—at God or at my mother upstairs, I'll never know. True or not, something had been said. It stuck with me, most likely because it was ungrammatical—I was that sort of child; I'm still that sort of person. What did it mean to be a lie, your whole self? Certainly something different from telling a lie or being a liar.

And this was what I meant about my mother and Vigil now. Not that she was a liar, not even in the sense we like to bandy about in therapy-speak—"She's lying to herself." I meant that Charlotte and Vigil—again, I thought of them as coextensive, mother and child, if not exactly the same—I meant that the fundamental grief, the hole out of which Vigil had sprung, was deceptive. A false hole, a black oval painted on the ground.

I tried to explain all this to my father as the pelican flew up and up, mounting strata of wind before it banked and dove into a controlled splash, then rose again with its prey—or perhaps empty-mouthed. His response surprised me.

"So. What? You think she's wrong for hoping her son's still out there?"

"I'm saying it's fucked—it's messed up that the Vigil pamphlets say he's *missing*."

There was a pause. Then he said, "His body is missing. We know that much."

I stared at him, saliva going salty in my mouth. "But they closed the case," I said.

There was a longer pause. Sometimes when we stumbled onto speaking about Wayne during our phone conversations, my father would say, *Remember how he used to . . . Remember when you two would . . .* This felt different from how it was at home, where only my mother's memories counted, were recorded and curated and distributed. And it felt different from how it was in therapy, where I often had to introduce Wayne as a new character to a new audience. My father's occasional reminiscing never occluded my own. It made a shared swing of a conversation where our memories could gently jostle, one foot or the other nudging the ground to keep us going. I longed for this way of talking about my brother but never felt brave enough to start it myself, and this time, my father didn't set it in motion.

Instead, he hunched forward and said, "You know, I looked for that man."

I immediately knew whom he meant but I asked anyway. "What man?"

"The man who was there that day. The man you told us about."

"How?" I asked, then clarified: "How did you look for him?"

"Well." My father sounded confessional. "There was that jacket."

"The windbreaker?"

"I don't know why but—remember how I had to drive it over to the police?"

I thought. Yes, only after the police had left had I given the blue windbreaker to my father. I had forgotten it in my shock, in the stalled panic of relating my account. I nodded.

"I drove on down to the station that night with it. I had it in a plastic bag. They had told me not to touch it. But before I went inside, I held it in my lap and—"

I pictured him in the parked Buick, the lights from the dashboard and from the street making a spectacle of his face while he made decisions, the way men always seem to, alone.

"—I wrapped my hand in another plastic bag and I searched the pockets. I found these candy wrappers—clear cellophane.

And a receipt. It was so faded I couldn't barely read what it said but it was for a 76 gas pump. And there was a dry-cleaning tag stapled to the inside of the collar, too. Red, two staples. Number 9-2-7."

He said it with the ease of something memorized. I looked at him, blinking through the new information.

"I wrote all that down. I took one of the candy wrappers but I left the rest. I thought the police would do a better job finding him with the evidence."

I nodded, frowning.

"Anyhow, it became something to hold on to. To do. Focus on."

This was familiar. *We have to investigate.* I saw my mother at the kitchen table, looking up from a hazard of Post-it notes. My father knew what I was thinking. He shook his head.

"I didn't tell your mother. I didn't want her obsessing over things till I got my hands on something real, something tangible. You know how she gets. So I did it on my own."

The pelican swooped and plunged, swooped and plunged, as if on a loop. My father's voice was soft and insistent, like the sea's waves slithering shoreward, like a thousand, a million gray worms. He steadily talked me through the leads he had followed over the years. He had gone to every 76 gas station within a hundred-mile radius. He had checked to see what kind of candy they sold, and had bought every kind at least once to check the wrappers. He had asked the cashiers about security footage, about erratic customers.

"I even bought a gun."

"What?"

He turned to me and tilted his head. "What d'you think happened every time I went into a place like that, looking like I do, asking irregular questions? I just knew some old white

man or some immigrant was gonna get jumpy and pull out a
shotgun on me. But you know what?" He turned back to face
the sea. "It turned out the possibility of some kind of justice got
them on board right off the bat. When I told them what it was
all about, they wanted to help me find that man. Especially the
brothers."

Some kind of justice. I had always thought my father was on
my side in the war between me and my mother. He had been
fighting another war completely.

"Gas stations were a dead end. But the dry-cleaning ticket,
I actually found the place. I thought I did, at least. Bubble
Cleaners. Only place around Bethany that double-staples their
tickets. 9-2-7. Red: special code for a tough stain. The ticket
was newish. That narrowed it down some."

I saw the man with the blue windbreaker—not his face,
which was by now featureless, smooth as sea-washed stone. I
saw the shape of him. I smelled his shadow.

"You found him?"

"No. The cleaners wouldn't give me his name. Didn't trust
me. You know how it is."

"What were you gonna do when you found him?"

"When I *find* him," my father corrected. But he didn't answer my question. He just looked at the water. The pelican flustered around once more, and finally away. We watched it go.

"Rain's coming," my father said.

In the distance, beyond the waves, where the clouds hung
over the horizon, you could see the thinnest mist hanging down,
with the slant of a cliff face but sheer as gauze. It swayed between the glum canopy above and the blurred line of the sea. I'd
never experienced that before, watching the rain fall without
feeling it plucking my shoulders.

11

≈≈≈

In the Metro station, the air felt greasy yet fresh, the way cleaning a gun might feel. The curved ceiling at Dupont Circle was like the concrete cast of a giant honeycomb, everything solid and smooth and hollowed with permanence. I was impressed. The underground tunnels in other cities I'd been to were sooty and scurrilous with rats and litter. I never touched anything. I turned my head when people coughed. I changed seats or stood if someone got too close. I didn't feel that way in D.C., though. The trains were not new but they looked less soiled and everybody seemed to know exactly how to stand at a point equidistant from everybody else—a physical etiquette, maybe even a political one.

I slid with relief into the slotted indifference of the train. The besuited business and government people stood and looked at their BlackBerrys. The regular people dozed, chatted, read. At the next stop, a group of sweaty, ankle-socked tourists stumbled on together, snailslow, huge backpacks for shells. I judged them unfairly—after all, I was here visiting, too, on my way to brunch with my college roommate, Reena—but I felt affection even for their ungainliness, and for not having to know them.

Right before the doors closed, a tall handsome man stooped

onto the train. There were seats open but he chose to stand. He touched the pole with his fingertips as a reassurance, grasping it only when the train lurched. He looked too young for his suit and his shoes, the toes of which were tapered into the oblique shape of good taste, the leather tawny and real. They looked off on him, though, like they were too narrow or too big, or just not sneakers. He caught my eye and I glanced away, catching the tail of his smile. I shrugged one of my backpack straps off, self-conscious of my co-ed gear. I gathered my courage to peek at him again but he was focused on a woman in a seat by the door reserved for the handicapped and the elderly.

The woman was neither. She was in her twenties, Hispanic or Persian maybe. She wore a gray skirtsuit with mauve heels, her black hair slicked back, and makeup subtle as a watercolor. She was blinking slowly at her BlackBerry, a manicured thumb lovingly stroking the scroll wheel on its side. The train coasted up out of a tunnel into bright summer light, a quick dawn through which objects outside cast swift blocky shadows.

The tall man sauntered over and sat next to the woman. After a beat, he spoke, his voice disappearing in the clattering sound of another train approaching in the opposite direction. I looked out the window and the two trains' parallel paths pulsed me backward into a brief illusion of stillness. When I turned back, the guy was peeping at me—did he want an audience? He tried again to chat up the woman. The woman smiled but her hand made a don't-worry gesture that was also a shoo-shoo. He continued his game, enough nervousness in his smile to tempt my pity. As a last-ditch effort, he gave his hand to her to shake.

"I'm Wayne," he said.

The train slammed to a stop, the floor seemed to crumple. Everyone leaned in one direction and looked up. Then the doors opened with the familiar clunk. Everyone looked down again. I felt dazed. At the last minute, I saw that it was my stop and I rushed through the open doors. I spun around, staring through the scratchitied window as the train departed. Then I zigzagged around the people on the platform, until, realizing that I was headed the wrong way, I turned and went with the crowd.

I shook my head. Too old. He obviously couldn't be *older* than me. And anyway, that name wasn't so uncommon. And any-anyway, Wayne was dead. My mind stopped here, as it often did, as though skidding to a halt at the edge of a cliff.

≈

I immediately felt the impulse to preserve this story about seeing "Wayne" on the Metro, and deliver it to Reena at brunch like a gift. In the past three years that we'd been college roommates, we had established this pattern. Perhaps it was because she always happened to be around whenever I woke up from the dreams of Wayne that still savaged my nights. Sometimes they were so bad—or really, so good, then so bad when I woke up—that I actually missed the more literal visions of the crumbling boy I'd had when I was younger: the "golem" (Dr. Rothman), the "imaginary friend" (Dr. Jacinta), the "manifestation of trauma" (Dr. Weil). Reena called it the demon and joked that what I needed was an exorcism.

At the end of the previous spring semester, she and I had discussed our summer plans while packing up our dorm room. I had found myself feeling relieved that she would be in Boca Raton working as a lifeguard while I headed down to Pikesville to help out with Vigil. Reena and I would do what we always did during the summer: chat on AOL now and then, and send long pretentious emails about our dull and dramatic lives. But I'd been home barely a month before I began to miss our late

nights together: smoking Marlboro Lights (her) and Camel Lights (me) out in the courtyard, teasing each other, elaborating our agreements and disagreements, the competing wonders of being the same and different, of being nearby versions of brown—like how we used the same lotion but not the same hair gel.

Then one day in June, my mother told me she wanted us to spend a couple of nights in D.C. Boosted by Grandma Rose's inheritance, she was trying to raise more funds and legitimacy for Vigil, which had fully grown from a maudlin, psychotic hobby at the rec center into a real nonprofit. She wanted me to shadow her at the meetings. When we arrived at our hotel, I mentioned that my college roommate was going to be in town, too. Reena and two of her high school friends from Florida were taking a roadtrip up to New York and she had offered to stop in D.C. to meet up with me. My mother didn't like Reena, didn't trust her. Telling her the plan only once we got to the hotel was one of those easy cruelties with which she and I bartered our passive aggression back then. When I left the hotel to meet Reena and the guys, my sense of freedom was buoyed by my mother's obvious irritation.

Within minutes of a wilted brunch at an overpriced restaurant, it was clear that my roommate had changed in the intervening month since finals, or I had, or both. While I had been spinstered at home doing secretarial work for Vigil, Reena's poolside stint seemed to have matured her. Her high school friends didn't even seem like they were from Florida. I know now that those two white boys couldn't have been much more experienced than me—just out of the closet, tender as babes— but they were well-coiffed and savvy. I could tell when they were being ironic but couldn't catch all the nuances of their gibes. Their repartee with Reena, honed to a certain rapacity and rapidity over the course of their roadtrip so far, was a wall I kept having to climb. I felt PMS-y and prim around them.

And as it turned out, I hadn't quite outgrown my tango with race. High school had been an immensity of whiteness, I, a lonesome brown pip bobbing in the sea of it. Many of my college friends, like Reena, were immigrants at least, or the children of immigrants: people who didn't feel at home here but didn't feel at home there either, not anymore. This was the closest approximation I had found to being mixed race—not knowing which foot was in place and which amputated. Or maybe it was that one foot was nailed down and the other was wildly kicking, running. That was one of Grandma Rose's favorite off-color jokes about child-rearing: "Stop running in circles, Johnny, or I'll nail your other foot to the floor!"

I still missed my glamorous French grandmother, who had finally succumbed to cancer earlier that year at sixty-seven. I'd always liked her more than I liked Grandma Lu. It had only recently started to bother me that this preference fell along racial lines. That summer day in D.C., navigating the city's anonymous civic spaces, I understood for the first time the sense of ease I feel around people who look like me. If crowds are like bathwater heated to different degrees, to me, a black crowd is the perfect temperature. This is changing now, of course, because of gentrification. But in the early 2000s, D.C. still felt like Chocolate City.

I smiled stiffly at my feet as coffee-shake Reena and her strawberry-milk friends jeered and sneered their way through our touristy day. At the Tibetan-cum-Rastafarian gift shop in Adams Morgan, I found I couldn't join them in their ridicule of the incense flavors, even the one labeled "Pussy." I didn't want to be part of calling Reena "homeless" when she squatted in an alley to piss because we couldn't find a Starbucks fast enough.

At the zoo, I wouldn't laugh with them at the "African American Heritage Garden," which was a measly patch of dust planted—according to the sign—with black-eyed peas, okra, and watermelon. One of the white boys philosophically noted the omission of the "rare, fragrant fried-chicken tree," which somehow wasn't the tipping point. I should have seen it coming that they would aim their snark on that woman and her three kids on the Metro.

We were sitting across from them. The woman had crammed her thighs into tight ripped jeans and was wearing giant gold hoops that the boys were agog at—"So heavy! She's gonna tear her earlobes!" I knew they weren't solid, but I didn't bother to correct them. She was asleep, her head tipped back, her mouth ajar. Every time the train stopped, her eyes would drift open and she'd reach automatically for her smallest, a toddler whose ashy cheeks looked like a recently washed chalkboard. It was those cheeks, or the kids running riot, or the mother's half-done braids, or her big earrings that made the boys start in. Reena cackled, and even though I might have thought the same things if I'd been alone or two years younger, I took offense. I didn't defend the family—who likely wouldn't have cared or even noticed if I had—but I sulked furiously until the woman and her kids got off the train. As soon as the doors slid shut behind them, I spoke up and accused the boys—lightly, I thought:

"You know, that was kind of fucked up. Racially speaking."

"Dear God, C," Reena scoffed with an eye roll. "It's not our fault that the National Zoo thinks your people are worthy of, like, botanical exhibition."

The boys laughed.

"Not the zoo. I mean what you were saying about that family just now."

I hated the petulance in my voice. For people of my generation, and of my class—aspirational middle—it was a time of bad-faith condescension when it came to these matters. To joke about race was to show how above it—how *past* it—you were. It was to defuse its offense in the name of a humor that nevertheless depended on that offense. And now I had broken the youthful pact, the one that swore that being edgy was better than being earnest. Worse, I had reminded them that I was not in fact one of them. The guys apologized exaggeratedly and changed the topic but there was something jagged in them for the rest of the ride and their spiky words felt sharper, more porcupine than cactus. I thought it was because I was being a burster-of-balloons, a rainer-on-parades. I hadn't yet come to understand that the worst thing for them to hear was that they might be racist.

When we got to their stop, I stood up and hugged the three of them goodbye with a close-lipped smile, then sat down by myself to ride the four more stops to the hotel. In the train, the AC hushed thinly and a polite robot told us to please stand clear of the closing doors, and we did, and of each other, too. Only then did I realize that it wasn't what Reena and her friends had said about that family that had irked me. It was the fact that they had said anything at all, that they hadn't stood clear.

Reena had never respected boundaries. She was intrinsically curious, which made her an excellent student—she's a professor now, of history—and an interesting roommate. But it also made her an insatiable gossip and a fucking welter of opinions. Living with her was both invasive and thrilling. I had considered moving out a few times but always ended up staying, I think because I'd felt bonded to her ever since we'd watched the Towers fall on our tiny dorm-room TV set. Our other two roommates were still weeping and whispering around us when she and I caught each other's eye—both of us mid-yawn—then caught a case of the stifled giggles. We had both yawned; we had both laughed; but later on, I found out she'd told everyone we knew that I'd made fun of 9/11.

I knew that this "Zoo/Metro" incident would be wrung of all context by the time it got back to our other college friends. Reena feigned an ironic attitude but took everything very seriously, especially her judgment of those who took things too seriously. Over the years we lived together, I had overheard her judge, among other things: my grades, our friendship, my skin, my sex life, and, twice, my mother.

"Oof. She's one of those too-thin women," Reena muttered to a classmate at a party, not knowing I was close enough to hear. "Hysterical." Moue. The clever girl meant the word in the psychoanalytic sense, of course. I confronted her about that first time but my anger always met Reena like water hitting ice: it either rolled off or froze into her own armor.

The second time she told me about my mother was on a rainy day in the quad. We had run into each other on the diagonal stone path. Our umbrellas touched, the wet silken edges brushing with a shiver.

"Why weren't you at breakfast?"

"Slept in."

"What happened to the Jung paper?"

"Got an extension."

"Another?" Reena smiled superciliously inside her popped collar.

"I got a note from Mental Hygiene." I ducked my head and pulled my lighter out of my back pocket. This was the name of the campus psychiatric center. "Can I bum a smoke?"

Reena wrangled her pack of Marlboro Lights from the pocket of her vintage coat and tapped out a little bar graph. I plucked a cigarette from it and lit up, sucking hard to fight the damp.

"And what was this brain-flossing note for, exactly?" Reena took my cigarette from my lips and turned it around to light her own with its tip. Our cigarettes kissed and smoldered. Our umbrellas creaked and thwapped.

"I don't know. I guess . . ." I looked out at the rain-slivered world.

Reena exhaled gray and handed my cigarette back. "Oh, that's right. Your brother's dead and your mom's batshit."

There was a smidge of surprise in her laugh, as if someone else had made the joke. I tried to laugh, too, and failed. We parted ways, waving our cigarettes.

How did she know how to wield her words like that, like weapons? When had she collected them into her curious arsenal? The fact of the matter is that I loved her and I despised her, this elegant girl who'd been assigned as my roommate freshman year. She was a stranger to me, always would be. But I've been trained my whole life to tell stories to strangers.

≈

When I got back to the hotel room, the door was cracked and my mother's wheezy laugh was wafting out into the hall. She had company. A freckled woman who carried her girth with great poise was sitting on the queen bed, her thigh hitched under a skirt patterned with paisley peacocks. My mother was lying on the floor. Her elbowed arms looked like wings attached to her head, reminding me of the angels I'd seen in baroque paintings at the National Gallery. She was too seized with laughter to see me come in. So it was the big, beautiful woman, the guest, who turned to the doorway and opened her arms wide, beaming.

"And this must be . . ."

"Oh, you're back!" My mother lifted her head, grinning. "Cassie, this is Evelyn."

"Call me Eve, sweetheart."

I walked toward her and she grabbed both of my hands. Her palmskin felt smooth and thick, like orange peel. She gasped dramatically.

"Gosh, would you look at that bone structure? A replica of her father."

"I know," my mother said wearily. "It's uncanny."

I threw my backpack down and collapsed into an armchair next to a table covered with Vigil documents. The moment I sat, I felt a deep inner twinge. My period had arrived.

"Evie and I know each other from Wellesley."

"High school," Eve corrected. "But Charlotte ignored me back then."

"Bah. You ignored me!" My mother pouted. "I was too 'out there' for you good girls."

Eve rolled her eyes. And so it went, the minibar drinks goading them to shared memories and contrary ones. I listened vaguely. I felt sullen and lazy. I was delaying getting up to put a tampon in, a kind of perversity—like skipping showers—that still descends upon me when I'm menstruating. I perked up only when my mother and Eve turned to the present, to Vigil.

". . . trying to expand," my mother was saying. "We've been local for years. Outreach in the counties. We used to just do counseling, you know, helping the moms get through it. But"— she raised herself onto her elbows breathlessly—"I thought, Let's get official! We're nondenominational but the name Vigil helps, you know. With the fundraising and all."

"Non-de-no-mi-na-tion-al." Eve articulated each syllable, one eyebrow cocked. Her index and middle fingers were set in a V, like she would take a drag on a cigarette if she had one.

"Yeah, well." My mother nodded over at me. "It was a Jewish neighborhood and you know I'm no believer but I sent this one to Catholic school. My mother would have murdered me otherwise . . ."

She rambled on. I wondered how different our lives might have been if we'd believed in God, if we'd had any belief system in our family other than her singular faith in my brother's eventual return. Eve asked after my father.

"Well," my mother sighed and lay back again, her hair flopping theatrically. "He's in Georgia now. He's remarried. A Chinese—a *Vietnamese* woman," she corrected herself, widening her eyes, "a lawyer with a daughter. But he's agreed to remain affiliated with the organization. Unofficially."

The flush in my mother's cheeks stretched down her neck. I hadn't realized she cared about my father's new wife. Eve smiled warmly as if to soothe me. I plucked at a hangnail.

"So his name and his face are still on the publicity," my mother went on. "They advised me that it would be more accessible, more . . . what'd-they-say? More *poignant* to have both parents on there."

"Ha!" Eve said. "They just wanted his mug on the cover—"

I looked up.

"—pretty as it is," she qualified. The room tingled faintly with scandal after this zooming tug back to a time before I was born, a time when my father had been so handsome that all the women around him had taken note.

"Somebody's always losing somebody." My mother was back on Vigil. "I want us to go national, you know? It's so important now, especially for our African-American kids. My mother left me a lot of money when she died, but we still need—"

"Oh my goodness, *Rose*? Rose is gone?" Eve sangsong sadly. "I haven't thought about your mother in ages, Charlotte." She clucked. "What a goddess. I worshipped her!"

"Didn't we all?"

I squashed my surprise. Apart from that disingenuous effort to get me to take her name, my mother had always been keen to disillusion me about Grandma Rose, to make herself look better by contrast. My mother had even told me that the week before I was born, Grandma Rose had referred to me with a French word that roughly translates to "half-breed."

Eve was talking about her own mother now, about what a hard woman she had been. "As they say, blessed are the barren. That woman should never have had kids! She didn't know how to *be* loved. And you need that to know how to love. You do." She turned to me. "You must be so grateful. Your mama is just the softest thing."

I smiled and said nothing.

"I don't know about soft." My mother rose up, her tongue poking out as she tried to crack the seal on another minibar bottle. "Evie, you have a little girl, don't you? Cassie, would you open this?" She tossed the bottle into my lap. "Don't look at me like that. *You* can have some, too, you little twit! Might help with the attitude."

My mother covered her mouth—she never spoke to me like this in front of other people—then began laughing so hard that Eve and I joined in out of sheer peer pressure. As Eve began to describe her daughter to us, I opened the little whiskey bottle and took a swig. Fingers of heat crept down my chest to my belly, which pulsed with cramps.

"She skipped a grade," Eve was saying. "She hates it. She's

always complaining about the older kids, how they stand in the hall like big ole trees and she has to walk through a forest of 'em . . ."

Lying on the carpet, my mother looked like a young girl with her hair spread wild like that, even though she had gone completely gray by then. Tears slid down her temples, creeping through her makeup—her lobbying face—shaping ghostly spectacle arms. She was thinking of Wayne, I knew. I stretched my leg out and nudged her with my big toe. She didn't acknowledge me, so I stepped on her hair, subtly lowering the sole of my foot onto the thin sweep of it over the carpet.

"I hope you never have to join Vigil, Evie," she said. "I hope your baby stays safe."

Eve paused. "I didn't mean—"

"Of course you didn't, Evie. And of course I still have hope," she said, moving to sit up. "My baby—" Her hair caught under my foot. "Ow!" she said with a wince. "What're you—?"

I lifted my foot, shrugged. Every piece of vengeance between us was small and deniable like this these days. My mother was too drunk to care and collapsed back again. After a moment, Eve returned to her complaints about motherhood. It felt like a penance for expressing her love for her daughter. *I'm sorry, I'm sorry,* she seemed to say. *Let's all feel bad together now.* I was just thinking that I should really go to the bathroom to tend to my period when I realized that I'd become the target of advice from both women.

"Blessed are the barren," Evie said again and again.

"Yes, they really are," my mother said.

They formed a chiming chorus of misery and warning: *Never fall in love, but if you do, never commit, but if you do, never marry, but if you do, never have a kid, but if you do, have only one, no matter what, you must absolutely never have more than one.*

12

≈≈≈

I'm on a plane. So dreary, so cold. I generally don't speak to people on planes. I'm the unfriendly woman gazing out the window, the wearer of earplugs, the bearer of novels, willful dozer, spurner of all contact. How docile everyone becomes in that chilly roar! But the truth is I, too, come when called, stand behind and before numbered strangers, move right along, buckle up, eat what I'm given, the moment it's given, sit and quietly endure. So much abeyance. So much obedience. Maybe that's why I don't say anything when the smell of shit breezes across my face half an hour into the flight.

I peer between the two seats in front of me and catch sight of the infant, its damp and hapless air. It reaches its hand at me through the gap, gurgling, flashing its toothless gums, which resemble the pink ridges of the mountains I saw out the window earlier. I turn to check—yes, they're still there, redder now—then glance at the passenger in the seat to my right. Does she smell it? The girl, earbuds plugged in, is engaged in a private battle with her broken touchscreen, which is crying white code down its black face. She doesn't seem to notice the aroma puffing toward us from the gibbering baby and I wonder why I want her to.

The girl looks like she's about seventeen. Earlier, she was reading a creased paperback of *To the Lighthouse.* No doubt watching a movie was to be a reward for finishing her homework. The book has vanished back into her bag and now she jabs at her dead touchscreen, her mouth flinching, and glances enviously at my functional one, which flashes advertisements. A minute's worth of tapping through a maze of menus already told me that nothing watchable is free except the news, and the news is always either a familiar disaster or an empty miracle these days. There's another world in which I offer to switch seats with this girl since I'm not going to use my touchscreen anyway. In this world, however, I tug my scarf up to blinker me from the smell as it thickens and ripens. When I look over again, the girl has returned to Virginia Woolf but is holding a tissue over her nose like a hankie. She widens her eyes at me and I shake my head to consolidate our commiseration. But I say nothing to this pretty white girl, who will waltz through life, I'm sure of it, who will be rescued at every falter.

I turn to look out the window again. There are fields below now, cast in the sunset's last gold, like shiny green scales on the face of the planet, this careful human portioning of the land. So clean and calm compared to the rumpled, gathered skirts of the mountains earlier. I lean closer to the window and my nose steams the glass like a puppy's and I feel a creaturely tenderness for myself.

Out of the corner of my eye, I see an adult's arm reach up to hand a folded white lump to a patrolling flight attendant. He receives it stoically, concealing the automatic crinkle of his nose by smiling up into it, and hastens to the back of the plane. I venture an inhale. The smell has dissipated. I feel grateful for the parent's disposal of the diaper, then incredulous at their presumption that someone else should carry their child's shit.

The man sitting across from my row stands up and moves into the aisle, casually stretching. He's lanky in a handsome way. His hair is shaved close and etched into precise corners. His skin, the color mine will be in the winter, looks healthy. This hints at money and time spent considering what ablutions to perform. He's wearing a dark blue button-down and has a salesman's smile—quick and promiscuous. He's standing ahead of my row now, his hand on the seat directly in front of the student of modernism beside me. He leans down.

"First kid, right?"

His voice is like fingers running through gravel. I can't hear the parent's answer.

"Yeah, that's tough," the handsome man replies with a politician's inflection. "I feel you . . ." He interrupts himself to beam at the baby, who is startling up. He reaches down and pats the little head. "Was that you earlier? Stinkin' up the whole damn plane?" Laughter. "It's an uphill battle, I tell you. But you learn. You do. You'll get the hang of it."

I roll my eyes up and away. I have no patience for this kind of folksy talk. What's the use of language like this, words you pass back and forth between your grinning mouths, clichés like the twice-chewed gum of teenage smoochers? The specific topic grates, too. I've spent too many years regretting being the specific daughter of my specific mother to feel optimistic about parenthood.

I was a psychology major but during my senior year of college, I took an elective course on women's rights. The course was difficult—the professor was concerned with presenting things "dialectically," she said, "not Socratically." But I remember the history: Sojourner's breasts, the raging fire and smashed glass of the suffragettes. The eruptive violence of feminism had surprised me and appealed to me. All that wounded flesh and antic activism added substance and color to a history heretofore trapped in black and white for me. I wrote my final paper about something Grandma Rose had told me once, cigarette smoke curling around her mocking voice: how these women in nineteenth-century France had called for a boycott on reproduction. No new babies, no new workers.

The baby in the row ahead is again standing on its parent's lap, ignoring the man in the aisle and reaching for me through the gap between the seats instead. I send a scathing look at its slimy hand but when I catch the young woman beside me doing the same, I feel annoyed with her and unaccountably fond—as I had of my own puppy nose a little while ago—of the baby's refusal of my disgust, its happy and plain indifference. How silly and cruel disgust is, how much it relies on what we assume to be disgusting . . .

"You can always tell who the other parents are," the man in the aisle says in a rough stage whisper to the parent. "Other people just don't get it. So quick to judge."

The man is looking directly at me over the back of the seats. He's already smiling but the second our gazes touch, his smile changes ever so slightly. I glance at his left hand pressing into the top of the seat. Ringless. He seems young to be a father himself. Is this man going to these lengths, talking all this baby-talk, just to flirt with me? Could it really be for my sake? I suppress a smile and look down. I feel my ears heating up, the only part of me that ever blushes. But when I look up again, he's back in his seat across the aisle, staring at his touchscreen, which lights up his handsome face. I guess not.

The possibility stirs me nonetheless, this sense that everyone on the plane is oblivious to a game for which I alone have been chosen. I feel buoyed by it. It reminds me of the man on the D.C. Metro that time, years ago, who wanted me to watch while he hit on another woman. It's like being drawn into complicity, being triangulated like a magician's assistant or a partner in crime. A web of silence and glances—*I know that you know that I know.* Where's he from? I find myself wondering. What's his name? I shake these thoughts off. I crumple them up and scold myself: You're too grown for this, C, each vision of Wayne giving way to another, and another, a rack of sharp thin images shuttling uselessly in the chasm of death. If you keep imagining him alive this way, those visions may take over. And then you'll be no better than your mother, with her grotesque and funded delusions. Yes, you, too, work for Vigil now—it was inevitable, wasn't it?—but at least you don't believe in it.

I look out the window and watch the outskirts of San Francisco at dusk rise to meet us. It's a tailor's heap down there now: smooth gray swaths of tarmac stitched with dashed lines, buttoned with cars, the highways' looped exits like masses of ribbon somebody forgot to tie. The rush-hour headlights are red and white sequins, and when the cars move, they loosen gently and fall.

≈

I find myself searching for the man from the plane at the baggage carousel. There he is, waiting about a dozen feet away. He seems thinner and taller, his skin duller in the fluorescent light. His clothes still look crisp and clean but there's a little street to his stance. Past the information booth behind him are the automatic doors leading outside, and above them, a sign inscribed into the concrete wall reading T E R M I N A L O N E, with massive, angled windows on either side. I tap my foot to summon my patience. Finally, the siren light above the carousel flashes. The machine grunts to life and starts to rotate, the silver scales grating over each other as they pivot. At the center of the carousel is a mouth, its black tongue the automatic belt that pulses forward now, vomiting up bags. The passengers crowd in, occasionally reaching forward as if to shake hands with their suitcase handles.

I recognize the child from the plane, in its mother's arms on the other side of the carousel. The mother, in cutoffs and a striped shirt, looks more tired and more attractive than I had pictured. She has her hand wrapped around the baby's forearm. She forces the clenched fist to wave at the man. He returns the wave with a nod, a smile. He turns his head and catches my eye. After a twinkling beat, he makes his way toward me. Surprise and anticipation skitter in my chest.

The carousel stops abruptly, with a shudder. An older white man in the middle of pulling his suitcase off the belt loses his balance and falls to one knee, and the handsome man pauses to help him up. Those nearby coo and assist. A child gleefully shouts "Whoa!" just as the machine starts back to life. It has reversed direction for some reason and there's a terrible screech and the black tongue buckles with a thumping sound. The flat lights in the ceiling shiver weakly. The anxious murmuring of the crowd rises a notch. The carousel is speeding up, shrieking unevenly, and is soon giving off a burning smell. Suitcases tumble off it into a cluster of passengers. A girl—the student who was next to me on the plane—yelps as a big Samsonite strikes her, knocks her flat. In the hubbub, no one helps her, no one rescues her. The carousel seems to tilt, but no—that's the ground beneath us, my own unsteady legs.

I reach for the column beside me to steady myself, gripping my purse strap to my shoulder. The escalators up to Departures slow to a halt, people stranded on the sudden stairs. The information screens go snowy and the automatic doors in the distance begin gnashing open and closed. There are titchy zapping sounds like electrical shorts. People are yelling. Babies are crying, at first in unison, then in a lopsided round. The intercom shouts fiercely and cuts out. Someone says, *What about the planes, what about the bombs,* and as if in reply, there's a faint boom. TERMINALONE trembles. The baggage carts rattle in their nested embrace. The overhead lights give a last spasm and die. All is dark but for the siren lamps.

We stand perplexed and hushed in the pulsing red glow, like we've accidentally entered a darkroom. The sound of sirens drifts in from afar as though the flashing red lights have beckoned them. Another boom, louder this time. The building shudders again. And now everyone is swarming, starting to run. Very soon, we are a torrid mass, cascading toward the automatic doors, which some brave souls have wedged open. I, too, am running to join the scramble out! out! out! when the ground before me ripples and I slip.

I fall backward into something, someone, who cradles me by the elbows until I regain my footing. I look up and see the man from the flight, who had been coming toward me when this all began and has managed to get in place just in time to save me. He lifts and spins me and I'm in his arms. His brown eyes look green under the swinging red lamp. A light twists between us, a gyred light, and I know. It's him. It's Wayne. This is our reunion.

Passing

≈≈≈

We take the same ambulance. We sit gingerly on thin ledges across from each other, on either side of a white woman on a gurney. The woman's skirt is riding up. Tubes and cords spill from her body like veins and there's a breathing mask over her mouth. The EMT is next to me, his hand on the woman's forearm, which is slowly, visibly bruising. I look over her body at the man from the plane. It seems impossible that we've only just met. The interior lights are palsied by jolts from the uneven road. Our bodies rock and sway as the ambulance swoops in and out of traffic. The siren is on but the sirens are everywhere now, in overlapping and continuous folds. We're lucky we got this ride.

At the hospital, we stick together, as if by habit. He's lost his wallet, so doesn't bother to fill out the forms but stands with me at the counter while I fill out mine. I managed to hold on to my purse but I stand tilted in my lone pump—the other one dropped somewhere along the way and I'm loath to lose this one. The pantyhose on my shoeless foot crisps against the linoleum. When I'm done with the forms, a harried nurse points us to a bench on her way through thick doors with crash bars. On the other side of those doors, it's clear, there are patients in far worse condition than we are.

Ambulances come and go, their sirens swelling then receding as they go back to fetch more of the wounded. Every few minutes, EMTs hustle in with their tempered panic, bringing in outside air redolent with smoke, and gurneys shuttle up and down the corridor, hospital staffers racing alongside like bobsledders. After a couple of hours, the helicopters and the sirens fade to a background like crazy birdsong. Now we can hear the hospital sounds: the tight buzz of the fluorescent lights, the muffled coughing, a lottery of beeps. There are still people busying about, staff and patients, but we're alone together. We're growing accustomed to it. In this pause between chaos and calm, it's easier to batten down now, to talk.

I tell him I feel the urge to look at a screen, to find out what happened. Our cellphones are dead and the TV looming from an upper corner of the room is off, too high up to turn on without a remote. I forlornly wipe dust from my watch—my father's old Seiko. The man is fretting over his lost wallet. He stares at his feet, elbows on his knees, hands clasped on the back of his neck.

"Without ID, I doubt they're even gonna see me."

"It'll be fine," I say automatically. "I mean, I could . . ."

He gives me a sidelong glance. He seems amused, even now. It's like a reflex, his smile. "You could what, exactly?"

"I could . . . vouch for you." I smile back. "I'm just saying."

"Vouch for what?" He sits up.

"He exists. He definitely exists," I say, practicing. It feels good to laugh, mostly. My leg hurts and blood has made a Pollock of my pantyhose.

"And where does he do all of this . . . existing?"

"Somewhere. Definitely somewhere."

"What's his date of birth?"

I look at him. He's covered in an offwhite powder, crumbled plaster maybe. It crusts into the creases around his lips and gives his hair a salt-and-pepper look. "Hard to say."

"What's his occupation?" He licks his lips and spits on the floor between his shoes. It doesn't bother me. It looks clean and delicate, like a cat licking itself.

"Judging by the makeup, I think he might be a performer of some kind. A mime?"

He gives his raspy laugh. "And what's my name?"

"Williams?" another voice says. We both look up. A nurse stands in the doorway, holding a clipboard. "Mrs. Williams?"

"*Ms.* Williams," I correct her as I stand up unsteadily in my one pump.

I lurch toward the doors. The nurse's uniform is rumpled against her skin, which is a syrupy brown. She doesn't say anything to me until we're on the other side of the doors in a small examination room. Only then does she remark that I *could* take off my shoe. It's the sort of perfectly logical thing one forgets to do in a situation like this but she says it as if she's been waiting for the two of us to be out of earshot. Womanly advice, the kind that defers to but cannot be spoken around men. Behind a green curtain, I uncup my heel out of my dusty pump, abashed but annoyed at her presumption.

The nurse motions for me to sit next to her and takes my vitals perfunctorily, avoiding eye contact. I feel chastised by this woman, who implies with every brusque gesture that I'm not injured enough for this much attention. The fingers resting on my wrist to take my pulse are polished neatly in a shimmery maroon, close to Grandma Lu's favorite shade. I stretch my sore leg out and wince as dried blood crinkles and unsticks the panty-hose over my knee.

"I see it," the nurse says, still looking at her watch. "We'll get to it."

"I just—"

"The doctor will be in to look at your leg." She stands. "Then you can join your friend," she says over her shoulder as she exits, her tone pinning the last word with quotation marks.

The door shuts behind her and heat streaks into my ears. I feel eighteen again; I sense the same judgment in the air I felt at that Vigil meeting at the rec center: coffee and doughnuts and sad women raking their eyes over my miniskirt and bloody nose piercing. The nurse is right. I have been flirting with that man. How surreal. Even in the rattling ambulance, glancing across at him, I'd been flirting. And I hadn't been aware of my leg back in the hallway only because it hurt.

"Let's take a look at that leg," the doctor says as she parts the curtain, startling me by naming my exact thought.

Fifteen minutes later, she tells me that I've bruised a toe. Nothing too bad. The most traumatic part of the ordeal is taking off my pantyhose, which is glued to my legs in places, bitty stones and broken glass crusting my purpling skin. The doctor, who smells of sweat and antiseptic, slowly wraps my second toe, binding it to its neighbor. She speaks peremptorily about how I should walk and stand, about salts and creams and heat and cold. I feel relief course through me. I realize only when she mentions it that I've been in shock for hours.

≈

I return to the hallway, my pump dangling from the hook of one hand, my purse from the other. The man is still there, reading a pamphlet about prenatal care, of all things. He's washed his face and there's only a smattering of white dust left in his hair. He looks up and smiles—there's something so familiar about the scimitar curves of his eyes—then stands up, tosses the pamphlet onto a chair, and comes over to me. He wears a concerned look that doesn't quite displace his obvious pleasure at being there to show his concern. I point down at the hospital slippers the doctor gave me.

"I got a busted toe," I say with a pout. "You?"

"All good," he says, running his hand over his head, spraying particles that hover like summer gnats. "The EMT that drove us came in. He found my wallet in the ambulance." He pulls it out of his pocket and holds it above one shoulder with both hands like a trophy.

"Really? Wish he'd found my other shoe." I laugh. "Not that it would fit."

When we reach a set of swinging doors with porthole windows, he holds one open for me. He jogs ahead to the outside exit as if to open the doors there, too, but they slide open automatically. Undaunted, he extends his hand to help me over the threshold and I take it, despite myself. Our phones are still dead, so a security guard hails us a taxi. We direct the driver to his hotel first. It makes a kind of sense, a returned favor: he waited for me; I'll escort him home. Plus his hotel is closer than my mother's place in Russian Hill. Plus-plus who knows.

In the taxi, I let my head fall back. After a minute, I swivel my eyes to the side without turning my head. He's staring at me, unabashed.

"Doctors wear me out," I say by way of explanation.

"Bad experience?"

"I guess . . ." I hesitate. "I saw a lot of . . . doctors when I was younger."

He's about to ask another question when the driver turns and asks which route we'd prefer, given that the roads are still tied up in knots. The man scooches forward to discuss this and when he sits back again, he reaches for my hand on the seat. Again, despite myself, I take it. The feel of his hand, dry and muscular, reminds me that I don't even know his name. It would be absurd to ask now. The driver flips through radio stations, trying to get more news about what happened. It seems nobody knows. I melt back into exhaustion.

I wake up when the taxi stops outside an old but dignified hotel. The man pulls out some cash from his wallet to pay, then opens his door and gets out. I'm trying to work out how I feel that he hasn't said goodbye when my door opens, too.

"Buy you a drink?"

I feel a tiny shock, a pinprick in the wider shock of the evening. "I don't have shoes—" I point halfheartedly at my gauzy hospital slippers.

"I'll get you some."

In the pause before I demur, he reaches in to take my elbow, proprietary now, and helps me out. He shuts the door and the taxi drives speedily into the night, as if in on this little three-card monte. We don't speak and I keep my head down as we walk into the lobby, as he registers at the front desk, as we wait for the elevator. My head feels fuzzy with doubt but also buzzy with kismet. When I look up again, he smiles, his lips parting in sync with the elevator doors. We get on together and I look down again as we ride up. I touch my hair, wishing I'd had the presence of mind to fix it in a bathroom mirror at the hospital.

His hotel room is softly stinky: ancient smoke, a lemony cleaning product, carpet dust. The closed vertical blinds shift against each other with a soft clipping sound when the door shuts behind us. I sit in an armchair, he on the edge of the bed.

He turns on the TV and the news is on every channel. We choose one and watch it replay itself, the footage on the screen displacing our memories of the yawning ground, the blows to our bodies, the flashing lights. We watch other people tell our story, of good fortune amid the unlucky dead. We watch the body count rise and the greater the numbered dead, the luckier we feel. One witness keeps saying, *Oh god oh god oh god. They took them away on baggage carts,* another witness says.

I don't realize that I'm crying until he turns off the TV. We talk for a while about nothing and my tears dry on my cheeks. He makes tea, boiling the water in the coffee percolator and serving it to me in a paper cup. He sits on the bed facing my chair and watches me drink. I bend forward to put my cup beside my ankle. When I sit back up, he's standing in front of me.

Our eyes meet and he leans down and kisses me, the first nip to the lips like a question, which I answer quickly. He grasps my nape with one hand, my elbow with the other, and I let him raise me from the chair, ignoring the ache in my toe. He kisses my neck, sucks it lightly, and runs his palm over my breast. I pull his face closer to kiss his mouth. Our tongues touch, passersby, and we moan at the same time.

Then I'm falling onto the bed, my skirt skidding up under his fingers, threads popping with the stretch. I stay his hands and we look at each other and break apart to undress fully, lying side by side on our backs. The tension dissipates as our clothes catch us up, the absurdity of this drapery we all wear every day, the slapstick comedy of removing it. Then we're naked, he rolls toward me, holds himself over me, kisses me, and we're back in it.

I encircle him with my limbs so that he collapses onto me. The weight of his body sets bees going in my thighs. Our hips part briefly and I catch a glimpse of his erection, the blessed clarity of its intention. I feel him trying to align us and I help automatically, the thought of condoms skipping over my mind like a stone that finally sinks and vanishes. I'm not ready but he goes ahead anyway, haltingly, and it's like water easing into a hole in sand, his skin catching slightly on mine until I'm wet and he's inside me and again we moan together.

For a while, I don't quite know where I am or who I am. Then he says something, my name maybe, and I understand that we're sitting up, facing each other, his hands grappling my hips, and we're moving in sync. He wants me to come, he says, and I let out a sound that would embarrass me if he didn't echo it louder, deeper. I swoop my head down and bite his neck. He winces but when I lean up again, he's smiling. A snarl puckers the skin above my nose, too, and there's a metallic taste behind my lips. My blood or his?

I close my eyes and try to come, rocking against him, my clit like a beacon. A stream of images runs through my mind, reels culled from the porn I watch: mostly gangbangs, a preference I try not to dwell on in my daily life. Now it feels oddly as if I'm on a train and the cabin I'm in is peopled with the regulars from my fantasy life, all those people doing their shaven, deadpan, tonguing, groping, choking, ramming thing, while I watch and sometimes participate. I'm getting closer and I can hear that he is, too—*fuck aw fuck,* he's chanting softly—and then for some reason, I glance out the window in the train of my mind.

And out there in the roar of time, horror, I see flashes of us—me and you, Wayne—in every permutation of our childhood: at the table, in the car, tucked in, woken up, ice-cream cones and skipping stones, swimsuits for summer, wool hats for fall, Christmas trees and kicking at puddles, green lawns and birthday cakes, crying for lost things, dustbunnies under beds, cuddling up and scuttling off, grabbing hands and racing to the shore, shrieking as the waves lick up our legs. That's where the scene outside the train window sticks, on repeat: you and me, holding hands, shrieking, waves leaping up our bodies like small animals.

I blink my eyes open, refocus to look at the man I'm fucking right now in this here life. I gaze at the jutting veins of his neck as I shove my hips rhythmically. I stare pitilessly at the stubble in his chin cleft where the razor didn't reach, beard hairs like threads poking from cheap cloth. I know I'm not going to come now—it has receded far away—but I feel another kind of hunger, monstrous, an open mouth widening inside me. The man lowers his chin, his face drugged, swooning. He guppers as if he might sneeze—I glimpse a dark filling—and looks into my eyes. *No.* I'm not going to come, I stop moving my hips, I see him, I see Wayne, I see him, I cover his face with a panicked hand, and when he starts to come, *No,* I say. *No.*

≈

It's gray out and I'm in the woods. I've got a towel in my hands and I'm walking a dirt path between the trees. The roots are like a ladder that fell down, broken rungs digging into my bare feet. I come to this clearing and past the trees, I see water, dark green, nearly black. The sky above is cement, no rays or clouds to break it up. Too cold to swim. I grip my towel, hunch my shoulders, walk on. Above me, the trees are hushing and creaking and leaning. The path opens out to a beach. I cross the sand, itty-bitty rocks biting my soles, and step onto the planks of a floating dock. Shifty but solid.

I look around. It's a lake. Water's choppy and there's nobody here but I can see the net strung between the buoys to mark off a swimming area. I drop the towel, sit on the edge of the dock, plop my feet in the water. Goosebumps spring up on my legs. My palms are gray as the sky. I turn my hands back over, put them on either side of me to steady myself. I lower myself into the lake, the goosebumps rising up my body as I sink down all the way until the water's chest level. As soon as I'm in, there's that quickness in my bones—I'm ready to swim—but I let my feet hit the bottom. Bumpy but silky. Mud? Moss? Hard to say.

Something brushes my thigh. I jump and step forward and I feel the ground slope down. Another step and it bottoms out. I drop an ankle like an anchor, close my eyes, and hold my breath as I go under. Something brushes me again, heavy and rough with folds. I push myself away from it. Waves suck at me—that's the feeling and the sound—and my heart's pumping, my body's trying to warm up or run. There's flashes of fear in my belly so I swim to swallow them—one stroke, two strokes, three. I come up, arms and legs frogging. These things in the water, whatever they are—they're hitting me from all sides now without much bounce or give, thick around me like some kinda nest.

I hold my breath and drop back down again, deep. I open my eyes under the water. At first all I see is a blue-green haze, the color of shadow. I wait for it to clear. I see logs and saplings and branches all around me, like I'm in a sea forest. There's a tree wrapped in moss. Another with a big knot, stringy seaweed growing out of it. A third rams into my leg and stays, my knee wedged in a fork. A branch scrapes over my face and my head turns and I see fingers, the fingers at the end of the hand that just trailed over my cheek.

I look up to the surface of the water. These aren't trees. They're bodies. So many I can barely see the sky above through them. The one trapped around my leg is still there, spinning slowly around my knee. Another glances off my back. I turn and I'm looking in its dead eyes. I shout, my mouth opening wide, wider, like it's hinged.

I'm in my hotel bed. I wipe my hand down my face and turn my head. She's on her side beside me, asleep, facing away. At least I didn't wake her. I breathe slowly, in and out, and find myself staring at her hip under the covers. I can feel myself getting hard, my dick changing its weight. I stroke it absently until the hard-on fades and my heart slows. What was that dream? Bodies underwater? Like a fucking cartoon. A murmur beside me—she's talking in her sleep, some kind of dream chatter. Her voice, even asleep, is low and lovely.

The sound of it turns me onto my side and I rock up to her ass but she shifts off. If it was another woman, I'd keep knocking. Instead, I remember last night. Her breasts, high and small, a chicken pox scar like a drop of sweat between them. Her breath in spurts like she was laughing or panting. When she took over—slamming her little hips against me like she could do me harm—it was almost cute. But it worked. It rose and rose and when I came inside her, it was like something she had built for me, then razed to the ground. Like sexual Tetris.

I think about how she let me hit raw, then said *No* right when I shot, but then brushed it off before we passed out, and also she *bit* me? It all makes me feel some kinda way. I know I'm not getting back to sleep now. I roll to my other side and sit up, put my feet down soft as a spy. I find my boxers and pants crumpled on the floor and pull them on. I look at the shape of her in bed. Three round hills: skull, shoulder, hip. There's a stain on the sheet. My blood or hers? We didn't shower last night and we're both still crusted up with plaster, glass, dirt. I can smell it, the disaster, under sleep funk and her perfume and the high note of come. I glance at the black face of the TV but decide not to turn it on for the news. I don't wanna wake her.

I walk across the room and find her purse on the desk. Her wallet is one of those long ones women always use and it's right at the top—a convenient, dumb place to put it. I crack it: Visa, Amex, a wedge of receipts, business cards, $46 and change, no pennies. I look at the license last. *Cassandra Williams.* Her name like a gift. I don't want anything more. Not yet. Just taking stock. But I feel a tingle in my wrists, so I take the cash—why not?—and stuff the bills in my front pocket, then take my own wallet out of my back pocket. I flip it open, slip her business card in, flip it shut. I hold it for a moment. The leather feels cool and thick, precious, like I lost and found it for real. I'd lied at the hospital about how it had gone missing and the paramedic found it—a big ole story just so I didn't have to fill out forms next to her. It was too soon to give her *my* full name, given that it's the same as her brother's.

Right up against it. Almost blew up my own spot. Didn't expect that end-of-the-world shit, for things to blow up so fucking literally. Well, nothing like a disaster to open a door between people, right? But then that other door opened and . . . I probably should've known better. This is gonna complicate things. I touch my neck again, finding where she bit me with my thumb. I press it, a punishment for giving in.

I walk over to the window, split two of the longways blinds open. It's night, the lights marking the shapes of the buildings and the lines of the streets. The city looks more like a city from up here. We're not far from where I first met Mo.

"Just weight and full measure."

First thing he ever said to me. He had to lean down to say it. I was on the ground, my back against a dumpster that smelled of Vietnamese food and piss. I was hurt and cold, shivering in the glare of that lying-ass San Francisco sun, heat promised and snatched back in one breath.

"You gotta keep the scales of loss steady," Mo went on. "Give something back."

"You crazy," I replied flatly.

Mo had been hounding me for weeks, showing up uninvited in all my spots: the Compass on Market, St. Ant's, the planters on the north side of Civic Center. I preferred concrete and commuters to parks, which were too crowded with meth heads and whiteboy backpackers—plus I've got allergies. But I'd been considering broadening my two-mile radius ever since Mo started tracking me. I was fifteen years old and had lived on the street for nearly two. Men had come at me before. But this? This was some stalker shit.

"Is this some stalker shit?"

"Yeah, I seen you around," Mo said.

"I seen *you* around. The fuck you want, bruh? You got short eyes?"

"Don't talk like that, son."

"Son? Fuck you mean, 'son'? Nigga, I don't even know you."

I sniffed and hitched my leg, using my sleeve to dab at my ankle. It had buckled under me on Larkin when I was running—from who or what I don't remember now—and blood was trickling out from where I'd scraped it on the sidewalk. Mo squatted next to me, in those fluffy boots of his, like cut-off teddy-bear feet. He was a big dude, spongy around the middle, strong in the thighs. Medium skin. In his thirties but forever young, especially in the cheeks. Hard and soft at the same time.

"I'm just tryna be like you." He smiled, running a hand over his cornrows.

"Fuck outta here, man." I let my face twist with disgust and looked past his shoulder. "You got on some *Uggs*? That's some faggot-ass shit."

It's like spitting in the rain, calling out somebody's preferences in the Bay. But Mo scared me somehow, made me antsy. I tried to stand up and walk away but my ankle hurt too much and I landed back on the ground with a wince. We looked at each other. After a beat, Mo reached his arms out with his wrists crossed. We clasped hands, leaned back, rose up.

"You can call me whatever you want. But I can *be* whatever I want," he said, putting his arm around me, his hand under my armpit. "You can too. Just gotta slip outside yourself."

I lifted my foot and we began a three-legged hobble together. Mo was a good foot taller than me then, but that would be flipped by the time we parted ways.

"We created them," he said, "and endowed their limbs and joints with strength but if we please we can replace them by other men this is indeed an admonition did he not confound their stratagem and send against them flocks of birds which pelted them . . ."

I shrank from him to get a better look at his face while he rattled on. His eyes were like stones in a stream. Then the waters sank and he smiled at me, gave a lazy wink.

"I'm just sayin'. You gotta always give just weight and full measure."

"Got your full measure right here." I spat and cupped my crotch with my free hand.

"It all comes around eventually, son," Mo said, easy as the breeze.

That was how Mo drifted in and out of crazy, like a car radio on a long drive. He had found this old copy of the Koran in a box on Dana Street in Berkeley. By the time we met, he'd practically memorized it. He spewed quotes from it, gave little sermons—weird metaphors, end-times shit. Everything in the Bay was inside out like that, though. Bedrooms laid out in storefronts, bathrooms where-the-fuck-ever, the crazy you're supposed to keep in your head bubbling out, frothing. But Mo was hella smart, the smartest man I've ever known. His pockets were full of scraps of writing and he was a numerological nigga too, could tell you all kindsa shit with his ciphers, knew all types of equations, knew every scam.

I remember one time we made us some Magic Dollars. We put our begging coins together and went to Kinko's and laminated a couple of dollar bills with a foot-long tail of cellophane so we could pull them back out of the vending machines once we'd paid for our chips and soda. "Automatic refund!" Mo laughed and laughed. Even then, he said we could take only what we needed, and weirder still, we had to leave trash, bits and bobs, in the receptacle under the swinging door of the vending machine to replace the pretzels or candy or whatever that we'd ganked. Tit, tat. Tick, tock.

Those years of living with Mo were like a rocking fever of *just weight and full measure.* He thought that eye-for-an-eye wasn't a weapon to use against people, it was a scale. He always said, "Not retribution, resti*tution.*" Eventually, eye-for-an-eye became an inside thing, his heart eating itself. He fucked it all up. But me? I've got my eyes on the prize. I'm as close as I've ever been to doing what Mo's Koran said to do. I'm gonna balance the scale. I'm gonna undo what was done unto me. I'm gonna find the man who tried to destroy my life, from back when we were just two boys in Baltimore, scrapping in the schoolyard.

But now, looking out this window at the grids of this other city, familiar as the lines on my palm, that man's sister mumbling in the bed behind me, I have to stop myself from thinking too hard about Mo. I know he would tell me that what I'm doing is wrong.

II

≈≈≈

1

≈≈≈

C's waiting for me outside by a trash can. She's just dumped her hospital slippers in it, and now she's looking away from me, out at the street, but in a way that tells me she knows I'm watching her. I'm still in the store—a pricey one, in Hayes Valley—waiting in line to pay for the new loafers she's already changed into. She starts shining the toe of one shoe against the back of her other calf, or maybe she's scratching an itch. I'm wishing she'd look back at me, let a smile sunrise up her face. Her smile is nice, and useful. But it's rare and it goes away quick, like something closing its wings.

"$51.76, sir," the cashier says, holding the scanner over the empty box.

I hand over my credit card, wincing inside. I'm not used to prices like this. When I leave the store, C's propped against the wall outside, like an umbrella, like something I could just pick up and walk off with. So I do. I hook her by the elbow, pull her off the wall and along the sidewalk, linking our arms. She's carrying her one high heel from last night in her other hand because it won't fit in her purse. She swings it as we shoot the breeze.

"It's warm today, I know, it's been so chilly, I never know

what to wear in this city, I like actual seasons, places where the weather has a pattern, yeah, I can never keep track of whether it's fall or spring out here, it's pretty much: folks, today it'll be somewhere between fifty and eighty, yeah, sometimes colder, but you can never know *how* cold, the seasons are just . . . unreasonable, totally, like *unseasonable,* and then there's the fog mixing it all up, it's mad unstable, any second could be a whole other world of weather, threats all around, it's hella shaky here, do you think that's what happened? I don't know, I mean, it could have been a lotta things, we're right up on the edge of everything, yeah, the ocean, the storms, the earthquakes, the weather, they say it makes these, what's it called? Micro—? Yeah, microclimates, right? They say we can see it in the leaves, how the green changes, the rhythm of when the flowers bloom and die, but don't they just bloom all the damn time?"

"Breakfast?" I point at a diner up the street.

"Oh, I don't know." A shy smile, lips closed.

She's been dragging her feet the whole morning. She insisted on bringing her one high heel from the hotel even though she's never gonna find the one she lost and I just bought her new shoes. Now she's tugging her arm out of mine, about to remove herself from the situation. That's when the kid pitches up.

"What it do, cuddy? You back? Where's Mo at?"

White Reggie. He ought to be less of a kid, ought to be White Reginald by now, but he's got the same skater-boy look. Drowning in jeans with a chain on the pocket and a hoodie two sizes too big. Up close, you can see his real age, though. Face like a mile of potholes and, like, three teeth left, tongue made of cotton, eyes kinda crossed. Meth's done a number on him. I glance at C but she's busy holding her breath.

"Hey man, wassup?" I give him a fist bump. It leaves an

invisible residue, an itch in the skin reminding me to wash my hand later.

"You know." Reggie sways his head side to side. "Just postin', regulatin'." He opens his palms to the blue sky, his feet pointing out, and for a second, he's a priest. Then he cackles and shuffles his rotten sneaks and turns back into a rat. His bloodshot eyes spin toward C, who's wearing another thin, no-teeth smile. She darts a look at me. I put my arm around her shoulders, ignoring how they tense up.

"Word. Listen, man, we should get going. Good to see you, though."

"I was just tryna say hi and shit. I ain't seen you in a *minute* minute, Wayne . . ."

Shit. But if C did catch the name in the slur of his speech, she doesn't react. Reggie's still talking: ". . . you lookin' all fresh and clean, almost didn't reckernize you, but you know, bruh, I ain't mean to interrupt nobody's *stroll* or nothin', uh . . ."

Fuck it. "Reggie, this is C. C, this is Reggie."

"Real nice to meet you . . . C!" Reggie sticks out both of his hands. C frowns but gives him her hand gamely. Shit. I know the little scrimp's about to make a move. I watch as he does this ridiculous two-handed shake that clasps her all the way up her wrist, dwarfing her hand. He's already halfway into one of his bullshit sermons.

"God bless your father and mother, who brought you into being into a world of sin and covetousness and evil, and God bless they grandparents, who brought them into this world too, a beautiful blessed benedicting world for all, and God bless *God,* who brought *errrybody* into this world, and God bless us all, specially you and yours and your family, C."

He stops abruptly and lets go of her hand and puts his hands back in his pockets. He sends another blissed-out grin to the sky, his mouth wide as a church with those crooked pew teeth. C laughs her thanks. Then Reggie starts in about some "wife" named Sue Ellen. C seems surprised he's still conversating but she follows up with a "How long have you been married?" and Reggie starts unspooling again. Is he actually high? Okay, well, it's on him if he doesn't know when to get out.

I sneak up to him, pat him on the shoulder. "You got married? Congratulations, man!"

He nods and keeps talking. He reeks of old and new cigarette, stale and fresh sweat. I let my hand slide down the back of his hoodie and hang for a beat by his pocket. C doesn't notice—she's nodding politely—when I slip her watch, still warm from her wrist, back out of Reggie's pocket and into the cradle of my hand. Reggie feels it go, though, he flinches and his energy dims some. But he keeps on answering her empty questions with his empty lies. What else can he do?

Five minutes later, we're rid of him and her watch is in my pocket and I'm planning the moment I'll "find" it for her—*It must have slipped off* and *it's a small mercy* and *I caught its shine on the sidewalk*. We walk on, talking, laughing. Getting away from Reggie is obviously a relief for us both. It's been a long time since I boosted a watch. I can still sense it in my fingers, a light vibration like I just strummed a guitar. I tap my fingertips against my thumb, one by one, pinkie to pointer, speeding it up. I guess I'll always love this feeling—slipping my hand in a pocket, skin dancing off the cloth, the *slink-clink* of a strap, the weight of the watch, the tiny heartbeat of its *tick-tock*. I guess no matter how high I rise, I'll always miss the day-to-day seesaw of good luck and bad out here on the street—the chance, the touch.

As I hold the door to the diner open for her, I even get the childish urge to boast on it. Boasting comes too easy to me, class-clown shit. The trick is to tell so many stories, people lose track. It makes the times when you have to come up with something on the spot easier too. Each version of a lie could be another joke. But it's different with C. This ease feels dangerous somehow with her, and turns out that it is—"Wayne, party of two?" the hostess calls out, and I realize I've let my guard down long enough to write my name on the clipboard. C stares at me this time but, again, she says nothing while we're being seated.

She pulls a small bottle of hand sanitizer from her purse and we share a spritz in knowing silence before ordering. She gets a mushroom omelette and I get something called a Lumberjack Special and after some chat about our jobs and a little riff on why mushrooms are clearly an alien species (the gills, the variety, the hallucinations), I change the topic.

"So what brings you to the Bay?"

"Um." She stabs at a mushroom and uses her teeth to scrape it into her mouth. "I have a family event to attend."

"Like a reunion?"

"No, it's a work event, actually. For my mother's foundation. A gala."

"A gala! Where do people hold a *gala* in this city?"

She shrugs—"Somewhere in Civic Center?"—then says an address on Van Ness.

I nod and memorize it as I take a swig of kumquat juice. "You said your mother's foundation? What's it for?"

"It's an organization for missing kids," she says, sounding like an infomercial. "It's called Vigil."

"Oh wow." I give a fake frown of curiosity. "How long has she been doing that?"

"A while now," she says. "Basically since my little brother—" She looks up. "Well, my little brother died and she got into helping other grieving parents and then it kind of spun off into this."

I give a real frown now. *Died?* All the Vigil publicity says that little Wayne Williams went missing. Why would C lie? Maybe she says this to people to avoid questions? Or is it to protect her brother? She's still talking about the organization.

". . . so we went national around then. I run the fundraising wing. My official title is 'Director of Development.'" She gives a wry smile.

"I'm sorry to hear about your brother," I say carefully.

"No, no," she says. "I don't even know why I told you—" She aims her fork at another mushroom, thinks better of it, drops the fork, nudges her plate away. She reaches for her purse.

I stay her hand. "I got you."

"You sure?" She looks at the loose eggs and rigor mortis bacon on my plate.

"Of course."

"Okay." She smiles. "If you insist."

She goes to get her jacket from the old-fashioned coat hook at the entrance while I wait in line to pay. As the customers shuffle forward to the old-fashioned cash register—I hate when gentrification gets nostalgic for inconvenient shit—I look down at the handwritten bill in my hand, stained with syrup from the cardboard pancakes I didn't even want to finish. Fucking $41? At least the tip's included. I reach for my wallet and it's gone.

I pat myself down, my tall tale from last night at the hospital haunting me. Did I actually lose it? No, I used my credit card just this morning to buy those ugly-ass loafers C's got on. Shit. Reggie. White fucking Reggie. The price for getting her watch back. His tit for my tat. I shake my head. I'm kind of impressed, to be honest. I'm used to my fortunes tilting like this, up and down all day, every day. But this feels like a premonition.

"That'll be $41.68," says the cashier, an Asian chick wearing green lipstick.

I look over at the entrance to the diner. C's already outside. Good thing I took that cash from her wallet last night—a small mercy, you might say. I pull the bills out, count them out on the counter, tell the cashier to keep the change, tell her to smile. I even smile back when she does, even though it's a horror show, it cracks her dark lipstick with pink flesh, like an accordion stretched too wide.

I'm still grinning like a fool when I walk out. I'm so swole with my own foresight that it takes me a minute to realize that C's gone. Her one high heel sits on the curb like a punchline. I look around but if I know anything, I know what gone looks like. I head back to my hotel, pressing the bruise from her bite on my neck. Shit. I didn't get her number, and I don't have my wallet anymore, which means I don't even have her business card.

≈

Back at the hotel, I call and cancel my credit card. They'll mail a replacement in a couple of days. I'm relieved: I had no idea they could do it so fast. Good thing I booked a whole week here—I can charge everything to the room until the new card arrives. I'd thought about shacking up with an ex or an old friend, but I figured I needed to stay as anonymous as possible for this. Reggie just proved my point. I'm gonna have to get a new ID somehow, and quick. Annoyed, I sprawl out on the bed, staring at the ceiling fan's sluggish spin.

I wonder—I sniff at the pillow—but no, housekeeping's

already changed our dirty sheets. I remember it, though: C smells like money and honey—metallic and sweet, a warm coin you've been handling. My mind runs over last night again. The way her hair, unwashed and gritty, felt with my hand tangled in it, gripping. How her lips looked, open and closed. Her thigh resting in my palm, the bone's weight and the muscle's pull. The memory begins pooling into a thick warmth at the base of my dick. The blades of the fan *wuck wuck wuck* through the air, slow enough I can make out the shape of a flower stripped of every other petal. *She loves me she loves me not she loves me.* I chuckle. Doubtful.

"And what do you do, exactly?" she'd asked me at the diner.

"You know. Tech. Like everybody else these days."

Her lips had pursed tight as a drawstring at that. Did she not believe me? All things considered, I thought I had pulled off this bougie look pretty well up to that point—my accent already being what it is, I'd mostly focused on my clothes, my hotel room, an ease with paying for things. Nobody likes the rich, but everybody loves a man on the up-and-up. Not her snooty ass, though.

I've been tracking one blade of the fan and my eyes are starting to whirl inward. I close them. I'm tempting myself. Back in the day, if a ceiling fan happened to tilt into view, I'd feel a rush of dizziness—what do they call it? Vertigo. Mine came whenever I looked up rather than down, though. It's more like a tease now, like jostling a loose tooth with your tongue tip. Or so I thought, because now I can see the white hotel fan slicing through the black behind my closed eyelids, and I sense it coming, rising up my back, and . . .

I'm there again. Ten years old, and the lawnmower is growling outside. It's the neighbor cutting his grass, that weekly shave that always made my nose runny. I almost feel the itch in my nostrils now as I come in the house, sling my bag on the landing—"Hey Ma! You home?"—walk to my bedroom, and flick on the ceiling fan, sensing more than seeing its slow, thick *wuck*-ing above me. The room is hot and murky, the curtains are drawn, the walls crinkly with the magazine cut-outs of MJ I've pasted on them. Mom should be home, maybe napping directly above me in her bedroom, but she doesn't answer and something feels off.

There's a pattering sound like rain and on my striped bed-spread, right in the middle, there's a stain, a messy red circle a bit wider than the radius of the fan above. I look up and see that the slow-spinning blades are red at their edges too, dripping with something that's drawing the circle on the bed. Where the fan is attached to the ceiling, there's a splotch, the same dark red, and it's creeping, spreading like a thundercloud. I try to read it—as I would later try to read so many clouds, so many days lying on my back outdoors, stoned or dozing—the red splotch on my ceiling could be the head of a dog in profile, a pair of scissors, a three-fingered hand . . .

I open my eyes with a cuss, slamming my hands against the plush hotel bed to wake myself up. I'm a grown-ass man but trifling shit like that still lays me out. The sound of a lawn-mower, a dog, a striped bedspread, a ceiling fan. All the details are carved in my mind, grooved there, sturdy footholds that let me climb down the stone walls into my past whenever I want, all the way down to the bottom, to the day my parents died in their bed and put me in the place that led me to that other kid named Wayne in the first place. I don't wanna remember today, but something about C, maybe the way she lied to me about her brother being dead, keeps dragging me back. *Hey Ma! You home?* Time for hide-and-go-seek.

2

≈≈≈

Friday night in the Tenderloin can get you high or get you killed, and can easily do both before sunrise. I stride along the sidewalk, headed toward Civic Center, threading my way between the tipsy types and the homeless folks bedding down for the night. Cars drive by, buzzing like bugs then hushing off, headlights skittering into the fog. There's a group of drunk girls on the corner, their outfits like plastic flowers. They lean and stalk in their heels, a posy for me to pluck.

Sometimes, when we were on the cleaner, saner side of things, Mo would pick up partygoers who'd just left the club. I'd hang back and watch while he finessed. "You a Scorpio? For real? Thass whass*up*." He was always slipping into their way of talking. Didn't matter if they were boys or girls or both, Mo liked them young. Not pedo-young but borderline. Thing is, they liked him too. Mo saw something in them and he called it out and they liked being seen, being named like that.

As I pass the pretty girls in their shiny dresses, their screechy voices set something off in me. Under my jacket, I'm wearing my new suit—purchased last month with the credit card Reggie just stole—but I don't wanna smile or flirt. I wanna yell in their faces, I wanna tell them they're destroying this city. I look away,

I think of C, I wonder if she's like them, then wonder how it is that I've gotten caught up in fucking this woman when I'm supposed to be finding her brother, and then I'm remembering the line of her spine, her ass curving up from it, just so . . .

I almost trip over a dude on the ground—his pants half pulled up like he fell asleep while taking a shit. Next to him, there's a plastic cup with a handful of coins and a cardboard sign saying YOU ARE PERFECT. A block down, some punk kids are clustered, their heads bobbing at a dude freestyling to the scratchy beat from a boombox tied to a parking meter: *You think you so slick . . . like pussy on my dick . . .*

Rain starts to fur the glow around the streetlights. I cut down an alley, a mess of graffiti on either side. Leaning into the wind tunnel, I jam my hands in my jacket pockets to help me hunch my shoulders and feel a cluster of hotel bar receipts in one, something cold and heavy curled in the other. I shake it, measure it, pull it out. A men's watch, a Seiko. I never got the chance to give it back to C after I stole it back from Reggie. I return it to my pocket. I can sense it now, there and not there, a weight on the body that belongs to the cloth.

I cross the avenue, glancing at the carnival colors—red, blue, green—lighting up City Hall, wondering what it's for. I track the address C mentioned at the diner to a hulking cube on Van Ness. There's a sign taped to the inside of a glass door: NO ONE'S ARK. I walk into the lobby, shake the rain off, jog up a short set of marble steps. A woman wearing cat ears and a velvet bustier is standing at a podium, its light casting a short dawn up her torso.

"You didn't dress up," the pussycat purrs.

I scan her breasts. "I can change now if you want." I touch the pull of my jacket zipper.

She smiles, her teeth too blunt for a cat. She seems

drunk—no, high—the angle of her flirt is off. Or maybe she's just tired of this gig. I grin and come around to her side of the podium to "help" her find me on the list as I patter on about how I lost my driver's license and how people are always mixing up my middle and last names. She looks at me from under raised eyebrows but, again, it's more weary than wary. I recognize a few names from placards in windows and on buses—local government, big business—as I page through the list to the end. There she is. Williams, C. There's no x by her name, but maybe she's running late. And look—I point at another Williams on the page, a male-sounding one.

"There he blows!" I grin again.

The pussycat knows I'm lying—*Your funeral,* her tired eyes say—but she nods me toward the wooden door that takes up most of the wall behind her. I lean into it and I'm in.

≈

Swing music wheedling, the shout of small talk in a crowd, splashes of laughter. The smell of damp fur, alcohol breath, and perfume. A jumble of costumes: stripes and spots and fringed shadows. It's like wading through a sewer on *Sesame Street.* I see a tiger clutching a bear, the couple swaying drunkenly at half the rhythm of the music. Next to them, dancing in time, though not to the beat, are two bunnies of the *Playboy* variety, a fairy in a lacy bra, and a full-on Big Bird, goofing off, making the best of her costume choice. A raccoon, a puppy, and a toucan are standing around a high cocktail table to my right. There are, for some reason, a lot of kangaroos and penguins parading around. One of the penguins waddles by, holding a tray of drinks—aha, waiters. I grab a glass of champagne and move into the crowd, eavesdropping on the light white chitchat.

". . . mugged by a gang of snails and the turtle says to the cop, *I don't remember, it all happened so fast,* an abomination when you think about it, the way they treat them, can't believe this is what it's come to, so what do you think it would go for now? In this market? The bubble's gotta burst, right? *The* Animal, like in Marx? No, dude, like in the Muppets, I'm sure he'll get the vote up in Napa, but, like, in the good part? But what *kind* of Japanese whiskey? Oakland is just San Francisco now, I work in tech, but what *kind* of weed gummies? Down in Palm Springs, yeah but that company ain't gonna survive the Big One, ugh don't remind me, yeah, in tech like everybody else, it's like the *old* Burning Man, but that's just like the *old* Burning Man, wait that's what she just said, all the tech bros are gonna lose their shit the second they feel a tremor, but what *kind* of sativa? This place has become so fucking unlivable, didn't *we* do that? Who you mean *we,* Sensei?"

Finally, a straggler. I sidle up to what seems to be a sea urchin—purple, spiky. He looks like he knows what's up, like those spikes are for catching gossip.

"Nice party," I say.

"A catastrophe," he slurs, then gives me a double take and a smirk. "What brings you here tonight?"

"You know, out on the hunt. Lots of prey around here." I smile. "How about you?"

He rolls his eyes. "Ugh. Aspirational networking. Drowning in contempt. This, apparently, is what 'philanthropy' "—he spits the word like seed husks—"has come to."

"Hmm." I nod. "Wanna smoke?"

"You angel!" The urchin's eyes widen. "That is my *favorite* song!"

He grabs me by the wrist and pulls me deeper into the party, stringing us through the furry, feathered crowd toward a balcony. We slip out through the glass doors. After the funk of the party, the cool air is welcome. It feels almost human out here. We share a couple of tokes from his weed pen, then I tap out two Kools from my pack, light one, and hand him the other along with my lighter.

"Menthol?" he mutters. "Fucking burnt Peppermint Pattie." He turns his back to the wind and lights up. The tiny flame casts quarter-moon shadows under his zits. "But *thank you*, honey!" He cocks his head and hands the lighter back. "So," he says, propping his elbow on his other wrist so the cigarette is within ready reach. "What's your *animal* costume?"

"I'm, uh . . ." I can't think of a better joke, it just tumbles out. "A Negro?"

He gives a shocked laugh, then rolls with it. "Yes! *Rare*. Exotic. *Wild*."

"Watch it." I smile around my Kool. "Don't say something you'll regret."

"My middle *name* is regret." He puffs happily, his attitude like a scarf around his neck. "So, you been to one of these pity parties before?"

"Pity party?"

He cackles, his urchin spikes quivering. "Peeee-ta party," he says, stretching his jaw forward. "You know PETA, the animal people? I call them PETA-philes." He snorts.

"Oh, right. I guess I knew it was a . . . 'save the animals' type thing. But I didn't know it was gonna be, like, a whole costume party."

"Everything has to be a *thing* these days," he says, rolling his eyes. "It's all so meticulously dull."

And for a second, I see it in his face—the same exhaustion I saw in the girl out in the lobby. It makes me feel sort of tender for him.

"You know, it reminds me of this party I went to once—"

"Mmm-hmm?" He shimmies his shoulders.

"It's kinda hard to explain but I was, like, homeless for a little while?"

"Really?" He tilts his head with interest but I see him flinch.

"Yeah, I was just a kid, but I ended up at this party in Berkeley and—" Goddamnit. I press the bruise on my neck. It's like C left a truth serum in me. "Know what? Never mind."

"Ohhh-kay, Mister Mystery." He coyly stabs out his cigarette on the railing, and we watch the sparks shoot up like ant fireworks. I pull my jacket zip up to my chin. The rain's stopped spitting and it's turned colder. The hills of the city in front of us glow in patches like the land's on fire and the lights are embers and the fog is smoke.

"Listen." I glance back at the party inside. "I'm actually looking for somebody."

"Mmm, aren't we all?" he smirks.

I explain what I know about Vigil.

"Oh, Charlotte?" he says. "*Everybody* knows Charlotte."

He confirms the story I've already got: she never remarried, she's been looking for her son for years, she registered her foundation in the nineties or early two-thousands, she's on all the charity boards in the city, from the Sisters of Perpetual Indulgence to City Arts & Lectures, she's fabulously wealthy. Then he adds some new info, as an aside: she lives in Russian Hill. I almost hug him—I've been trying to get that address for months.

"Oh, my weed goddess told me that," he says with a laugh. "She delivers exclusively to the rich and *un*famous."

But then he goes quiet. I'm starting to get the feeling that nobody really knows Charlotte Williams, and that she and Vigil are either too saintly or too sad to mock.

"Yeah," I try again. "So this, uh, PETA thing, or whatever. Is she on the board?"

"Well, I haven't seen her here . . ." he sighs. "I doubt she'd show up for something like this." He purses his lips. "This is pretty small-fry."

Shit. So, this wasn't the gala that C meant after all. I must've got the date wrong.

"Wanna head back in?" He's bored, looking over my shoulder through the door.

I figure it's pressing my luck to ask about C, so I nod and follow him inside. I watch his hips waggle as he raises his arms, dancing toward a tall, beautiful woman—Iranian or Indian—who's wearing a giraffe costume that fits her like skin. She smiles at me and I move to join them but a kangaroo cuts me off.

Floppy ears, saggy pouch, big-ass haunches. He asks me something—I can tell it's a question but the words are the reverb of the sea in a shell.

"Excuse me?" I shout, and promptly regret it. It sounds hostile at that volume.

The kangaroo head leans in. "See some ID?"

Shit. Security. I almost protest, then I remember where I am and who I am, so I say, "Sure," and reach for my wallet, which, of course, is gone. White fucking Reggie.

"Ah, man, I'm sorry," I say. "I lost—I left my wallet—"

"C'mon, guy." He shakes his head, ears waggling. "First and last name."

I should say whatever name pops into my head. I should say my own damn name. But I hesitate, trying to remember the one I'd told the receptionist. The delay dooms me.

"Right," he barks. He tugs a paw off his costume, uncovering a hairy but human hand, and shoves the paw in his pouch. He takes my arm. "Time to go."

≈

I relent, letting him drag me out of the room, his pouch pushing a path through the party, his foam tail knocking into my leg with each step. Out in the lobby, he nods at the pussycat, who shrugs at me. Traitor. The kangaroo shoves me awkwardly down the marble steps, then even more awkwardly into the revolving doors along with him. We inch forward, pressed together in one humid slow-moving wedge. As soon as it cracks to the outside, he pushes me ahead between two giant potted cacti on the sidewalk, but he's still holding on to my arm, which hurts. Now that we're out of his domain, I wrench it away and say, "Fucking get off me, man." In fury, he pulls off his kangaroo head and tosses it on the sidewalk. His hair stands in salute like a plume. I suppress the instinct to raise my hands.

There's a cluttery bang behind us and we both turn. It's a bunch of rubber duckies inside the lobby, throwing themselves against the glass windows, quacking hysterically. They waddle to the revolving door and squeeze themselves in. It churns them out, one by one. We watch them, hypnotized. They quack stupidly as they emerge—two of them, three, four—and waddle up the street, bouncing off each other. It almost breaks the tension but then the last one yells, "Mall cop!" and waddles off into the fog. The headless kangaroo takes a step toward them, fist raised like he's gonna do something, but then he stumbles into one of the cacti. The pot tumbles over with a thud and a crack.

And I guess that pisses him off because now I'm laid out on the ground, and my head's being smashed against the pavement, and I should probably be focused on the pain pulsing from the back of my skull to the tip of my nose, a rhythm steady as sonar, but I'm thinking instead about how quiet he's made this whole scene, about how his plume wobbles whenever my head bounces, about the spray of spittle from his mouth, and I should probably be fighting back, but it's difficult because of our positions—I'm on my back, he's straddling me—and I find myself remembering that moment when C looked in my eyes and put her hand on my face and said *No*. I almost see her, right there, to one side of him, and maybe that's why, right before everything goes black, I feel a weird kind of peace.

3

≈≈≈

You can call me Will. That aint my real name. But close enough. Plus my real name's brought me a whole lotta trouble in this life. I aint that man now anyway. That name's dead to me. But I don't wanna talk about what I did to get inside here anyway. You already know, and besides, it aint worth the spit. Everybody up in here got their boasts and excuses on why they hurt somebody—they was broke, they was riled, there was some woman. Some of these niggas up in here, they'll tell you—and I believe em—they will straight up tell you they did it for *fun*. But what happened to me never happened to nobody else. I'm in here for life. I'm only talkin to you cuz I don't wanna leave this earth with no misunderstandings.

Most niggas get into street shit slow, bit by bit. For me, it was like I gave up all the good in me at the same time. Just pulled it off and dropped it on the floor. It was petty shit at first, like we all do when we young and raw. But really and truly, darkness entered my life one day. You know. You look back on it and you can see where somethin stepped in. *Right. There.*

I always had that chaos in me. I will acknowledge that. I showed signs even back when I was fresh in the foster system.

Social workers said it, doctors said it. ADHD, all of that. I remember grown folks talkin bout it—how it was in my blood and I couldn't escape it. But I aint even know who my blood really was, feel me? They found me on the street when I was but five-six years old. It weren't my fault, but I couldn't do nothin about it. So when they said *it's in his blood,* it put this feelin all up in my chest. Like an animal was in there, slammin up against my ribcage, tryna break out.

I really only started buckin when I was thirteen-fourteen. You know how it is, more bark than bite. But shit was real hectic where I came up. Mostly I was just tryna make people do exactly what I said—that way I always knew what was comin.

The school in my hood was this big-ole fallin-apart building, church-lookin windows and thin-ass walls. A real ding-dong bell between classes, not one of them buzzy ones. Halls like a maze. I still dream about it sometimes, wander round, get lost. Even when I'm awake, if I get to reminiscin bout that school, I start grinnin and shit. Cuz that was the last place I really felt known—like I was *me* and not somebody else. Yeah, this whole story, how I got here? It started right there. Not "in the streets," or in some locked-up bedroom with the curtains closed, but in that school.

Remember recess? That's where the shit went *down.* Yeah, we'd be out on that playground with the seriousness. Teachers would walk us out there like the guards do here, but back then they'd let us ramble or rumble. No grass out there, just concrete with cracks so big, your mama's back stayed broke. Weeds so tall you could pluck em and use em for jump rope. High walls on every side, broken glass up on top to keep the animals out—or *keep the animals in,* Coach liked to say.

That school, man. There were these water fountains with old signs—permanent fuckin signs—saying DON'T DRINK

THE WATER. The desks were so dirty, so carved up with tags and dicks and titties, they looked burnt. They were bolted to the floor. Some of the doors was nailed shut too, so sometimes you had to walk through one classroom to get to the next.

There was this sound all the time, kinda soft. Like a rustlin sound. So, I had always thought it was comin from the big-ass trees outside the school. It was mad dark and cold inside because of those trees, but they couldn't cut em down—they was "historical" or some shit. I remember, you know, lookin out the window at those trees tossin and turnin out there, then lookin back at the classroom, and I was thinkin the trees out there looked so alive, but the doors and desks inside looked so dead. Like chopped-up tree bodies.

I was weird like that, always dreamin up weird shit. I guess you could say I was innovative. Like, this one time, me and this kid Ramsey got some screwdrivers and we opened up a closet door. We was lookin for supplies in there to sell, or some old tests with the answers or some shit. Anyway, we bust that door open and—shit, I will never forget it, man. Ramsey nearbout screamed his head off. That rustlin sound weren't no trees. It was rats! Came streamin out like a river. Turns out they were all up in the veins of that old-ass school.

Most niggas leave those schooldays behind—it looks to them like the shadow of their real lives. Not me. The things that went down in that school, they feel like forever. Like this ink I got all up and down my arms. I remember all of it: the pranks, the brawls, the rumors, the jokes, who was topdog and who was under—I got so hyped on that shit! No need for physical contact, feel me? Niggas just knew. On the playground, that shit was clear as day. Naturally, I got a reputation right quick. I can see now it was all nonsense. But those young bloods really looked up to me.

≈

Except for this one kid. New kid. The wildest thing? He had my same name. What'd I say to call me before—Will? Yeah, so let's say this new kid was called Will too. They said his parents got shot dead in their beds—it was over some H, I heard, they was using together—and he got put in a foster home in Gwynns Falls, so he ended up at my school. Now, this kid was young— plus fresh out the county with his corny ass—but he did not buy what I was sellin. He weren't about to do what I said just cuz I said do it.

And the thing is, that was it, that was my whole entire game back then: buckin up to tire everybody out, gettin up in your face nasty enough that I aint really have to swing, feel me? But with a game like that, all it takes is one person to kinda insinu-ate, like, *that nigga ain't shit.* That was Will.

I aint gon lie, I was uneasy about him from the get. It was like he had decided in his mind that he had beef with me. So I told him step outside so we could squash it. And this pussy-ass nigga just walked off! Nobody really saw it happen, so I couldn't even shout on it. Hmb. That boy was sneaky. He would step to me between class, when the hall was loud as hell: lockers bangin, dudes yellin, girls screamin, Jordans chirpin. He would say some shit in my ear—mad corny, like, *I'm just tryna be like you, man* or *I just don't wanna see you play yourself, man*—and then he would wade right back out into that mess of kids in the hall. Irked the fuck out of me. The thing is—and that's why it riled me—he aint really *wanna* be topdog, far as I could see. He just didn't want *me* to be.

He was always raggin on me, checkin me, like we was blood. Some of the other kids even thought we was family for real, especially us having the same name. And because of the alphabet, they put us next to each other in nearbout every class. I did dumb kid shit to him. Wedgies. A dead rat in his desk. Took the screws out his chair one time, so he fell on his ass. He brushed it off for the most part. The only thing that got to him was when I made fun of his voice. It was kind of rough, crackly, like somebody done punched him in the throat.

I started pickin fights with him on the playground too. Real fights or whatever real fights means for kids—coupla swings and a knee to the chest, the other kids standin all around, yellin like demons. I always won. Or he always let me. He got me back in his own way. He was slick about it. See, I always hated my name, even back then—too easy to make cracks on. By middle school, I had crushed it out of everybody but the teachers. Made em call me by my nickname. Then this nigga shows up and I gotta hear my real name *twice* every other hour. That shit vexed me. And he knew it. He started sayin it all the time— his name, my name—like, incidentally. My back rose up every damn time.

And *then,* this nigga starts dressin like me. Wearin my labels. Same belt, same kicks, same puffer coat. Dude was all up on my jock. Walkin like me, tryna talk like me—but with that ugly-ass wheeze in his throat. You ever have somebody play that echo game on you? It's like—I can't even describe it. It gave me the heebies. It was like he wasn't just tryna be me. He was tryna to do me *better* than me.

Musta been seventh grade, I had occasion to beat the fuck outta him one last time. I remember it exactly. We was out at recess. I was swingin and he was layin there, playin dead like always, mouth all dirtied up with blood. Then somethin shifted and we was lookin at each other. Dead in the eye. I look him in his and he looks me in mine and I *see* him. And it's like—I *know* you. Like, I *been* knowin you, for a long-long time, from before I was even born. It was like all this dumb kid shit, all this craziness—the way he was actin like me, the way he was tryna look like me—had one purpose: to make me kick the shit out of somebody who been with me since birth.

4

≈≈≈

How long before sunshine does its thing, slips a hand through the blinds, and reaches toward my pillow? A couple hours? A day? The hotel elevator chimes outside my door as a ray of light hits my eyelids. I open them to a pale buzzing quiet, like moth wings. It's hard to find myself in or under or around the pain. I lie as still as I can and try to think.

Did the rubber duckies come back and save me? The last thing I remember clearly is their yellow asses wobbling into the fog. Then darkness. A triangle hovering into view before multiplying like a fly's eye. Wetness on my neck. Rolling. A black circle inside a white oval. A gray paw. A car door slamming. Darkness again. How'd they know where to send me? It takes a minute before I remember the receipts in my pocket from the hotel bar. How'd I get up to my room, though? The hotel doorman? Poor dude. I laugh, which is a mistake. "Ugh," I say to the sunlight and roll my eyelids back down.

After a couple more hours of ignoring the muffled clock of housekeeping's knocks, I sit up, stagger to the bathroom, take a piss, chug two glasses of water. I realize I've had my shoes on this whole time. *What's the plan now?* I ask my reflection. First things first: I clearly can't be going around without an ID. I need to get official again. And for that, I need Sticky.

≈

An hour later, I'm at the bus stop outside Rockridge BART. The fickle sky's gone gray but I can't tell if it's fog or cloud. I hate the bus, hate being on it, hate waiting for it. I hear Mo's voice: *Does there not pass over man a space of time when his life is a blank?* Before I met him, I used to scrounge around here between Berkeley and Oakland, the borderland like a threshold, like that big H E R E T H E R E sculpture on MLK or the striped awning at Black & White Liquor on Adeline. It'll feel like you're in the suburbs, everything covered with rainbow flags and P A Z signs and T R E E S A R E B R O T H E R S scratched in the sidewalk. Fly-ers like fossils on the telephone poles, bumper stickers with jokey politics: M I N D Y O U R O W N U T E R U S! You'll stroll along, feeling protected by Berkeley's good intentions, and maybe you're a little likelier to ask for change, but then you cross a line and you blink and you're in the hood. That's how close "good" streets and "bad" are, how neighborly *here* and *there*.

There's a white dude at the bus stop with me now, holding a stack of old soul records. He keeps grinning over at me like he wants me to ask about them. When I don't, he asks what time it is. I pull C's watch out: 2:37. The guy says, "Fuck AC Tran-sit." I look away. I'm not about to commiserate about public transportation with a man who actively chooses to dress just this side of homeless. Insult to injury, it starts raining. At first it's light, leaving bamboo patterns on us, but soon it's a down-pour. I tug my collar up and the white dude opens an umbrella, janky as a broken kite. When the bus finally pulls up, its wheels cast a short gutter wave that splashes over our shins. We cuss in unison but I avoid swapping smiles with him.

The doors hiss open and the white dude makes to get on but the driver motions for him to wait. An old lady inside the bus, bent nearly in half, slowly comes down the stairs, a long purple umbrella in one hand, a small pink purse in the other.

"Young man, would you hold my umbrella?" She stretches it toward the white dude.

He shakes his head. "I've only got two hands and I'm already using them."

"Who raised you?" She starts berating him, waving her umbrella like a wand for curses. After a beat, I move in front of him.

"Excuse me," I say, and take her outstretched umbrella. "Here you go, ma'am." I even open it over her as she clambers off the bus in her tan stockings and her gray skirt and her lavender hat. When I pass her the handle of her umbrella, she nods at me.

"Thank you, young man," she says, then turns to the white dude. "No thanks to *you*."

"Look, you can ask me to help," he snarls and shuts his own busted umbrella, showering us all with rain. "But I don't have to say yes. My hands are fucking full."

"Well, what are you good for?" the old lady calls out. "What are you good for then?"

He hops onto the bus, ignoring her words, ignoring the driver's glare and mine. The old lady heads up the street, the rain hitting her umbrella giving off a spray like an aura.

What are you good for? Her question stays with me as I board and move to the back to avoid the white dude, who's still steaming in a handicapped seat up front. Is there anything more than being polite to your elders, anything like being *good*, in how I acted with her? Maybe. But as the bus heaves its way through the rain toward Sticky's crib in the hills, I feel a twist of regret in my wrists: what if she'd asked me to hold her purse instead?

≈

I met Sticky for the first time on the 51. About a year ago, I was riding this same bus, minding my business, sitting across from a gaggle of punks in the back. They wore nineties-retro clothes, looking like Salt-N-Pepa Smurfs: neon blues and greens and pinks. They'd wrapped a strip of yellow-and-black caution tape around themselves, a loose chain binding them at the wrists and ankles and necks. The girls toyed with the bumblebee strip and murmured and smiled. The boys raised their arms to cheer roller-coaster-style at various landmarks outside.

"There goes my spirit animal!"

"Wheeee!"

"There goes the good Peet's!"

"Wheeee!"

I watched them. They were nothing like the East Bay punks I knew coming up. Like Mo's boy, Brontez. Nineteen, five foot flat, platinum blond fro, skin dark and smooth and covered with tattoos: x x x on his neck, a crop of cotton plants growing up his side, and a placard on his wrist that said: T O D O: 1. T H R O W A B R I C K. 2. W I N. He served lattes, sang backup for a glam-punk band, made intricate zines, cruised the White Ho, and had a heart so broken it was always leaking love. He had run away from home when he was twelve and lived in an abandoned building in Emeryville with a bunch of other punks. Me and Mo would visit him in the middle of the day to get high—meth, dust, powder, whatever—and watch porn. "I would sit on that dick," Brontez would say to Mo, "I would *rotate* on that dick," showing us how with his little bubble butt. Mo would laugh shyly with his hands on his cheeks, the three of us high as the noon sun outside the big, cracked windows, the three of us pleased as day. I think they did fuck a couple times maybe, while I was taking a nap. But that night, or another one, I found myself confessing to Brontez about my schooldays back East, the shit that got me sent out here in the first place. He's the one who put the idea in my head that I needed to get justice. I thought Mo would agree, with all his tit-for-tat talk, but he lost his shit, beat the fuck out of Brontez—some kind of jealousy thing—and that was the end of that.

Anyway, so these kids on the 51 were nothing like that. They were healthy, drug use more like a tic than a lifestyle. I used to duck townies like this whenever I was out in the East Bay: mostly white—or gray with tattoos—with armpit hair that looked and smelled like mold. They'd lay on the sidewalk outside Rasputin or Amoeba, playing their own music on their boomboxes, leering at Cal students just to fuck with them even though they were the same, really. Gentrified punks, with homes to go to, numbers to call, pets.

One of the ones on the bus that day, skin like milky tea and sporting an orange mohawk, started watching me, his eyes swooping over me at a steady beat. I knew this method of spying well, so I did the same thing, offset: I was looking at the kid when he was looking away. The whole time, he was still talking to his groupies about his lame-ass trespasses. Another generational difference: Punks back in the day would rattle off the letters and numbers of the laws they broke. This kid just named them outright.

"Yeah, I mean, 'intent to distribute,' what the fuck? The pigs knew it was bullshit. I was kicking it with them and shit. Officer goes, 'What drugs do you do?' and I go, 'Um, everything?'

and he's like, 'That's not a very smart answer, young man.' But he's laughing like I'm kidding and what he doesn't know is I've got two Klonopin in my shirt pocket. I mean I forgot they were there but when they put me in the cell, I was like, 'Oh, shit! Look what I found!' I mean, I'm pretty sure they can't charge me for, like, *anxiety*, right?"

"Nah," said a mixed girl with hair like a bouquet of question marks. "Thass legal."

"But I can't flush 'em—if you put pills in the toilet they go *tink-tink* and they'd be all like, What the fuck is that? So I look left, look right, look left. Gulp. Ten minutes later . . ."

He glanced around and the boys raised their arms and this time everybody chimed in: "Wheeeeee!" They cracked up, falling over themselves, making the caution tape rustle. The bus whooshed to a stop and they untangled themselves and tumbled off, all but the mixed girl and the mohawked kid. When the bus started moving again, he caught my eye.

"Sup, homie!" The kid leaned forward, elbows on his knees, hands dangling. His knuckles were tattooed: E-A-T-V on the left, E-G-A-N on the right. "You lookin' for some?"

"Nah, man. I'm good."

The girl traced a raindrop on the outside of the window with her finger.

"I said you *look like* someone," the kid enunciated. "Someone I've seen. You Asian?"

"Asian?" I'm used to being taken for other races but I hadn't heard this one before.

"Not *Asian*. You know, like, from . . . hay-dee?" the kid said uncertainly.

"You're asking am I *Haitian*?"

"That's what I said!" the kid shouted and the girl giggled.

I shook my head. "Nah, man, I grew up around here."

"Yeah, you don't got the accent. I swear I've seen you before though!"

His name was Sticky and he stuck. By the time I got off the bus—parting with a fist bump as he canoodled up to the shy, sweet mixed girl—I had Molly in my pocket and his number penned on my wrist. We kept in touch, traded connections, did each other a couple of sideways favors. I was slowly climbing the steps up out of life on the streets with Mo at the time, and Sticky was like a landing in the stairwell—a rich kid with broke friends.

When I get off the 51 today, the rain's stopped but the sun's still speckled with gray clouds. It looks like the tip of a giant cigarette waiting to be ashed. I walk a few more blocks to the old bungalow, which has those brown shingles that look like velvet and a lime-green trim. I send a text and wait across from the front yard, which is wild but in a manicured way. It's overgrown—wildflowers, an apple tree in one corner pummeling the ground, these two cacti like a couple: a thin man and a fat lady, both covered in spiderwebs that make them look old. The gardens in the East Bay always humble me: gigantic plants fed by the fog and the sunshine, leaves too green, petals too thick and bright.

The front door opens and a woman in a navy suit comes out, her phone to her ear, her mouth in action. A few feet behind her a teenage boy limps along, knock-kneed, dragging his foot. One arm is folded at the elbow and pressed across his chest, the wrist drooping, the hand crumpled up, his head at a tilt. Next to the woman's fast-paced clip and chatter, the kid's movements seem even slower. She glances over her shoulder at him and without missing a beat, she reaches back, smacks his head, and heals him.

Sticky's next step flows smooth, like he was just kicking out a cramp. Shithead. His mom shakes her head at her silly little boy as she dashes to her Saab, which is missing its bumper—Sticky's doing, no doubt. Through the open car window, she tells him to have fun and feed the cat and he sticks his tongue at the back of her head and I hate him because she loves him and it's just that easy. She doesn't see me as she pulls out and drives off. Sticky jogs across the street. His mohawk is purple now, brighter under the clouds.

"Whaddup, G?" he says and our hands meet in a clasp. "How long you been back?"

I dodge the question. "So where's your boy at?"

"Around here, just a couple streets up." Sticky points up the hill. We start to scale it.

I take a guess. "Cal student?"

"Was."

"Lives alone?"

"With his mom, but she's never home. She's a lesbian." Sticky snickers.

"Is that . . . why she's never home?"

"I dunno." Sticky shrugs. "I just kinda wish she was hotter."

I know he's rebelling against the Bay's old-school rebellion but I hate him again.

We climb up and up into the Oakland hills, high enough we can see them spreading below, strung with roads, crusted with houses, fringed with trees. When we get to the guy's building, it takes some work to find our way to the apartment itself. The place is like a maze, random stained glass windows casting spots of color on the white walls. Stairs and walkways and gates spring up like we're in some kind of video game.

Sticky finally knocks on a door with three blue diamonds built into it. An Asian dude my age opens it. He's wearing fancy-shaped glasses and he's handsome under the baby fat.

"Sup, Quentin." Sticky reaches out a fist.

"I hope you didn't have a hard time finding me," Quentin says in a surprisingly deep voice, ignoring Sticky's fist as he turns to lead us inside. "This place used to be a hotel, I guess? Back in the forties? And they cut it up really weird? I'm upstairs."

We follow him up a narrow staircase to a carpeted loft. The roof is pitched but I can still barely stand full height. A stained glass skylight makes the room glow green.

"I fucking love this place," Sticky says with a grin. "It's like being inside a frog!"

He strides over to a bong standing beside a quicksand sofa. I toss him my lighter and he bubbles up, and the room soon dims to the murk of an old aquarium. Apart from the sofa, there's an unmade bed, a desk, and a rolling chair with a mesh back. The computer dominates the room, its screen painfully bright in the greenish fog. Against one wall, there are two sinks scalloped into a cabinet with a tiled surface, seashell sconces nailed to the wall above.

"This used to be the bathroom, I'm pretty sure?" Quentin says as he sits at the desk. He spins to face me and hands me a sheet of paper. "I take PayPal."

I scan it. It's a whole-ass business contract: dates, the nature of the job, lines for the "person of interest" and for our signatures. His is already in place in dramatic black ink.

"Is Quentin your—"

"Real name? Are you broken?" He blinks at me. "But trust, it *will* hold up in court."

I raise my shoulders. "Okay, okay, man. Just asking."

"Contracts are standard." Quentin hands me a pen. "I'm not about to, like, get got."

"Oh my God." Sticky guffaws a cloud of smoke. "Did you just say *'get got'*?" He's stretched out on his stomach on the sofa now, paddling his arm as if he's on a green boat drifting down a green stream. I look at him, the pen in my hand hanging over the contract.

"He's goofy." Sticky nods. "But he's good. He can print you an ID in, like, an hour."

I lean over the desk, write W A Y N E W I L L I A M S in all caps, then scribble a choppy signature underneath. It looks like a gravestone floating on an ocean. An idea strikes me. On the back of the contract, I write the gist of what my sea urchin told me at the PETA party.

"I also need an address in Russian Hill for Charlotte Williams," I say. "I know that the Goddess Dispensary delivers there."

Sticky overhears and perks up but I give him a shut-the-fuck-up look and he does.

Quentin eyes me. "That'll cost extra, depending on how hard it is to find."

I nod and hand over the sheet of paper. Quentin puts his headphones back on and spins in his chair.

I crouch over to Sticky and take a hit from the bong, then sit with my back against the sofa and light a Kool. The cigarette smoke curls into the marijuana haze like milk in dishwater.

"So," Sticky leans down and whispers in my ear, "you found Mom?"

5

≈≈≈

Going from Mo to Sticky was like going from having a father to having a son. Sticky had run away from home a couple of times, but sleeping rough and doing drugs and misdemeanors had done opposite things to us: it made him older than his age and me younger than mine. Sticky knew about the paper world, the world of bank accounts and legal aid and government names. I could finesse the basics, which I knew from my folks, from foster care, even from Mo. But it was this scrawny sixteen-year-old who first helped me put a résumé together—riddled with holes and lies, of course—and get an ID, a credit card, a cellphone.

Sticky taught me about Craigslist, where I found cash gigs mowing lawns and moving boxes. Sticky taught me about OkCupid, and the bedrooms of the artists and baristas I dated became my rotating hotel—"a Ferris wheel of IKEA beds," he joked. All he seemed to want from me was to get high and talk shit. I think he thought I gave him some kinda "street cred"—I didn't want to break it to him that I had never really been "street," except in the sense of sleeping on it. In any case, he was clearly fond of me. Every time we kicked it, he'd shake his head and say he swore he knew me from somewhere.

A few months into our odd-couple friendship, Sticky asked me to meet him at a coffee shop in Temescal. I thought he was gonna hook me up with a new job. It was one of those deadland stretches of Oakland where auto shops and liquor stores congregate. Jah'Va seemed out of place but maybe it had been here first. It looked old in that Bay Area way, archaeological layers of a seventies vibe: an encrusted bulletin board, rickety tables under Afro-print tablecloths, slanted floors, and sky-blue walls painted Caribbean-style with a giant parrot, a hand-sized palm tree, and a sunset with rays like a lion's mane. There was only one other customer in there when I arrived, a grad-student type with a pixie cut, big glasses, and a tattoo of a flock of birds like shrapnel in her shoulder. She stared at her laptop, her Converse tapping, her fingers skittering over the keyboard with the fluency of personal business.

Sticky was already at the counter. He waited for me to join him there before he ordered a cappuccino and a slice of pumpkin bread. He didn't ask, and we both knew he had more money just from his allowance, but I always paid. These were the terms of our friendship. The barista—Somali or Ethiopian, judging by the purple shimmer in her skin—flashed me a smile as she handed me my change.

Sticky sat at a table and started goofing around, gripping his cup with his teeth and tilting it up to sip. *Look Ma, no hands.* The froth gave him a mustache and made his lip piercing look rusty.

I sat across from him. "So what's this about? This place looking to hire?"

He leaned in. "No, I remembered where I saw you, how come I recognized you on the bus. It was here!"

"Here? I never been here before, Sticky."

"Not *you*—the guy that looks like you!"

I had reason to be doubtful—they can't always tell us apart—but I had reason to wonder too. Just then a man came out through a door behind the counter. He was a bantam-weight, dressed in a full denim suit—pants and a jacket, covered with a rash of metal studs. He kissed the barista on the cheek—"chérie"—then opened the register and started counting out his money, his lips and hands shuffling. When he was done, he shut the register with a *ding* and looked out over his tiny kingdom.

I eyed Sticky, like, You think I look like *this* dude? Sticky ignored me and saluted the man, who grinned, spread his hands like a pastor, and brought them together in a loud, happy clap. The grad student looked up with a start, then returned to her typing. The man came and sat down at the third side of the table, between me and Sticky. He had a tattoo on his neck of a bow tie, the knot sitting right on top of his Adam's apple. Classy.

"Steeckee. You bring me bizness?" The accent was heavy—not heavily foreign, just heavy in itself, as if a bass drum boomed in the middle of each word.

Sticky leaned forward. "You're from Hay-dee, right?"

"Eye-tee," the man corrected with a pout. He tilted his head, curious. "From where you come, Steeckee? Your color: in Paree, we call you beurre, like budder."

"Oh, uh. My mom's . . . Portuguese?" This seemed like a fact that Sticky knew but didn't quite understand.

"Ha! Perfect. Alors. What is happening with you?"

"Okay. So. 'Member that missing kid? The flyer you guys used to have up?"

"Yes."

"*He's* from High-tee too, right?"

"Non, non." The Haitian frowned, interlaced his fingers. "French. It was many years ago. Rose, the boy's grandmother—

she have come here always for special gâteau à l'orange and speak about him. After she is dead, I send small thing, fleurs. And her daughter come to say thank you and bring us the brochure about the boy, and she ask us to put it up. What a shame, enh?"

"Oh, okay. So the boy was French?"

"Non, the boy Americang. Why you ask?" Only now did the Haitian turn to look at me, his friendliness retreating into the dark caves of his eyes as he asked: "You are who?"

I glanced at Sticky, who shrugged, but before I could speak, those caves lit up again.

"Mais non!" the Haitian said. "It is not possible!"

"Right?" Sticky grinned, nodding wildly. *"Right?"*

"Chérie!" the Haitian shouted. The door to the back moaned open and the barista came over. He spoke to her in French. She nodded and headed to the bulletin board up front, where she unpinned something, unpinned something behind that, and a third thing behind *that*—only in the Bay—then finally returned and placed a pamphlet on the table.

REMAIN VIGILANT! it shouted in a corny font.

"I thought it was a dope-ass band name when I first saw it," Sticky said with a laugh.

I opened the pamphlet and read aloud: "The Vigil Foundation, a San Francisco–based national nonprofit dedicated to the safety of all children, the recovery of missing children, and public policies that keep children safe in their communities, was officially founded in 1999. But its pulse began to truly beat when a young boy went missing in—" I closed the pamphlet. This sort of thing rubbed me the wrong way. People sucking on pain like vampires.

"What's this gotta do with me?"

"No, no, dude," Sticky said. "Flip it over."

I didn't move, so he snatched it out of my hands to do it for me, then slid it back across the table. The picture on the other side of the pamphlet was blurry with xeroxing and creased with folding. On the left was a white woman in a boxy suit, a curtain of hair hanging in front of one shoulder: a mall-photo pose. Her face looked hard but she was smiling. Next to her, his arm around her shoulders, was a man: tall, grinning. I leaned in to read the caption: *Charlotte and Bernard Williams, Still Seeking Wayne.* Whoa, Wayne?

"Okay, that's weird about the name but—"

"Look." Sticky tapped the man's face.

I looked closer and put my hand over my mouth. The only difference was in the skin. Bernard Williams was darker than me. Otherwise, it was like when you see somebody's face on a train, then realize it's your own reflection in the window. The lips, the nose. It was me.

Something swarmed up my back. My eyes crossed and the face in the picture tore into jagged layers. I blinked and it came together, came clear again.

"See?" Sticky was saying, sounding victorious. "You see?"

The Haitian and his chérie were smiling with wonder, with pride. Resemblance always pleases people that way. In a daze, I flipped back to find the missing boy's birth date.

≈

That was how this whole thing with the Williams family had started. Sticky had helped me plan it out. I used up nearly all the money I saved from Craigslist gigs and side hustles. At first I thought maybe somebody in the family might even know where he was hiding, or at least the last traces they'd been using to hunt him down. When I looked into it, the boy's older sister seemed like my best bet for getting some info on the man he'd become. So I'd tracked Cassandra for a while on her work trips, up and down the coast, then ended up tracking her here like some kinda foolish boomerang. I almost maxed out my new credit card booking all those flights and hotels. I have to admit, when I found out she was flying back to SFO anyway, it felt like fate—like a curse at first but then like a clue, like I was on the right path. The fucking her part made it feel like a curse again.

I don't tell Sticky about all that while we wait for Quentin—the kid talks too damn much—just that I've got a new lead for the family, and that the daughter's in town. I tell him about running into White Reggie, though. The story's too good to pass up. Sticky laughs sagely—or just slowly, he's already stoned—and heads downstairs to hunt for snacks. A moment later, Quentin spins in his chair and gives me a new California license, warm to the touch. While I hold it up to the light to admire his work, the printer whines and ejaculates a sheet of paper. Quentin hands it to me.

"The address you asked for."

"Wait, are you sure?" I say, seeing a suite number. "This looks like an office building."

"Could be an office." Quentin shrugs. "It's pretty close to the Financial District."

"An office? For weed delivery? That's . . . bold."

"We live in the future out here in the Bay," he says with a smirk. "Right on the edge of time."

By the time I've folded up the contract and the address and slid them with the ID into my pocket, Quentin's already put his giant headphones back on and fired up a bonanza of CGI on his monitor. He lets go of the controller long enough to wave goodbye. I make my way down the narrow stairwell and find Sticky in the kitchen, sitting in lotus position in front of the open fridge, somewhere in the no-man's-land between the vagues and the munchies. I leave him there.

≈

The sun's come out just in time to set. The world is still watery, light splashing out of the sky, puddling across the rooftops, across the heads of trees. A waste of light. I walk down to the BART station and catch the train back to the city and it's night by the time it rises up from the tunnels under Oakland. We can't see the rails and we can't see the other trains, so it's like we're in the sky, blue and white and orange lights around us like stars. *When the sky is rent asunder, when the stars scatter,* I hear Mo's voice like a storm in the distance.

Past West Oakland, the train dips under the water and we all rotate our jaws in sync from the change in pressure. The train lets out its banshee scream as it scrapes the bottom of the Bay. On the other side, it slides to a halt and sighs open to let out the passengers, their faces lit blue by the screens in their hands, their earbuds plugged in tight, in denial. They scurry through the turnstiles and into the night. Civic Center Station grows lonely, just me, a bum sleeping on the stairs, and three women strolling to the escalator that leads outside.

Two of the women are wearing jeans and baggy sweatshirts. They look related, sisters maybe. The third woman is skinnier and darker, in an African print dress, hair dreadlocked and amber-colored, wrapped so it looks like grooves in clay. The women get on the escalator and I do too, to dodge the smell of the bum, which is awful and familiar. I immediately regret this. The women are standing offset in a triangle ahead of me so I can't pass.

"Just give it to her." This from the dreadlocked friend. "It's only ten dollars."

"Yeah, well. You best shut yo mouth 'cause nobody axed you, LaShawn." This from the woman whose back is closest to me. "Ma, you hear me? You said the train would get here at 7:50 and it got here at 7:56. So we neither us won the bet."

"I thought you said you *both* won."

"Nobody *axed* you, LaShawn," the daughter says. "Always in errybody business." She sucks her teeth. "A'ight, Ma, you can *have* it. I'm just saying. We *both* won. We neither—ugh, just take it."

She squeezes her fingers into her pocket and pulls out a $10 bill and holds it over her mother's shoulder, waves it like a muddy flag. Her mother, facing away on the upper step, shakes her head. The BART entrance gapes above and something fizzes in me—some itch from that old lady's purse at the bus stop or from stealing that watch back off White Reggie. I climb the escalator stairs and press two fingers into the daughter's back.

It's like a kid's joke, cops and robbers, but she freezes, her hand with the money still in the air. Ma and LaShawn don't even turn as I snatch the bill from her fingers, wriggle my way between the three women, and race up the last four rising stairs of the escalator. The pigeons roosting at the BART entrance take flight with a sound like applause.

I hear the women's voices crying out behind me—*Did y'all see that? Motherfucka had a gun, oh my God oh my God oh my God, I ain't even see his face, call 911, you better not call nobody, goddamn this fuckin' city*—quieter and quieter behind me as I run.

6

≈≈≈

Musta been the next year, eighth grade. One day after school, me and my boys was out on the playground—throwin bottles, sparkin up. Dumb shit, all of it wrapped up in ganja smoke. And I looked up and saw Will—the other Will—standin outside the gym door. I stood up, blunt cupped in my hand, chest out, like, *c'mon now, roll up or snitch.* I know he saw me, but that lil pussy-ass nigga turned around and went inside the school. So I followed him in.

I went through the gym and started walkin classroom to classroom, huntin the flash of his back, the squeak of his steps. I know I had a plan—to fuck him up, probably—but it kept driftin off the side of my head cuz I was blazed. Anyway, I turned a corner and he was gone—couldn't see him or hear him anywhere. I stood there in front of this closet door just starin at it, wonderin if he had went inside, thinkin on those rats, tryna figure out what the fuck was happenin. I was about to bounce when the closet door opened and he came out. Except it weren't him. It was Coach.

Coach was our basketball coach, but he was the principal too. Basketball at that school weren't nothin to brag about—I don't even know if we played any away games. It was more for school spirit and shit, and you knew that because the principal was doin overtime to coach us. In the mornings, Coach was this dignified dude, cleaned up like for church, wearin these shiny-ass wide-lapel suits, walkin all slow and serious up and down the halls. But come afternoon practice, he was this ratchety old nigga in a crumpled tracksuit, playing ball, talkin shit, draggin us for being dumb and lazy, complainin about his bad knees.

That day, he looked surprised to see me, but not mad.

Coach, I said, tryna keep the smile from meltin off my face.

He scoped the hall, left-right, said *Come inside, I need to talk to you.*

So I went in behind him. Turned out it was an office, not a closet, but about as small and dark inside. One window with the curtain half-closed, the light from outside stripped to the bone. There was only one chair up in there and a desk with a bunch of old TV monitors up on top. Coach told me to take a seat facin em and he stood behind me, talkin about how *he needs to show me something and he can't account for it cuz he knows life's been hard for me but I aint never seemed the type and it's important that I look real close at what he's about to show me.* And then he shut the curtain. I was dizzy as hell and I had that choke in my throat—you know how it is when you blaze and you feel like you gotta swallow, but aint nothin in there but more throat?

Coach pressed some buttons and the TVs snitched on, all showing the same blurry black-and-white tape. Old-school security. Mind you, I aint even know the cameras at that school was workin. Us kids always thought the eyes in them corners was dead, but apparently . . . So, this tape's from behind the school, the playground. No sound. Nighttime, so it's pretty dark, just a coupla streetlights. And you can see these two young Gs. You know how we dressed back then, it was all Timbs and chains and puffy coats, and they was standin under one of those big-ass trees out back. They dap, swap words. You can't hear what they're sayin because no sound, but that time of night, you get the idea. And then—

OK. Wait. Lemme say somethin.

You gotta understand, I was what? Fourteen-fifteen years old? I weren't a bad kid. I weren't no criminal out there breakin the law and shit. I was just a boy. I was mad all the time, sure, but in that regular teenage way. My foster mom Kima used to call me Feisty for Nothin. As hard as growin up in the hood was, I aint never really seen this kinda shit *live* before, feel me? Not up close. I saw some shit go down in the homes and I got in scraps at school and I did favors for my cousins, a lil trade— just kid stuff, though, weed, loosies, that kinda thing. OK, so maybe I *had* broke the law, but I still aint never really seen nothin like what was on that tape, except maybe in the movies and shit.

So, after the young Gs spit, shit gets heated. And this one nigga—you could see the fire rise up his back and across his shoulders. His fist pulls back. *Blam.* Right in the gut. Other nigga hits the wall. Too late to square up now. First one sets on him with the fury, and they're on the ground. *Blam-blam-blam,* gets him in the face. Other nigga's head is straight-up bouncin off the concrete. And just like that, it's over. Twenty seconds max. Champ's done. He's won. He stands and looks up, like he's takin his glory from the leaves of the trees, from the streetlights, from the whole gotdamn sky.

And then he lifts his foot. You know, casual-like, like he's about to walk up some stairs. He's not even lookin down at the kid on the ground. And he slams his Timb down on that nigga's face. There was no sound on that tape but you could still hear it.

Coach hit pause. I remember my head was turned, and I

was like peekin at the screen from the side. You wouldn't think it but that kinda shit turns my guts. Coach hit rewind then pause again, right before the stomp, right when Champ looked up at the sky. The screen was kinda jerkin from the freeze but you could see the streetlight on his face. I leaned in—and man, it was like my blood turned to ice. Couldn't catch my breath, knees locked. Couldn't hear nothin, my ears blocked like I just came out the water. Black starts creepin in from the edges of my eyes.

You already know what I'm bout to say. The face on the screen? It was mine.

Thoughts start goin off in my head like gunshots. This kid shows up at school with my name my face my walk my voice my threads my flow, but it's just a game, right? We just kids, right? But now? Nah nah nah this shit don't make no sense. Coach opens the curtain. I'm shakin. Jabberin, like, *that aint me that aint me Coach that's that kid,* but when I say the name— *not me,* I say, *the other one*—Coach looks at me like I've lost my damn mind. Thing is, and I don't even know how to explain this now: It coulda been me. It just wasn't.

I stopped yappin. Closed my eyes. Tried to breathe. Then Coach put his hand on my shoulder. I'll never forget that. The feelin of a hand that's not beatin on you or strokin you or pattin you down. Just . . . there. When he spoke, it was slow and quiet.

I've got no choice in this, son. You understand that, right?

He took me down to the precinct. They called my foster mom but she was workin her shift, so I was hours in the holding cell. One toilet, no seat. I was up in there with five-six grown-ass niggas, half of em in withdrawal, the other half ready to pop you in the face if you so much as sneeze. The officers finally pulled me out, cuffed me to a table, and asked me a whole lotta questions I couldn't answer. I just kept tellin them to find the other Will.

It took a week, but my foster mom scraped together enough for bail. We ended up with state counsel and my arraignment was like a drive-through, man—in and out. Public defender came in all hassled-lookin—white lady lookin like she half-scared of me. Nothin she could really do about that video, though. That nigga on the ground? His face got fucked up and he was in a wheelchair for a minute. But he aint die. So I just got sent to juvie.

≈

I done enough since then that I can see how maybe I belonged there. But not for the reason they put me there, feel me? And that makes you feel a certain kinda way. I was in juvie for two years, fifteen to seventeen. Dropped my name for good, got a crew, got a tag. It aint worth the spit to tell you the shit we got into in there. We aint sneak past the rules or even bend the rules, really—we just took em and turned em right around, on our terms. Crime, punishment. Big fish, little fish. In the end, everybody drinks the same poison in juvie. Outside, maybe you trip and fall into the system. But once you get inside, you swim-min in it, tryin not to drown. You aint even got time to see what it is.

I was a week from eighteen, about to get a sentence hearing, when I saw him again. Will. My boy J, we was from the same hood, and he had brewed up some pruno and the guards turned an eye for us. So, we was in J's room, actin up, gettin messy, that vomitty kinda drunk. And at the bottom of the night, right before dawn, I went to the john. I don't remember all that much about juvie but I remember the john cuz you had to watch your back. That night, I remember gray light, bars on the windows throwing shadow stripes on the floor, the hiss of my piss in the urinal. I was shakin off when I felt it. There was somebody in there with me.

Now, I aint see or hear nobody come in. It was nothin but shadows and the smell of piss and shit in there. But it was like this . . . heaviness came in. Like one of those shadows was creepin up and leanin over my shoulder, breathin on the back of my neck. I zipped up and was bout to turn and square up when I heard it. Felt it in my gut, almost. That gravelly-ass whisper. All up in my ear. Sayin my name.

That voice—and like I said, I never use my real name if I can help it. I even had the guards in juvie callin me by my tag by then. It was him. I always knew I could take him—we were the same size, welterweight. But middle of the john, middle of the night, this nigga all up my back with my name in his mouth? That kinda shit crushes somethin in your chest. Makes you a kid again. I froze up. And that's how he got me in a chokehold. I heard that raspy breath in my ear, like a bull before they let him in the ring. Then everything went black.

I woke up back in my bunk. Bruised, burnt—I got smashed into a radiator. See how this line on my ink kinda warps right here? That's a burn mark. Now get this: They said it aint happen. Nothin on the security tape. I'm like *Do you not see this fuckin third-degree burn on my arm?* And you know what they said? They said *I* did it! Now why the fuck would I do this to myself? I aint even have a lighter! I don't even smoke! But I *had* been drinking that weird-ass pruno that J always made so I thought *OK, maybe you passed out, maybe you trippin.*

Day of my hearing, like clockwork, guard comes in my room, says warden wants to see me. Man, I tell you, the minute I stepped in that office, my head was shakin like *nah nah nah,* cuz the warden had my kit and it was open, my toothbrush and washcloth on his desk and a baggie sittin right next to em. I was like *Nope*. Will planted it. It was him. I *know* it was him. But nobody knew who I was talkin bout! *Will who? Will you?* Not J, not the guards, not even the office manager I used to flirt with who registered everybody that came in there.

I was like *Who the fuck is this nigga?* I couldn't pin it down. How'd he find me? What'd he want from me? I asked the other boys in there from around the hood. *Member that grandpa-talkin nigga from middle school, look just like me?* Most of em aint even know who I was talkin bout. But J said Will had left the school and gone out to Cali right around when I got sent to juvie, I don't know what city—I aint never been out there. J said it was cuz Will's foster mom had got fired for sellin pills from her job. But that felt like another mix-up or another setup, cuz that was what had happened to my foster mom Jackie.

You see it, right? I'm *this* close to gettin out? And *that's* when this shit happens? Cuz when my sentence hearing came up, you best believe I got a promotion—felony narcotics possession. Three more years. You get a rap like that, eighteen years old? In *Baltimore?* It's a wrap. Straight up. It's like you dead, and now you gotta spend the rest of your days as a ghost to the life you was sposed to be livin. When I got out, what was I sposed to do? Move back in with Jackie or Alicia or Kima—after all the shit they been through? All the shit I done *put* them through? Or what—get me an apartment and a job? Aint nobody hirin an ex-con. Nah, man. Truth is, there aint no life but The Life once you done a nickel.

7

≈≈≈

I head down to the Financial District, to the address for Charlotte Williams that I got from Quentin. Stony skyscrapers shadow the streets, their sunlit windows tossing gold in the air. I walk the black and bright streets, roaming in knights' moves. Mo told me once that whenever they dig up the ground around here, they find the ruins of ships from the Gold Rush—not wrecks from the sea, but the ships they dragged to shore to make hotels and brothels. Now, whenever I walk around here, I see the buildings as big old ships, ready to sail off if the landfill crumbles or the earth opens up. I buy a baseball cap and a pair of shades and swap a few coins for a *Street Spirit.* Then I lean against a wall across from Charlotte's building and skim it, peeking over the paper's edge now and then. As the afternoon passes, time starts to fold under its own weight like honey.

That sounds like something Mo would say. He talked about time a lot, mostly when we were playing chess. When we made that Magic Dollar, he got a printout of a board laminated too, and it stayed with us over our years together, though over time, one corner got chewed and the other three curled up. We used a hodgepodge of pieces from different sets. I remember one white bishop was markered black like a bad spy. Mo always gloated his way to victory, knees moving like window wipers as he hounded me across the board just like he had across the city, fingers delicate as he picked up each piece and dropped it in place with a

"Check.   Check.   Check.   Check."

Like a slow tap dance toward the inevitable.

"Mate." Mo dropped the word soft as cotton and immediately started scooping the pieces into a baggie.

"Fuck," I groaned. "That's the fourth time. It's not a fair fight! It's like you already know what I'm gonna do."

"I *don't* know what you're gonna do. I just contemplate the possibilities, son."

"But how do you always know which one to choose?"

"I *see* 'em. The threads of possibility. The choosin' happens on its own, like a riff in a song. That's why we call it *playin'*. Lemme show you something, son."

Mo took a scrap of paper out of his pocket and smoothed it out on the now-empty chessboard. Then he took out a pin-striped Bic pen and sketched two vertical lines in parallel.

"See this? This is time."

"Aw man, not this shit again. Breakfast time is what it is. Can we go eat?"

"This right here? This is time," Mo repeated, staring me down.

I sighed. "Okay. What's time today?" I looked at the picture. "Some kinda tube?"

"*Nooo.* It's a rope. And what's a rope made of?"

"I don't know, string?"

"String. And what's string got? *Threads.*" Mo sketched diagonal lines inside the tube to give it the twist of a rope. "So, this is what time looks like to us. A rope, a line pulled tight. But that's just the *past,* the things that already happened, one after the other, in a line. But the future?" Mo drew a fan of lines at the top end of the rope, like it was unraveling. "Threads of *possibility. Infinite* threads. But you see, when time goes on, they get twisted together *into* the rope. The coulda-woulda-shouldas get twisted inside of what we *did*."

And I actually saw it: a fist moving slowly up the frayed rope, threads squeezing tight in its clutch. I leaned over the picture, frowning.

"So what twists the uh . . . future threads into the past rope?"

"God. The Law. Don't matter."

"And we're right here?" I pointed to where the tight rope met the spray of threads.

Mo was already rattling off more notions: ". . . like the future threads are just waitin' for us to tie 'em or pluck 'em or use 'em to make people do things, like puppets, like in the space war Reagan started before the future could even *get* to us. It was at the convention when they set up the board, I'm not talkin' 'bout nineteen eighty-seven, I'm talkin' 'bout *seven*teen eighty-seven, and we know they set it up, with Madison on the inside, castling, makin' the early moves so they'd never line up in our favor, see, no matter how much the devils at General Electric sell you at the current rate, you'll never find a way to buy no sandwich, no land, no conscience, which is . . ."

He was falling down his rabbit hole. This happened more and more toward the end of our time together. It was like watching an old black-and-white movie—ladies weeping, staring out windows—and then a Looney Tunes cartoon would bust through, bright and wild. And like a cartoon, it would have a kind of logic to it: Tom chasing Jerry, Coyote chasing Road Runner. But the rules of the world would be just a little off-kilter. Rules like gravity and speed and pain. I could generally only wake him up by interrupting him.

"Looks like a mop to me," I said this time, my voice loud enough to stop him.

". . . but that's a fallacy of . . . What?"

"Time, man." I pointed at the page. "Looks like a fuckin' mop."

And Mo fell out laughing, his big hands cupping his cheeks. But *Time is a mop* just joined all his other crazy theories. Watching the facade of Charlotte's building change shade as the sky does, I try to remember them all. *Time is a hinge. Time is a heap. Time's got grooves in it. Time is the juggling of coins, the rise and fall of change: a penny for the sunrise, a gold dollar for the day, a spinning dime for the moon.*

≈

I don't know how much real time passes before I see someone I recognize come out of the building and it's not Charlotte Williams. It's her daughter. I wonder if I'll feel some kind of vibration, see some kind of aura. But no, C's like everybody else around here, decked out in white and gray, strutting the ruts of a lucrative life. She looks up at the percolating clouds, down at her phone, then heads east. I put my shades on, tug my cap down, and follow.

At the top of the escalator at Montgomery BART, she turns up her white collar and glances over her shoulder, like she senses me. Then she glides forward and down and vanishes. After a few seconds, I look over the edge and see her step off the escalator toward the ticket machines. I wait a beat, then race down, gritting my teeth at the jolts to my spine—I'm still tender from where the kangaroo beat me down. The machines are deserted but for a tourist family, all in hats. The dad pokes a screen, filling the air with chimes. I dip my hand in the reservoir of the machine to his right and peek at the receipts. No clues there.

I roll up perv-close behind a woman as she passes through the orange jaws of the turnstile, then run around her and race down the second escalator. The lady robot announces a train departing for Fremont in seven minutes; the gentleman robot cuts her off to say the train for SFO is now arriving. I march beside the train coming in, scanning the platform as the doors open and people step on. I don't see her but the doors are about to close so I leap in, catching my shoulder on the edge of one before they shudder shut. I sneak a peek around.

C's not on this car. Is she even on this train? There's an old dude ranting about the Vietcong and a group of deaf kids signing to each other, their hands beautiful, like versions of water—quick and icicle-sharp, loose and lazy, stream-twisty. At Powell, I stick my head out the open train doors and scan the throng on the platform for C. No sign. I duck back in. What if I miss her? I'm still kicking myself for letting her out of my sight when the train reaches Civic Center. I look out between the doors and catch the back of her white jacket moving up the escalator. I go to get off the train but the closing doors hesitate around me with a clunk, which makes me hesitate too. By the time I'm out, she's gone.

I take the stairs three at a time, my legs bouncy with the hunt. I burst out of the exit into daylight that seems nuclear bright after the subway. There she is, her white jacket like a dove in the forest of people on the sidewalk. I catch my breath and trail her down Market, keeping my distance until she turns up Hyde. As we pass the UN Plaza, I wonder why she didn't cut through it. She doesn't seem to know where she's going but after all, she's not from around here. She walks slowly, looking up at the buildings like a tourist.

Past the law school, the Tenderloin starts to swarm with its calls and barks: *What you need? How you doin'? Where you goin'?*

She ducks the hyenas but stupidly turns right on Turk, deeper into the hive. Dodging a woman squatting to piss on the sidewalk, I speed up, trailing C a little closer but keeping to the shade under the store awnings. At the liquor store on Turk and Taylor—a cluster of men outside brown-bagging it, batting shouts around—C turns in a circle, her hand on her hair. She looks to the left: two kids carrying guitar cases, running down the street from a crackhead who's shouting *Yo, let me play that!* She looks to the right: an old man in a wheelchair wearing a grimy but dapper suit, a cat on his lap, a red hankie flapping from his breast pocket like a tongue. C chooses left, up Taylor.

After two blocks, she makes a right on Ellis. But just as I turn the corner, I see that she's spun around and is heading straight for me. I duck into a corner store. Through the sticker-covered door, I see her profile tip back to look up. She turns and goes back down Taylor. I come out of the store and we retrace the path we just took, together but apart, tin cans on a string. At the corner, she makes a left on Eddy. She's going in circles.

"The fuck?" I mutter.

A Tenderloin shadow echoes me and cackles. We walk another couple blocks. I'm wiping sweat from my nose with my sleeve—more from nerves than effort—when I see that C has stopped. She's standing in front of a building. It's the hotel. *My* hotel. The doors slide open to swallow her. I look up and shake my head, as if the sky knows what's going on. I pull off my cap, my shades. I follow her in and right as she hits the bell at reception, I tap her shoulder and it's like I made the ringing sound with my hand on her.

She turns. "Oh!"

"Hello there."

"I was . . . I was just looking for you."

"Were you?" I say in my smoothest tone.

"Yeah," she laughs. "I, um," she says and swallows. "I lost my watch? And I thought I might have—but I couldn't remember the name of this hotel or where it was exactly. That night's still kind of a . . . blur."

She looks in my eyes. Her blouse billows like a sail between her drawn-up shoulders.

"Yeah, I know what you mean," I say. "That morning too."

She bites her lip, looking caught.

"So, your watch. I haven't seen it," I lie. "Would you like to come up and look for it?"

"Oh, no, no," she says with a glance up, as if at my hotel room, the things we did there. "That's okay. I must have left it somewhere else. I'm sure I'll find it. I'm sorry to bother you," she flusters, the tips of her ears going pink. "I should go." She turns to leave.

"Hey." I catch her arm. "How about a walk?"

She looks down at my hand on her arm and when she looks up again, I see the ghost of a smile around her lips. We step outside. Up and up, Jack and Jill, we climb toward the sun together. It's still warm enough that she takes off her jacket. I peek at her, little nibbles of looking. Gold hairs fuzz her forearm, which is a color that feels deeply familiar to me but that I'd be hard-pressed to name. Our shoes make a two-tone beat, which is drowned out now and again by passing cars, then swallowed completely by the sound of a jet overhead. Our feet still stepping, we look up and watch the jet unzip the sky.

"So, where are you from?" I ask, even though I already know.

"Baltimore. Well, Baltimore County. My parents don't live there anymore, though. How about you?"

"Uh, here and there. I never really knew my folks. They died when I was a kid."

"Oh no, I'm so sorry—" she says sincerely.

"No, no, no," I say lightly and our voices jostle for a tone.

"I'm sorry," she says firmly, winning the battle. There's a pause. "You have other family around here?"

"No." The back of my neck heats up. "I mean, yeah. Well, no, not really." Why is it so hard to remember to lie to this woman? My words are usually ready, stored under my tongue. But with her they crumble to dust, they turn to air that I move through, toward her. At the top of the hill, we come to a natural stop and she turns to me.

"His name was Wayne," she says.

"Who?"

"My little brother," she says. "The one who died."

Died. This again. "For real, he was a Wayne too?" I fake it pretty well.

"I know. Synchronicity, right?"

She doesn't know what I know. She's searching my eyes and it feels like she's scouring them out. My dick stirs like a pet seeking attention. There's the truth I need and there's its source, right here, cradling her jacket, her leg muscles tense because of her heels and the slope of the hill. The ground trembles— "Excuse me," I say, turning—it's just my phone buzzing in my pocket. I pull it out and answer. It's the hotel. My new credit card has been delivered and is waiting at the front desk. "I'll swing by to pick it up," I say. Perfect timing. I hang up and turn back to her with my best smile. "Hey. Have dinner with me."

≈

So, Cassandra and Wayne go on a date. We don't know what's good around here—she's not a local and I'm not exactly a connoisseur—so we end up at a stuffy place called Burt's, which has carpet on the walls, and stark lighting that deepens the shadow between her breasts and casts a shine over her skin. I still want her but my thoughts feel blunt—I'm tired or nervous or bored or all three. Or maybe "perfect timing" is too fixed for me and C. Maybe we can only fall into a rhythm if we stumble into each other first. There's no easing in tonight, no ease at all. Silence interrupts and carries on like an unwelcome guest. We trade lackluster speeches about good food, bad weather, terrible real estate, and maybe I'm too spent to keep track, to keep up, but somehow we end up arguing.

"I don't know why they don't just change the laws, well, it's not like that would actually work, rent control is a good thing, yeah, but tenants' rights backfire, don't they? I wouldn't know, the laws are meant to protect us, redlining happens anyway, the neighborhood watch? My god, it's like slave patrols, in the realtor's office if not in the court, slave patrols? I mean the police rose out of that, they did? You've seen the videos, right? They've been around since King, since Martin, what is there to garner? It's not like it's gray, it's right there in black and white, everybody's seen the videos, that doesn't mean, they think we're animals, you really think that? It's the twenty-first century, and so? It's so awful, I mean it's not something someone like *us* has to worry about, are you fucking kidding? They do it to *all* of us, there are a million ways to die, sometimes I hate being black, I love being black, they always look at us funny when we say that, like it's shocking that we'd *choose* to be black, it's not like it's really a choice, yeah, but it's not even about that, we do have a lot of privilege, have you seen the videos? I stopped watching them, they just make me feel so terrible, so sad, you know sometimes they make me feel ashamed."

That word ends it. Our eyes stay locked for a second, our chests raised. Then C plucks the little dessert menu from the middle of the table. While she blinks at it, I breathe out and look around. The only other diners are a man and his daughter.

The girl's five or six—her head barely clears the table. It's clearly a "special occasion": the pink dress, the white tablecloth, the single flower in a vase. But the man's been tapping at his phone while she plays on a touchscreen this whole time. They don't seem to have heard any of our conversation.

The girl sighs and says, "I'm hot."

Without looking up, the dad says, "Well, take your sweater off, honey."

"I've *already* taken my sweater off. I should take my tights off."

"Okay," he says, still tapping. "We'll go to the restroom in a minute."

"Dad, it's fine. I'll just do it here."

C and I trade a look. Her eyebrows rise, I smile with my mouth closed. The man doesn't seem to notice his daughter scuttling down in her seat, putting her ankles up on the table one by one to tug her shoes off. C's eyebrows rise even higher. The girl reaches under her dress and starts rolling her tights down. C says *Oh!* and catches her laughter in her cupped hand. The dad finally blunders to his feet, screening the girl with his napkin.

"What are you doing?" he says to her, his eyes shooting sorries at us.

"Dad!" She glares at him. "I'm a *kid*. It's fine." She turns to me and C. "Right?"

"Of course," I say.

"*Thank* you," she says, handing the wadded-up tights to her father.

The tights are just an occasion, a way to escape whatever mud pit C and I fell into with that argument. The little girl at the next table lets us fall back into flirting again, lets us make up without really making up. We chat about her as we head out of the stuffy restaurant into the cold city fog. We use her, take turns inventing a life for her, the Chicana housekeeper she treats like a mother, her futuristic toys and old-fashioned books, her well-bred shelter dog with a name like Jerry or Steve, the eco-humble car she'll drive someday.

We're still talking about that little girl when we reach my hotel. We joke about her in the elevator. We chuckle over her antics as we sit on the edge of the bed and take off our shoes. We laugh especially hard when C pulls down her own tights, which aren't white like the girl's, but silver-threaded black. I look down and see that C's knees are still speckled with scabs. I lean over and kiss them and our laughter falls from the air and a seriousness comes in and soon enough, we're fucking again, fucking like dogs, fucking like people.

8

≈ ≈ ≈

I look down the length of myself at C. She just got out of the shower and she's standing at the hotel window, peeking out through the blinds at the noon brightness. They tap in the upward breeze from the floor vents and light dips between them and casts the skin of her thigh in gold, bringing out a spangle of droplets or goosebumps. She's naked, her shoulder blades rippling, that golden thigh . . . I'm getting hard again and I almost feel sick. It's ridiculous that I want her to come back to bed, to take me in her hand, her mouth, her pussy. My body doesn't feel like my own. I'm spent. We've been in this room for days. It would smell awful—sweat and smokes and sex and half-eaten room service, all mingling now with sweet shower steam—if we'd left long enough to come back and notice.

I lean up to call C to bed anyway—I want her and she's a stone's throw away—but her phone's buzzing and she's turning to the bedside table to see who it is.

"Shit," she mutters at the screen and picks it up. "Hello?" she answers. "Hey . . ." She listens for a moment. "Oh no!" She springs taller. "When?"

I shift so I'm sitting on the edge of the bed, looking up at her. I watch her face move through feelings—shock, hurt, anger—like one of those videos of a flower blooming and dying.

"Oh no," she says again. "Of course. Yes. I'll get the next flight out. I'll text when . . . Yeah. Okay. And, Dad? I'm so sorry."

She hangs up and sits next to me on the bed. I wait. Then she throws her arms around me, one breast pressing to my chest. I let her sink into me, wondering what Bernard Williams wanted. I sense her looking over my shoulder at the wall. After a moment, she speaks to it.

"My grandmother died."

It hits me in the sternum, which surprises me. "Oh wow. C, I'm so sorry." I pull her closer. I feel a little guilty for trying to find the play here.

She nods into my neck like a child confessing misbehavior. "She was a vile woman."

I slouch away from her to take a look at her face. "Really?"

"She fucking hated me," she says and releases me. She stares down at her naked thighs, kicks a foot, swinging her plastered toes.

"Mmm, hate? That can't be true."

"Fine. Maybe not *hate*. But you can have really dark feelings about your own family."

I lean over and pick up my pack of Kools. I pull one out, light it.

"*Everybody* knew Grandma Lu loved Wayne and hated me. That's why they only just told me. She died three days ago!" She looks at me. "You don't believe me."

"It's not that I don't believe you," I say, making a keyhole with my lips to blow the smoke away from her. "But family hate has got some tenderness built into it."

She shakes her head. "This was hate, pure and simple. And

you can't explain it as, like, not getting along or rubbing each other the wrong way. It's, like, your worstness person. The person who brings out the absolute worst in you. Grandma Lu was mine. Or I was hers."

I try to sound reassuring: "She's gone. Can't stay hating on somebody who's gone."

"I was a kid, you know?" Her cheeks are wet. "When you're a kid, you love them. But you start to hate the fact that *they* hate *you*. Loving in the face of hate—it feels endless."

I stay quiet and smoke my Kool. After a moment, she leans against me again and traces the inked lines of my rose tattoo with her finger.

"How old were you when you got this?"

I peer down at it. "Teenager." It looks like something in muddy water.

"It's your only one, right?"

How she says it makes me feel some kinda way. "Yeah, one was enough." I chuckle.

She goes and sits her bare ass in the chair at the executive desk and picks up her phone and taps at it for a minute. I pull on my boxers and pants and sprawl in the armchair.

"Such a nightmare," she mutters. "The timing is ridiculous." She sees the look on my face. "I just wish they'd *told* me sooner. Now I have to book a red-eye to Baltimore . . ."

I watch her, sort of taking in her complaining, sort of not. One of her nipples is hard from the AC blowing against her side.

". . . an early-morning flight back the next day for this fucking gala."

She gives a final tap, puts her phone facedown on the desk, and looks at me. There are questions all around her eyes but I don't say anything. After a beat, she gets up and starts to put her clothes on. I watch her pull up her business-y gray skirt and string her bra on, clasping it in the back by feel. She pulls on and buttons up her shirt, tucks it in, and shrugs her jacket on.

I reach into my pocket and pull out some change. For some reason, I want to touch money—not cash but coins, with their smell of blood or burnt things, their cut-off heads and crimped edges, the clipped sound as you slip them between your fingers. So, like some pervy boss, I fondle coins and stare at C's ass as she bends to pick up her dirty panties from the floor. She folds them neatly—lace panties like a veil, barely there—and puts them in her pocket, which makes me smile. Then she heads into the bathroom.

I feel so tired, dead on my feet, lead in my bones. I sit in the peace and loneliness of being away from her. It lets me think a full thought, then another. A gala here, a funeral there. A funeral, I think, is more likely than a gala to be the kind of situation where somebody who's been missing for years shows up. Long-lost grandma and all that. Can I really weasel my way into a family function so soon? C's right—it does feel ridiculous, like some high-flying business-exec life, cutting back and forth across the country, sea to sea, tracing grooves through the air. But she has her reasons and I have mine.

I join her in the bathroom, where she's fixing her hair. We smile in the mirror as I pass. I get in the shower and pull the glass door shut. I bow my head and let the thrumming water decide. Afterward, I wrap a towel around my waist and embrace her from behind. She's putting on makeup, quickly, lightly, like she's dabbing at stains on her face. I kiss her neck.

"I could come with you," I say.

She looks at my face in the mirror again. Mo always used to say you can see everybody's truest self in the mirror. Hers looks funny, lopsided in the reflection.

"To *Baltimore*?"

"Yeah. You shouldn't be alone right now."

She frowns and scratches her nose. This is a lie that she can't call a lie. I can tell she's weighing being rude (saying no) against being inappropriate (saying yes). Women.

"The flights are really expensive," she says, "because it's so last-minute."

I ignore the implication. "BWI, right?" I press my ribcage to her shoulder blades.

"Yeah." A smile slinks around her lips.

"So?" I kiss her cheekbone once, twice. "Can I come with?" I sound like a baby brother asking to hang with the cool kids. She doesn't say yes but she tells me the flights she's booked herself on. I leave her in the bathroom and find my phone by the bed. "You should check if you have miles," she calls through the doorway. Right. Airline miles. The sort of thing you can't fake knowing about.

≈

I buy a ticket online. My new credit card worked fine at Burt's the other night, but I still feel relieved when it goes through. C heads out to Westfield to buy herself a black dress. I iron my suit and brush off my jacket, then put them on. When I order the car to SFO, she doesn't offer to pay, and at the airport, she waits with an absent look while I print my ticket at a kiosk. Is this grief? Regret? We walk through the giant, airy Departures hall silently, without holding hands. Some honeymoon.

It's only the third flight I've ever taken, and my pulse pitter-patters when I hand my new, unofficial ID over at security. But the sirens hold their peace, the officer nods me on to the X-ray machines. I take off my shoes and belt and when I go to empty my pockets, I realize I still have her Seiko. I drape my jacket over the bin, but C is too busy taking off her new black heels to notice anyway. She looks brave in her bare feet.

She leaves me at our gate while she makes a call. A little peeved, I board without her, then feel bad and persuade a Silicon Valley type to switch seats with me so I can sit next to her. But when she finds me in her row, she doesn't seem too appreciative. She gives me a weak smile, buckles in carefully, pays attention to the safety instructions. The plane rumbles along, gathering vibration, then tilts to the sky. We rise into darkness pricked with light. C shuts the shade. Since she's acting like a random seatmate anyway, I play along.

"So, you travel a lot?"

She nods at the joke, sends it back.

"I guess so," I reply. "I moved around a lot, you know, growing up."

"Oh," she says, remembering about my parents. "Right."

"But yeah, you know," I say lightly. "Backpacking. Touristy stuff."

"Seeing the sights, doing the locals?"

"No, not like that." I laugh. "More like, one time I slept in the back of a truck."

I enjoy changing the details. Camping (homeless). A truck parked near a lake (the deserted lot of a U-Haul facility). Stars in an indigo sky (broken glass on the tarmac). It was fear, but I tell her it was the cold that sent me into that empty, echoey chamber.

"Ooh, extreme camping," she says. "I'm impressed."

The flight attendant asks for our drink orders and we settle into a silence interrupted only by the tapping of plastic cups and ice. After a bit, C puts in earbuds and turns on her screen. I tilt my seat back and sleep, off and on, in a cramped way that parches my joints. I wake as we're landing in Baltimore. C's

asleep. I reach over her to open the shutter. We're moving down through the dawn, rose-gold clouds going from marble to smoke as the plane pierces them.

≈

My legs are riddled with knots and I'm still exhausted, even after we grab coffee at an airport Dunkin' Donuts. I live in a cotton-wool world until my ears pop in the cab we take to the inn that C booked for us a few blocks from the funeral home. It's decent, but the pale wood, cursive lettering, and hipstery decor can't hide its old bones. The bathroom has pink tiles and moldy floorboards and pipes that bang on about being used.

The morning is cold and gray. C's jacket and the dress she bought at the mall are both thin, both ill-suited to the weather out here. There's no ice on the ground but the sidewalk is scabbed with snow too sooty to melt and the walk takes longer than it should. We've missed the funeral service and the reception's already started by the time we get there.

The funeral home is a new building annexed to an old church. The inside smells of dust and air freshener. C heads to the bathroom by the entrance. I linger like a butler, excusing myself out of the way, scoping the door, watching black bougie Baltimore arrive. With the women dolled up and the men in suits and everybody in hats, it could be an old-fashioned cocktail party. I see a couple of Asians in more casual clothes—staff, I'm guessing.

"Hey, mister." A boy of about six stands in front of me. "Can I tell you something?"

"Sure."

"I think—" He stops and heaves a dramatic breath. "I think I swallowed my toof." He flings his head back and unlocks his jaws wide, revealing the tiny red gap.

"Aw, I'm sorry, little man. I can see where it was. Gum's looking kinda raw."

"Ong fung," the boy says, sounding like he's already in the dentist's chair, then closes his jaws to say it clearly: "I'm fine. S'just blood." He opens his hands to show me. There are red stains on a couple of fingers and a red crease in one palm, like a river on an old map.

"You should go wash up. Can't have blood on your hands." I smile at my own words.

He nods, looking forlorn. Then he looks up at me and says, "But if I swallowed my toof, I won't have nothin' to trade with the toof fairy."

"Oh." I frown. The tooth fairy. I realize I remember that, from some childhood in some other life. "Well," I say, reaching into my pants pocket. "How 'bout a quarter?"

He looks at me like, *Really, nigga?*

"Okay, okay, I got you." I go back into my pocket, dig out the rest of my change, and count out most of it into his bloody palm. "How 'bout . . . seventy cents?"

The kid solemnly accepts, his mouth a grave line. Then he says, "Hey, mister?"

"Yeah?"

"What if, when I swallowed it, my toof got stuck in my *heart*?" He gazes up at me, hand on his chest.

That's when I know the little punk is hamming it up. I grin with gritted teeth and hand over the rest of my coins, then pat his shoulder and take my leave.

But I can't quite get rid of the idea of a tooth in the heart while I'm strolling around, eating stale food, drinking flat soda, hunting for whiskey. I feel a tightness in my chest, like when you see a close-up of porcelain tiles in a movie and you know

there's gonna be blood. Everything is calm in here, though—
the aftermath. The room is all soft noises: the hiss of the heating, quiet munching, hushed chatter, gospel at a low wail from
hidden speakers.

I drift over to a blown-up photograph propped on an easel.
Grandma Lu, I learn, was Louise Corrine Williams, born 1934.
She doesn't look vile to me. She looks like someone who lost a
whole lot in life but in waves rather than one fell swoop. I'm
reading about her upbringing, her education, who she's left behind, when a woman joins my side. We smile at each other.
She's in her forties—maybe, it's always hard to tell with us—
and stands so close to me, I can see the acne scars denting her
makeup, so close I could reach out and touch them, read them
like braille. She gives me her condolences.

"Oh," I say, a bit confused. "Thank you. Uh, you too."

The kid with the missing tooth darts behind her, yelling,
"Howdy, mister!" and she hushes him—"Where are your man-
ners, Darius?"—then smiles at me and shakes her head fondly
and I know her. Or it seems like I do. I realize that our ease
together is because we're family—or we could be. I scan the
room again, with new eyes. I've got the same reddish undertone
as half the people in here. But even with all the likeness around
me, I don't see *him,* and deep down I know that I won't, and I
suddenly wonder if this woman thinks *I'm* him, and something
in me wants to lean over and whisper in her ear: *There's been a
mistake.*

I walk away and look for C. It takes a while before I spot her
in an adjoining room. An older, dark-skinned man is stooping
to put his arms around her. They finish their long hello and
C looks over her shoulder and gestures me toward them with
a jittery smile. The man squints to find me in the distance

and I feel a tightness in my chest again—something's about to happen—when I recognize him from the Vigil pamphlet at Jah'Va. It's C's father.

I walk over, eyes around me coming to life, not staring, just observing. It is a funeral, after all. As I approach C and Bernard, I notice that their coloring is reversed: his dark skin and white fade, her light skin and black hair. I can see the resemblance in the forehead and cheekbones.

"This is my dad," C says to me, touching her ear, its tip red as a stoplight. The price tag of her dress is still dangling under her armpit.

"Bernard Williams." He smiles and reaches out to shake my hand. His grip is fatherly, riding the line between welcome and warning.

"Wayne Williams," I say and his brow flinches. "I'm so sorry for your loss, sir."

He cocks his ear toward me. "What did you say your name was?"

"I know, right?" C laughs foolishly. "Isn't it uncanny? I—"

"Wayne Williams, sir." I cut her off but I don't look at her. What the fuck is this little loopy show? Didn't she think it through, bringing me here? Not that I did.

"What are you playing at, son?" Bernard steps toward me.

He and I have been making eye contact this whole time but now our looks strike each other like match to tinder. You can almost hear the tearing sound of the flame coming alive.

"Dad—" C objects, her voice coming from somewhere far away.

"I don't know what you mean, sir." I say it politely but I'm holding the flame.

"Where'd you get that name?" He hears the heat in his voice and stops. He looks down to collect himself and when he looks

back up, the flame has dimmed. "I'm sorry. I know that's an odd question. I'm not myself today. But—is Wayne a family name?"

"To be honest, I don't know, sir. I didn't really know any family where I came up."

"I see. You can understand why I'd ask. My son had the same name as you."

"*Dad—*" C seethes.

He doesn't say anything, shuts her down by just looking at her. She falls silent and I watch her become a child again, girlish shame dawning in her face. Her lower lip rises to cover her upper lip. Then her phone starts ringing, loudly.

With a look of horror—"I'm so sorry"—she unzips her long lady wallet and fumbles it out. "I'm so sorry," she says again at the screen, then looks at her father. "It's Mom." She's pivoting away to take the call as he says calmly, "Tell her I send my love." C nods over her shoulder even as her mouth exclaims questions into the phone, quieter as she walks away: "What do you mean, *animals*? That's not possible. Who—?" She moves out of hearing range.

Abandoned, distracted, Bernard and I nod grimly at each other, less like strangers who just met at a funeral and more like two brothers passing in the street.

"So. Wayne." He returns to my last comment. "Where is it that you 'came up'?"

You can hear the quotation marks around the last two words. I find myself looking over him—his pocket handkerchief, the tassels on his shoes—to squash my irritation before I speak.

"California. Oakland, mostly."

"I see," he says.

And I feel him back off—his body, his voice, his eyes. Maybe I ought to ask him some questions too, go back to that name,

feel out if this man knows something the Williams women don't about the son who bears it, the monster he became. But now Bernard is cupping my shoulder—again, a tad too tight for comfort—and thanking me for coming.

I watch him walk over to an Asian woman and take her hand, then glance back. The woman turns to look, and I can tell they're talking about me. Beyond them, C's stalking back and forth, whispering fiercely into her phone, the tag under her armpit swinging. I see the mourners in the room move together and apart, a loose braid of guests and kin. I feel eyes on me, landing and flitting off like flies. Something rotten comes up my throat. Time to go.

≈

My hand's already on the bar of the door at the back of the funeral home when a squeaky bang stops my heart. To the side of the door, there's a window and there's a bird outside it, a seagull, rising, like it's trying to climb up the side of the building, its wings furious on either side of a body the shape of a bowling pin, its black eyes fixed but scared. I hear its frantic fluttering, then a hoarse sound comes from it like an old-school modem. It's weird to see it so close, so low down. Is it injured? Before I can do anything, there's a shriek and it's off, white against the off-white sky, trying to find the ocean, and I see my reflection in the window. *Of course he's not here, son. And what would you have done if he was?*

I shove the door open and find myself in an old graveyard behind the church. I clench my fists in pulses as I pick my way across the frozen dirt, skirting tombstones and flowers, fighting the bitter wind. At the far end of the graveyard, I find a low black gate that opens out onto the main road. I push through it

and look up and see the skyline of downtown fucking Baltimore, which I know like the back of my hand, the buildings like the shapes of my fingers. They're not so different, I think, that city in the distance and these headstones and monuments. Built on death. Death is everywhere around here.

9

≈≈≈

They're all covered up in this jumpsuit, but I always say my tattoos is like rings in a tree, just on the outside of me. You could read my whole life on my skin: all the shit I done did or didn't do just tryna get by, specially when I first came out the joint. Odd jobs in the hood, deliveries, favors, and yeah, soon enough, sellin again. Started off small. Pills for the College Park kids and whatnot.

Then that snowstorm hit, around '09—remember that? Everybody in the D.C. metropolitan area walkin around sniffly and glassy-eyed, like flu season was forever. And I got lucky. I got a connect on some product. Straight from the source. Pure.

Look, I aint never wanna get into that shit. That baggie in juvie weren't even mine! But I always knew how to stunt. And being locked up taught me a lesson in how to mismatch what I do to what people see. So I thought *Lemme flip some product with one dumb nigga and retire. Maybe Kima*—she was the only foster mom I was still in touch with—*maybe I'll buy Kima a house out in the county. Maybe we can live in peace, take a damn breath.*

I musta waited almost a year on that plan before this dude

came around. Everybody called him G.E.D. Now, that nigga aint have no high school diploma—that nigga's head was half meat, half jello—but he went around tellin everybody he was plannin on gettin his G.E.D., and I guess the name stuck. He moved with this crew of Miami niggas that ran his security—all of em shooters. And when he came up to Baltimore, he got himself an army of runners—mostly kids from my old school, now that I think about it.

It was laid out like the yellow-fucking-brick road, man. All I had to do was let him win and pull him in. So I made some introductions, sold him pills a coupla times on a discount, then hit him with a proposition. Now, G.E.D. weren't just sellin, he was usin too. Bad business model. Plus he was paranoid as hell. So, I got him to meet me at this club where my nigga T was management. That way, I told him, we had privacy and we had security.

So, we get there, T waves us through the metal detector—which was honkin for G's boys cuz they was packin heat—then up to this VIP area above the dance floor. The club was new so it was like a big-ole house party. You could look over the railing and see all the bottles and bitches and all that music-video shit. But up here in VIP it's empty, just us—me, G, and his three boys.

An hour goes by and G's deep in a bottle of Henny, kinda slurry and jumpy, snortin like a bull. I knew he was gon bite on this deal but I was still reelin him in, droppin the price bit by bit, even though it was way too high to begin with. The product was real—I aint stupid. But I was polishin it to a shine, feel me? So, I'm talkin and talkin and he's sweatin and noddin.

And all of a sudden I feel it in my gut: somethin aint right. The music starts takin over my heartbeat and I get this tingle in my neck, a squeeze right about here. And right then, like a switch: music shuts off, lights go out. Somebody downstairs screams.

And then shit just goes crazy: niggas shoutin, bitches screamin, glass breakin, furniture crashin everywhere. I lean over the railing to look and it's pitch-black down there but I can see the lights from people's phones, bouncin all around like a pinball machine. I'm like *Fuck, I aint got my piece on me!* G's yellin *What the fuck what the fuck.* I turn back to him and that's when I see it.

It's like this . . . shadow. It's risin up behind him, darker than the dark, and it's like a wasps nest or some shit up there, this buzzin everywhere. And then that shadow—I don't know how to say it, but it *shifts.* It shifts its focus. It focuses on me. And I know. It's him.

I jump for him but there's hands on me already—security throwin me on the ground, turnin me inside out. By the time they pull me up on my feet again, G's gone, T aint nowhere to be seen, and Will's gone too. I don't even know how he got up to VIP in the first place—it's like he oozed out the dark and back into it again.

Now I got G's security holdin me on either side, third one facin me, starin me down. He's in a suit, funeral sharp. Swoops down to pick up somethin from the ground where I was just laid out. Turns it over in his hands. It's a piece.

Now, I know I said that shit turns my guts, but I had a piece—everybody had a piece—and mine was just like this one, same make, same model. Dude looks it over, looks at me. I'm like *I aint bring that in here with me, man. I don't know who did but I aint got no death wish.* Dude drops the clip and pockets it, then hands the piece over. *I'm gon have to ask you to take your property and leave this establishment immediately,* he says. So I take it, real nice and slow, and let the other two beefy niggas basically carry me out to my ride.

I get in and watch em walk away, just happy to be alive. Then I open the glove box to put the piece in. And here's the wildest shit: my real gun is still in there, twin to the one from the club. And that's when I know. That nigga been watchin me. How else he know where I was gon be? How else he get a piece tricked out *exactly like mine*? Shit, man. I shut the glove box, turned the key, and got the hell outta Dodge.

≈

You can run, but whatever's behind you is always gon catch up. Like the OGs say, in the end, the game plays you. When Kima passed, I aint even make it out for the funeral. I had lost track of damn near everybody by then. I was city to city, just tryna make it to the next day. N'Orleans, Detroit, Atlanta. It seemed like everywhere I went, somethin came in to undo me. Some kinda hex. And I don't mean the law. That's always there. I mean somethin else, somebody watchin me, houndin me, gettin in the way of shit. Tryna fuck me up.

I weren't on the straight and narrow, no doubt. I was survivin. I did some shit. But I aint never get caught for the shit I did, feel me? It was always on some random-ass thing. Everywhere I went, somethin would go down. Like clockwork: some old warrant or some bitch callin battery on me, a broken taillight, assault charges.

So, yeah, I started usin. Mix that with the blood I come into this world with? I was, like, on the *brink,* all the time. Man, that shit made me feel *ready*. Amped. Made me feel like a free man— even though I was still in and out the joint all the time, like a gotdamn yo-yo.

People outside think it's hard to get your hands on product inside but it's not. What's hard is finding a place to use it where you won't get jacked. So what you do is, on laundry or kitchen duty, you got these face masks on anyway, so you just dab a little at a time inside your mask and sniff it from there. Keeps it off your hands.

The day it happened, I was on laundry. This nigga had followed me out into the hall where we take breaks. Me and him was sitting with our backs to the wall. He's sniffin in his mask just like me so I figure he knows the drill, must be an OG. I don't know why, but we start talkin about this bitch that had just come in. Pretty bitch, eyelashes like a horse, flashin purple lace panties at everybody, purrin. Laundry was always hot and loud, plus I was high, so I was already riled up. And me and this nigga start arguin about this purple-panties bitch.

It was just one of them hyped-up dumb-ass squabbles you get in when you're high. But it got heated. He put his hand on me and I smacked it off and that's when he said it. My name. His voice all low and rough. It lit me right up and I tore off his mask. It was him.

I say *I got you this time nigga* and grab him by the neck. I stand him up and push him against the wall. My mouth is up against his ear and I'm yellin but quiet-like, like *Bitch why you been houndin me, you gon square up or what?* I drag him to this supply closet where we keep all the mops and buckets and shit, and I shove him inside and I shut the door. I tell him again *Square up, nigga!* I can feel my heart going so fast it's like I'm vibratin.

Then I feel that shadow creepin in again and I shake my head like *nah nah nah*. Man, it's the worst feeling. It's like—it's like you about to faint and the black behind your eyes starts shootin fireworks but there aint no light, just electric black on black. Or like a storm's comin and it's night and you can't see it, but you can feel it loomin up on you. Or like a hoodie's droppin over your head but mad slow—the darkness crackin wide and swallowin up everything, everything goes black and—

Hold up. Hold up. Just gimme a minute.

OK. They say—they say I stabbed him. They say I broke a mop, broke the handle over my knee, and stabbed that nigga in the side of the neck with it. Now, what kinda sense does that make? Stab a nigga for what—for sayin my *name*? I don't remember none of that.

What I remember is, the guards came in. They musta heard the fight and started tryna open up the closet door. They was bangin on it, yellin, so I pressed my back against it to keep em out. And that's when I saw the light cuttin in from behind me. Comin through the cracks around the door, under the door. Light catchin on things in the closet, makin em shine—tools and buckets and puddles—and Will too, his eyes and his teeth flashin in the dark.

But then it was too many damn flashes and movin too damn fast and I could hear scratchin sounds and things fallin over. I lost my shit and I must have let up from pressin back against the door cuz it slammed open and shoved me inside and I stumbled over him.

He was laid out on the floor, all crooked, at funny angles. I smelled the blood before I saw it. Nearly choked on my vomit. But maybe that was the rats. Cuz when the guards bust in, the light came in with em, and you could see the rats runnin around, slippin in the blood.

You wanna know the wildest thing? When I saw him there on the floor, his body—the way it looked from above, lyin on the ground all crooked—he looked like somebody. He looked like that kid that got curb stomped, the one that—the one that I saw on the videotape in Coach's office.

That's how this shit gets you. Haunts you. Everything that ever happened to me started back then, with *him*. I aint got no reason to lie. Why would I lie? What's a man like me, in here for life, gain from tellin a story like this? I just don't want no misunderstandings on me fore I die. Sometimes I feel like I'm already dead. Sometimes I tell myself: *You won. You got him.* But sometimes I'm like *Man, you aint got nobody but yourself.*

10

≈≈≈

Back at the inn, I watch old cartoons on my phone and contemplate the possibilities. "My son *had* the same name," Bernard had said. That means that, like C, he has either bought into the idea or is sticking to the story that the other Wayne is dead. If Charlotte Williams is the only one keeping hope alive, she must know something that they don't about him. The gala will be my chance to find out. I just hope I haven't fucked my chances of an invitation.

When C gets back to the inn that evening, she doesn't ask why I left the reception early, just eyes me warily when I bring her a glass of water. I sit next to her on the edge of the bed, in another room that belongs to neither of us. I notice the price tag on her dress is gone and wonder who told her.

"How was the burial?"

"No burial." She sips the water. "I told you. She wanted cremation."

She puts the glass down on the carpet and picks up a small, sealed cardboard box. She places it on her lap. There's a blank white label stuck to the outside.

"They divided the ashes up between the family."

"Guess Grandma Lu didn't hate little C after all, huh?"

"My dad gave me his box," she says stiffly.

"Oh," I say, and as an apology, I lie: "It was nice to meet him."

She doesn't respond to this. Instead she asks, "Do you like animals, Wayne?"

"Animals?"

"Yeah," she says, looking at me. "You know. Like the zoo. Like, Save the Whales."

"Sure." I smile. "You wanna go to the zoo with me, C?"

She looks down again. "Maybe."

"I guess we should get some sleep?" I say finally.

She nods and moves the ashes off her lap, onto the bed, and puts her hand on mine. I stroke it with my thumb and she strokes my hand back. After a moment, her touch running over my skin starts to feel different, restless, and there's a long pause that speeds up until it feels like falling. Then C's turning to me and clambering up on my lap, kissing me deeply. Her lips are chapped, her tongue still sugary with funeral home gin. Her craving for pity, her quirky animal questions, are off-putting to me. But me and I are apparently divided on the question of this woman, and I'm hard again within a minute.

So, under the wild-eyed geese in the painting above the bed, we start over. We take off our clothes and roll onto our sides, facing each other. I'm gentle at first, which is like an inside joke given these last few days. As lightly as I can, I run my hand down her side, sloping in for her waist, out again for her hip, and down along her thigh, all the way to the knee. She rolls onto her back and my hand wanders over her breasts and her belly. She shivers whenever I skim a nerve. It tempts me and I dig my fingers into her sides, tickling her. She squirms, and then we're playfighting, laughing. I pin her down and kiss her hard, squeeze her breast harder. Her laugh catches and thrums in her throat like a plucked guitar.

I slide my hand down her belly again and she lifts her hips, parts them to let my hand in. Homesickness gathers inside me. We're teenagers. We're grown. She's hot and swollen and wet and I finger her, slow, then fast. Time skips like a record and I'm sitting with my back to the wall under those flying geese and she's in my lap, facing away, and we're fucking. The angle is new to us and a little awkward—she can't take me all the way in—and it takes longer for us to come, but it's just as good.

≈

An awkward thing to carry, I think the next morning as C tucks the box of ashes under her arm on our way out. Can't be too casual about it. Can't be too solemn, either. I watch her dart ahead of me through the rain to the cab waiting at the curb, its wipers waving goodbye. C just about pulls it off, carrying death like a purse. She has that kind of grace about her.

We get seats next to each other at check-in this time. I take the one by the window. C plugs in and zones out, so we don't talk or touch until we hit turbulence three hours in and start tumbling around like dice in a cup, and C reaches out and clutches my hand. When the plane levels out, I show her the dents her nails made in my skin, half circles like hoofprints.

"I always think I'm gonna die this way," she explains sheepishly. "Some sort of vehicle. A plane. Or a train. Sometimes when I'm driving, I think, *Did I just die?* I'll change lanes without checking my blind spot and it's like what if I just . . . skipped the collision part? What if I died back there but immediately moved into a parallel existence, in the next lane, without even knowing it?"

I snort. "That's some woo-woo shit. You think heaven's got freeways?"

"No." She smiles. "Just. What if it happens when you're not paying attention?"

"If it happens right now"—I gesture around at the other passengers, dozing, snacking, watching their screens in a trance—"you think you'll drag all these people along with you?"

"I guess that's a reason not to die alone," she says. "To make sure you're really dead."

The plane dips and sways. She shuts her eyes and grips my hand again. For some reason, her fear makes me think of her face when she's coming, and I feel a new tenderness for her in my stomach. It's hard to believe they're kin.

"I had this . . . mentor once," I say. "He used to talk about things like that—parallel existence and all that. He'd say, *Time is a mop.* Or, *Time is a rope.* He'd say, *The world is made up of threads of possibility, all the coulda-woulda-shouldas, but only some get caught in the rope.*" I shake my head. "I'm not explaining it right."

"No, no," she says, nodding, her eyes still closed. "This is good. It's distracting me."

"Okay. One time, he told me, *Time's got grooves in it. A moment is a needle and time can skip like a record.* I mean, listen, he was kinda nuts. He said things like, *Time is like the ground, and when something big happens, it's an earthquake, and when it's little, it's ripples, like those rows on a farm.*"

"Furrows." She nods faster and the plane spasms and she laces her fingers in mine, tight. Everything grows warm and wide and round, a bubble around us.

I lean over and say into her ear, "It's okay. Nobody wants to die alone. I wanna be next to somebody too." I'm not sure I mean this. Sometimes the words just follow themselves. The plane dips again and the wing outside the window shifts wildly. C turns to me, our noses almost touching. She opens her eyes, so close it's like they're inside mine.

"What would you do if this was the end?" she whispers.

I'd kiss you. The thought comes easy. But something tugs me back and I don't say it and I don't do it and she looks away as we even out again. The minutes pass and the plane hangs in its own hum, as still as the sky outside the window. C's head drifts slowly, then all at once onto my shoulder. I smell her hair grease, the coffee on her breath. Her eyelids shiver. Her white jacket is laid over her like a blanket but her dress rises one millimeter at a time under it as she slumps deeper into sleep. Her thighs are wet sand under the tide of her hem. Her thighs are smooth and bare and just within reach.

But I leave her be. I let her sleep through the pilot's crackling apology for the Rockies and her announcement that we're landing, through the lights coming up like the end of the party, through the flight attendants' final march down the aisles— "Trash? Trash? Trash?" they say like an accusation.

C wakes as the wheels kiss the tarmac. She turns to me, shocked, then remembers who I am and her smile swings to life. Then it falls again, like she's remembered something else. She reaches down to get the ashes and her purse from under the seat in front of her. She takes out her phone and turns it on. The second the seat belt sign pings off, she stands and rushes down the aisle until she meets the back of another passenger eager to deplane.

I slide over slowly, unfold my sore bones, and stand. I yawn and get myself together: tuck my shirt in, rebuckle my belt, pull my jacket on, put my watch on. C is already six passengers ahead of me now and as others inch into the aisle and pull down their luggage, she darts forward so the distance between us grows and grows. I decline to hurry. I shuffle forward in the halting queue, the rhythm like traffic at a stop sign. By the time I reach the tunnel from the plane to the airport, I can't even see her white jacket among the stagger of backs ahead of me. I feel a bit unappreciated. I went all the way out there for a damn *funeral,* met her *father,* held her *hand.* Didn't even find *him.* I know my sulk doesn't make any sense. But what sulk ever does?

I'm still nursing this boyfriendy grudge when I emerge out of the tunnel into the pale glow of SFO, the spinning wheels and striding shoes and TV news on low, toddlers screaming with joy or pain, the overlapping echo of flight announcements. I search for C among the pools of seated passengers, the streams of walking ones, and I finally catch sight of her going through the exit to one side of security. I break into a jog through the automatic doors and almost trip over her. She's standing at the top of the escalators down to baggage claim, her back to me. And she's with a white lady and two cops.

Something inside me starts leaping and slamming like a dog trying to jump a gate. I look behind me but there's no going back through those automatic doors. So I duck my head and turn left, looping around the escalators where the three of them stand, walking quickly but steadily toward the exit in the distance. I'm trying to work out how to get the fuck out of here, trying to figure why the fucking cops are here, when I hear one of them call my name.

Freeze or run? Mo always said a man who's gotta ask the question is already dead. I decide to freeze, but I do it smoothly, more like I heard a barista calling out my order than the police calling out my name. Then I turn, squashing the instinct to raise my hands, which bougie don't do. Instead, I smile broadly, I tilt my head in a confident, interested way, and I walk over to them, my heartbeat a bass drum in my chest, my nerves electric.

C's flushed and stock-still, clutching her phone at her side like a weapon, the box of ashes tucked under her arm. Next to her, Charlotte Williams has a washed-out, drooping look—she doesn't dye her gray hair or wear makeup to cover her age. She's got that space between her legs that women get as they grow older, an emptiness around the crotch. Her linen get-up is expensive—I know because it somehow has no wrinkles—and as I reach the four of them, she digs into a fine leather purse to pull out her glasses. I focus on the cops.

"Yes, Officer? What can I do for you?"

The Latino one addresses Charlotte: "Ma'am, is this the man you were telling us about?"

Charlotte nods as she wrangles her glasses open.

"What seems to be the problem, Officer?" I ask the white one.

C jerks ahead like somebody pushed her. "You didn't have to call the cops, Mom!"

The Latino one ignores her and says, again, to Charlotte: "Ma'am, is this the man threatening your daughter?"

"*Threatening?*" I blurt.

"I believe so," Charlotte says as she puts her glasses on and turtles her head toward me. "A man who claims that he has my son's name has been going around to events in the city, to parties, asking questions about my family, about the foundation I run. To be honest"—she shakes her head at the cops—"this isn't the first time someone has tried to take advantage of us. And my daughter informed me that he's been following her too . . ."

Following? I look at C. She swallows but doesn't deny it. The edges of her lips are still white from plane sleep and for a second I picture licking my finger and wiping them and then kissing her, the kiss I didn't give her on the flight. I can almost feel the bones of our faces colliding, my teeth mashing her soft lips. So much for the gala, I think, and there's laughter in my chest, but I can't let it out, its corners are too sharp and my throat's too tight, already choked with what I thought I knew, and with what I now know that C doesn't know about what calling the cops would mean for somebody like me, like us.

I look around at the passengers coming through the automatic doors, their attention catching on us briefly before they walk to the top of the escalator and disappear down one by one, like they're falling in slow motion off a cliff. Of course, most of them are frowning at me, not at the cops or the Williams women.

"Hold on, hold on," the white cop says to Charlotte. "Where's your daughter now?"

There's a pause while we register his confusion. Then C sighs.

"*I'm* her daughter," she says. "I know it's hard to believe because she's *white* but—"

The white cop looks at her blankly, then nods and pats the air—*Okay, okay, calm down.* Before he can say anything else, Charlotte moves toward me, fingers gripping the frame of her glasses. I know why they do it but it's still amazing to watch the cops ease back. They know who she is, the power of her claim. Charlotte is aware of it too. Her steps are sure as she comes closer, and her eyes don't waver—they're puffy and gray and her glasses make them huge, suffocating. Is the world holding its breath or am I?

When she breaks into the invisible ring around me, the span of my body, my own human space, I feel like I've been struck. I lean away as Charlotte reaches for me, as she folds back all her fingers except for two, and . . . cocks her hand? I almost laugh again. She's making a play gun with her fingers, like I did with those women on the BART escalator, and now it's aimed right at me—no, not at me. At my wrist. She's pointing at my wrist.

"Where did you get that watch?"

I look down, past my rolled-up sleeve at the old Seiko. I must have put it on without thinking when we landed. I look at C. Her mouth opens and closes. I can't speak or move either, but something big and broken in me starts pounding again, throwing itself at the gate. It's not even about the cops. It's about the gaping chasm they guard, circling its edge, tossing some of us in outright, keeping others out. Charlotte is already walking back to the uniformed men. She stops and turns, as if sheltering under them.

"I don't know what this man is trying to do," she says to them, still facing me. "Using my son's name, crashing a family funeral, stealing a family heirloom. I believe it's a poor effort at identity theft. I think he's trying to impersonate my missing son."

C cries out: "That's not possible! Wayne isn't *missing*—I mean, there's been a mistake. This isn't—" She looks at me helplessly. "I didn't mean for this to happen."

Charlotte frowns and starts scolding her daughter. "What is wrong with you, Cassandra? This man is trying to manipulate us! To deceive us that he's our Wayne."

Three bystanders stop to watch.

"No!" C's voice is jagged. "You *know* that's not possible. Mom, *please*. Just *stop!*"

Charlotte seems taken aback and she turns away, shaking her head, but then looks around and seems to gain strength from our audience. I can feel eyes itching up my back.

The Latino cop sighs testily. "Are you *presently* in any danger, ma'am?" he asks C.

"No!" she shouts.

"Okay, okay," he says patiently, then turns to Charlotte. "Ma'am?"

We all look at her. After a moment, she lifts her chin, shakes her head.

"All righty then." The white cop sounds frustrated. "I'm sorry, but we can't really do anything here. This is out of our jurisdiction. You'll need to go in and file—"

"So we're good now, right?" C interrupts to say to her mother, then barks at the cops: "And yes, you fuckers can fucking go now."

No no no no, I reach out and clap my hand over C's mouth and—of course I don't. But I almost see it happen, like an acid trail: my arm reaching, the sound when my cupped hand hits her face, her scared eyes. I stare hard at her instead, this black woman who has somehow never learned the cardinal rules of blackness. It's too late. It was almost over but C's cuss has flipped a switch and a kind of static swarms in over us now. The cops shift their feet and swivel their heads and more bystanders gather and the backs of phones start to rise.

Then the Latino cop, because he's a cop or because he's a man, and needs to have the last word, places his hand on C's shoulder. It could be to reassure her, to calm her down, but I can tell from how she flinches back that it's heavy with threat. And because I'm a man too, I guess, I step between them and I say, "Don't touch her."

The white cop comes at me immediately, one hand moving toward the zip ties at his waist, the other toward my forearm.

"Mr. Williams," he says as he grabs it. "You don't want to make any trouble."

Freeze or run? *What are you gonna do, son?* Nerve and muscle and bone make the decision this time. I wrench my arm out of his grip, turn away, and book it.

"Stop!"

I make it maybe four steps before it explodes across my back: a hundred bees, a thousand bees, a million bees, all roaring to life. My body twists as I fall and in the distance beyond the roar, I see the white cop, his teeth gritted, his legs apart, his arms in front of him, his hands meeting at his bright gun. I hear Mo's voice again. *Just like target practice,* he says and I hit the ground, bucking. Then it's just pain. Pain growing wings, so many quick wings, beating down sound, sight, everything, beating down on me through the dark.

Past

≈≈≈

The room in 7D is plain and white, blank with light. I'm the mess at its center, wounded flesh and a bunch of machines and a bed like spacecraft. The hours are food, piss, food, meds, shit, food, meds, piss, and sleep that's straight chaos—I wouldn't even call it dreaming. Only my name is a constant but it's censored around the edges like songs on the radio, dissolving into a *shh* that blends with the sound of the machines I'm strapped to. Charlotte's eyes drown me in gray. Grown folks smile at me with kindly faces. *Well, if it ain't Wayne,* they say. *Hush now,* an old woman says, then bends to rebuke me: *Well, what are you good for then, Wayne?* Two bodies, wheeled out of a house, naked on the gurneys, a man and a woman, their mouths sealed black with flies. The old woman rubs my back. *Hush now. It ain't your fault, Wayne.* Mo puts a joint to my lips. *It ain't your fault, sweet boy.*

I wake up, missing my friend like a splinter in my palm, and I hear the machines bleating. The glass in the window on my door is threaded with wire. *A prison everywhere,* Mo always said. *A prison everywhere for you and me.* I should've seen it coming. Should've known that man was crazy the second he told me that his real name was Gary, and that he'd changed it to

Mohammed in '01. But Mo was always muttering apocalyptic shit from the start, so it wasn't obvious right away when it started coming more often and at a higher pitch. Especially because the words were the same—*admonition, blazing fire, rent asunder*—all of them ganked from that beat-up Koran he carried everywhere, its cover faded from his fingers and the sun's, its pages so glued together you could barely crack it.

One morning, I woke up under a tree by Lake Merritt, a million dawns on the water. Mo was already awake, doing his morning prayers. But they were out of rhythm, too fast, he was rocking, plucking at his graying beard, mumbling about *calculation, reckoning.* I tried to interrupt him out of it but he turned on me. He was shaking, his words clogged up with spit, said that he knew that I was going to *carry vengeance to excess,* said I had got it all wrong, that what happened to me wasn't by man's hands but by God's, and that there was no undoing whatever force had pitted me against that other boy named Wayne, that the scales of *just weight and full measure* were God's hands, left and right, not mine. And then Mo showed me his own hands, left and right, and then he laid them on me.

But this time, I fought back. I was a boy when we met but now I was a man, nearly twenty years old. I beat the man down, ground his face in the dirt, spat on him, told him I would find *just weight and full measure* myself. I took all his money, what dollars I could shake out of his pockets and out of the caked pages of his Koran, and I used it to start over, to start my life over, with Sticky's help down the line. I left Mo behind, left him bloody and dirty and mumbling by the shining lake. But it felt like—and I don't know why—but it felt to me like he was the one who'd gone and left me.

≈

My nurse in 7D is a cheerful petite woman named Abigail. She ignores the officers milling everywhere like they're just part of the furniture, bustles into my room and greets me the same way every time: *And how's every little thing?* She's from Texas and doesn't like to be called Abby. I'm a little bit in love with her. Abigail is methodical and breathless and I imagine that she'd be that way in bed too. I relish the click of the plastic spoon against my teeth when she feeds me, and I sink into self-pity when she goes on her rounds, leaving me with the silent, irritable officers on hospital watch.

Day two, Abigail tells me I have a visitor and my lawyer comes in. She's young and seems bone-tired. But she's smart and on top of her shit. The fact that the cops brought me to the jail ward at S.F. General was already a concession. She tells me they still had to charge me with a misdemeanor to account for tasing me, to cover their backs. But even Code 148, which they tried to pin me with—evading and resisting arrest—can't quite justify the extent of my injuries. Trauma to the head from when I hit the ground (blood had come out of my ear, which looks dramatic on the cellphone footage), plus a broken arm and three broken ribs from the Latino cop kneeling full force on my back to cuff me even though I was already unconscious.

I answer my lawyer's questions. *No, I'm not using a fake name. No, I'm not impersonating anybody. No, I'm not gonna sue. No no no no,* I repeat like a two-year-old, the morphine in my veins making a steady fog in my head. In the distance past it, I see my lawyer close her notebook. She tells me she can appear at the arraignment in my stead. I'll have to show up in court again but—this is news to me—somebody's already paid my bail. I'm no longer in police custody. As soon as the doctors say it's safe, I can go home.

Home. I laugh, but one corner of my lips digs into my cheek.

Something in my chest turns over in waves, starts to roll out of my eyes. It's just the meds—Abigail explained this the first time I burst into tears—all the opiates chugging into me from the machines, my pet robots. I'm like a girl on her period, a man on his deathbed. My lawyer frowns. Abigail scurries in like a little bird, says it's lunchtime and I have to eat, and escorts my lawyer from the room. When Abigail comes back without a tray, saying *And how's every little thing?* with a knowing smile, I give a mock swoon, hand over my heart.

They monitor me for one more night. Mo hovers over me in my dreams again. *Well, if it ain't Wayne,* he hums. He doesn't sound like himself but it's him, he's wearing his Uggs and his du-rag, the naps creeping out the sides like mildew. *Fuck you,* he says to passersby, *You can't have him. He's mine. Look at that buttery skin, ooh, you gotta let me suck on that baby-boy dick, Wayne.* I stare at him, I try to find his daytime self, but I feel my dick swelling against my thigh anyway. *I'm gonna tell yo dead mama, I'm gonna tell her you looking for that other boy when you already got me,* he says. *Fuck you, Wayne. Fuckin' nigga.* He turns away in a huff and I move up behind him, press my hard-on against him, but when he presses back against me and looks over his shoulder, it's C, and she's the one that says, *I'm glad, I'm so glad, I'm so glad it's you, Wayne.* I bend her over and fuck her and after, she rises up again and she's a giant now and she takes me into her arms like I'm a baby. *Hush now,* she says.

≈

I wake to my sparrow, my love, fluttering around the room, preparing it for me to leave. The officer who usually sits at the door is gone. A white sun seeps up behind clouds and the room is like the inside of a fridge. Abigail trails the smell of apple and pepper.

"I didn't want to wake you," she whispers. "You have another visitor."

"Who is it?" I croak.

"Looks kinda like you." She shrugs. "Your sister, maybe?"

And just like that, I fall out of love with Abigail. She leaves us alone in the room at least, me and my visitor. I know it's the rules around here but I still take note that Cassandra Williams comes to me bearing nothing. No gifts, no flowers. Only herself, and not even that entirely. She leans against the wall, wearing tall boots and a trench coat. Her hair is tied back but springing to life from the damp, spangled with rain.

"How are you?" she asks.

"How you think?"

"They said you were okay. That they're keeping you for observation because the—"

"How's your ma?"

"She's—" C crosses her ankles and looks down. Her chin is almost to her chest. "She's okay. She sends her thoughts. She's very sorry that you got hurt."

"Oh, *she* is, is she?" I laugh once and wince.

"Are you in a lot of pain?"

I don't say anything.

"I never wanted this to happen."

"Really?" I ask. "Because, far as I can tell, you're the one who *made* it happen."

She huffs, like this is some lovers' quarrel. "You're the one that pitched up in the middle of my life! Out of nowhere!"

"You called the fuckin' cops on me, C."

"No I didn't." She's furious. "My mother did. She called me when we were at the funeral. She said Vigil security told her a man was going around, saying his name was Wayne, asking about us online. I figured it must be you, so I told her, and she decided that you were trying to impersonate my brother. I couldn't convince her otherwise because—well, I didn't know what the hell you were doing either."

I swallow. My mouth tastes like sewage. We look at each other for a minute, tense, snakes in the same pit. I look away first.

"Fuck this. I don't need to answer to you."

"I shouldn't have come," she snaps back.

"Maybe you should go on ahead and leave then."

I feel a howling in my gut and I'm not looking at her, but I sense her walking toward me. I feel trapped in cords and tubes like a bug in a web. I'm about to call for help, but in this place, that's calling the cops, and then I smell her—not her perfume, but her—and the words melt under my tongue anyway. She sits on the edge of the bed, then rises briefly to pull a gadget from under her thigh—a pump for the pain meds. She looks at it, looks at me. Before I can nod, she presses the button. The meds stir into my arm. I exhale as their pressure pushes into my veins and calms the urgency pulsing through me.

"We made sure they brought you here. We paid your bail."

"I know." She can't possibly think I'm gonna thank her.

"I told them that there's no way you could be my brother, no way you were impersonating him, and—"

"I mean," I say with disgust, "it would be kinda fucked up if I was pretending to be your brother. You know, given that we've been . . ." I bob my head.

"Fucking?" She laughs. "Well, yeah. That and the fact that my brother's dead."

At first it's like she's telling a joke, truly so silly that a laugh rolls up my chest. But C doesn't notice. She's rattling on and her gaze is fixed on a point on the other side of me now.

". . . twelve when he died. He was seven," she's saying in this mechanical way. "I saw him die. We were alone, just the two of us. But it was allowed. It's what we did every . . ."

It suddenly feels like Mo is in the room and I put my hand on top of hers. *Come back.* Touching her closes her down but it opens me up. And I hear what she said now. *I saw him die.*

"I didn't know your brother *died*," I say. "I thought Vigil was for missing kids—"

"Vigil is a lie."

I feel like I'm slowly being dragged out of my own body.

"My mother built a fortune out of looking for a dead boy," C's saying. "Imagine. All that love for a child." She shakes her head. "What kind of a person turns that into—"

"I was looking for him too."

"What?"

"Your brother. Wayne." I laugh. "I guess we've all been looking for him."

"*You* were looking for *him*?"

I nod.

That's when it hits her. "You thought he was alive. Because of Vigil. But—why were you looking for him?"

Sleep is calling out to me from far off, like it's summer and it's late and I've been outside playing too long and it's time to come inside.

"Listen, C. I need to tell you what happened to me."

There's a pause.

"Okay," she says. "Tell me."

My eyes are spinning inward, my chest aches, my broken pieces drift to the bottom of what's left of me. I pick them up and start over.

"I was born in Baltimore."

I feel her lean forward but she doesn't saying anything.

"Well, the county. And my parents got killed there, shot in their beds."

I feel her flinch and I turn my head from her. I know I won't get through it otherwise.

"I was ten. I never really found out why or by who. I think it was drugs. They were using heroin, which I didn't know at the time, but it explains some things. After they died, I was a ward of the state and I moved around a lot, you know—different foster homes. Then when I was thirteen, they moved me to a home right near Gwynns Falls. You know the area?"

I'm still not looking at her but I feel her nod.

"So I started going to this school. Pretty rough, you know, metal detectors and stuff—this was middle school—and I was a new kid and I was shy. I didn't fit in too well. And there was this other kid. And he had the same name as me."

I feel her sit up.

"I don't know, at some point, me and him, we kinda got into it. You know. Arguments. Pranks. Jokes. Tripping you up in the hallway, messing with your stuff. I guess they call it bullying now, but it was actually worse than that. We started fighting at recess all the time, beating the shit out of each other."

I hear her *hmm*.

"I was mad about a lot of things and it got in my head that this kid was out to get me. And then this thing happened. Back of the school. Drug deal gone wrong kinda thing. And someone got curb stomped. You know what that is?"

I'm drowsy and I forget myself and look at her. C's flushed but calm. She nods.

"And the other kid accused me of doing it."

She inhales with a hiss.

"And you know, they never get things right with boys like

us, even when a mistake happens. So, I got put in a correctional facility until they figured it out. When I came out a month later, I ran away. I didn't want to go back into foster care, and I'd found this address, in Oakland, for an uncle or somebody who'd paid for my parents' funeral. But when I got out here, I couldn't find him. And I had spent everything I had on those Greyhound tickets. So I started living—" I breathe out slowly. "Yeah, I mean, I was living on the street. I only got back on track with a job and everything a few years ago."

"So . . ." she says. "So, you thought that other kid? You thought that was my brother?"

"Yeah, I did." I sigh. "I mean, it's been years and I haven't seen him since, like, middle school. When I started looking into the public records a couple of years back, I found a lot of men he could be. Wayne Williams isn't exactly a rare name. I found men who'd been arrested for drug deals, for broken taillights, for DUIs, domestic violence. Some of them still incarcerated. It could've been any one of them. But then I learned about Vigil. And it . . . fit, you know? The name. That he went missing in Baltimore—that kid from my school was in foster care too, so I thought maybe, when he went missing, he got pulled into the system. Then I saw your dad's picture . . . and I mean. You can't deny it. There *is* a resemblance."

She nods, taking it all in. "Were you . . ." Her voice is so faint I can barely hear her. "Were you just using me to get to him?"

I smile. "Not *just.*"

A frown flickers over her face. "What were you gonna do when you found him?"

I see Mo's eyes, the pain in them when I was kicking him in the gut, and the love in them. Truth be told, I never had a plan for after. I just wanted to find that boy—that man—and look him in the face. But maybe what happened after would have ruined us both. Maybe that's why I found her instead. "It don't matter, right? Wrong Wayne anyhow."

"Yes," she says, not loud but crisp. "It must have been another Wayne Williams. My brother died when he was seven. I was twelve. I was there. We were alone together."

I pat her hand and she falls silent. I don't wanna get her going about it again. It feels too much like a hand on the stove. But then it comes to me that she needs to tell hers the way I needed to tell mine. My blinking is slowing anyway, so I let my eyes close when I say it.

"Tell me what happened, C."

There's a pause and then she says the strangest thing. She says, "I don't wanna tell you what happened. I wanna tell you how it felt." She keeps going, and it's like she knows it by heart, like it's a poem she's memorized and she's reciting it. I let her words swirl around in the dark behind my eyelids. I see a beach with sand the color of her skin, the color of my skin, the water rippling and rushing at my toes, like fingers scrambling to tickle them, but out to sea, the water looks sluggish and dull green, and the waves are long rolling bars like the shadows of trees, and in those grooves out in the water, I see a man my height standing, facing away, his back to me, and the waves are rolling up to him and making a pocking sound whenever they hit his legs, and he stares at the horizon, and I stare at his back until he turns his head to look at me, but no, he's looking past me, and I remember I'm in the water too, it swishes warm and frothy at my ankles, and I turn my head to look at the shore and I see a boy standing there, it's Wayne, and his feet are buried in the sand, I see a boy a boy a boy—

C gasps like she's coming up for air. "And it's funny. You know what my dad said to me the other day?" Laughter chatters through her. "He said, he said, 'Cassandra, for *us,* death is everywhere. Didn't you know that?' Like I didn't *know* that. And I said, 'Of course, but . . .'"

My eyes slip open and in that snapshot before I pass out, I see her hectic, happy face.

"'. . . in the end, what does knowing that get you?'"

≈

When the whistling evenness of your breath convinces me that you're asleep, I reach over and stroke your silken eyelids. A curious intimacy. When I get up from the bed, you seem to wake briefly. "More," you murmur, but your eyelids stay trembling with REM. I stand and watch over you. I collect your face and hold it close. Then I leave your room and wave to your nurse with a fake smile. I find her disagreeably plain and condescending, but I want to maintain friendly relations so it'll be easier when I come back to check you out of the hospital, which is also checking you out of jail, a double institutional goodbye.

As I exit onto Potrero, I look at my phone. My mother wants us to meet in the Castro, a couple of miles away. I'm an hour early, so I decide to walk. The sidewalks are still leprous with puddles but the rain has stopped and the sun is burning the clouds from a blue sky. I head down 22nd.

I feel unbearably sorry that you're hurt; I've never felt more powerful in my life. How to express this twofold feeling? Everything is twofold with you. I've never been with someone like you. It feels like some deep, atavistic déjà vu. The last time we had sex, in the inn after the funeral, a Saturn-ring feeling like this took a loose lap around my mind, nearing my awareness, veering off, nearing again, until it came clear. Two sets of words, pressed against each other like competing palimpsests: *Hit me. I love you.* I think of your hip bones thudding against my sit bones and feel a snap of lust under my navel. Dr. Weil would say I'm fixated, that central *x* of the word like a stitch binding me to you. I'm in your thrall, those tall letters on either side of the word imprisoning me.

Just as I cross Bryant, it comes to me, the way to express it: *I submit myself to you.* The wording is faintly religious in a way that feels familiar to me—though it's doubtful someone like me could ever be a nun or a penitent. The sentence captures what I feel when I'm pressed against you: screaming light and searing heat and rips of darkness. As I approach Folsom, I hear the cries of children and the amateur jangling of guitars. I look up from my foreshortened shadow and see pop-up tents and balloons— some sort of street fair. Dreadful. I'm resisting checking the map on my phone. I know the general path. I push on until I reach Mission and make a right.

This neighborhood feels old and new. It's a bedlam of businesses: nail salons and butcher shops and thrift stores. On every other corner, bodegas spill out onto the street, selling every imaginable fruit in every life stage: fresh, juiced, dried, fermented. Within a few blocks, I'm weaving through throngs of locals with their hodgepodge browns and melee of Spanishes. The repurposed buildings along the street have vestigial storefront signs. Chinese food is being served out of a taqueria, haircuts are advertised in the windows of a hardware store, but most disconcerting are the old movie theaters, with their signs rising grandly like the prows of ships—El Capitan is a parking lot, Cine Latino a climbing gym.

There are traces of resistance to the gentrification. WE NO GO flyers, riflesights scrawled on walls, sidewalk graffiti saying QUEERS HATE TECHIES. Someone has turned a cash machine into a protest sign by scratching an E on either side of the ATM. But the trees give a historical correction to the idea that any of this is new. These exotics, too, were imported long ago, palm trees like eyelashes and evergreens like eyebrows. And over all of this, the sun bears down, too sharp, too bright, too close. It makes me think again of fire, and of you. This city is you. You are its issue.

How could love be anything other than a rapture? "You should *date*," my mother says. "Meet someone *nice*." As if there's any correlation between this force, this feeling, and *dating*. Oh, the interchangeable men on the Google Calendar—Chris, Pete, Rob, Malcolm—like so much bland litter; taking Ubers and Lyfts to restaurants and bars; doing the math to split the bill and match the tip with men who own bicycles more expensive than their furniture, men who are oddly puritanical about hops and vegetables, men who are boastful of their neuroses—the trauma, the therapy, the meta-therapeutic rejection of therapy. One told me in earnest that it was important that I know right away, from the start, that he hated his mother. I just nodded over my Korean short rib, sipped my orange wine. Men so weak that I have to break up with myself for them. *Sperm on crutches,* Grandma Rose would've said.

I turn left on 18th and see a sidewalk inscription—THIS IS WHERE I DRAW THE LINE—and it's true, it's like I've crossed an invisible force field into wealth. A city divided unto itself from its faultlines up. I cross Valencia's spangled sidewalk and a mural on a condo swoops into view: a trapeze artist hanging upside down, arms reaching, reaching. I pass subdued lines outside the famous ice-cream shop, the famous bakery, the famous pizza place. Across the street, white tennis players pock the air dialectic. I see a white stone building with round crusty towers, teens sprawled on the steps—not a church, a school.

I think of your story about the boy in school. Of course I knew there were schools like that in Baltimore. They were the darkness that made my father light out for the county. *Education is the most important thing,* he said. *They can't do anything to you if you have your mind,* he said. *They.* More and more before he left us, the unnamed *they.* By the end, he didn't even bother to qualify this *they* in front of my mother, stopped saying *present company excluded.* But before I knew what he really meant, he was gone, leaving those little cryptic warnings. For what? A trail of breadcrumbs to find my way home?

Home. *You called the fucking cops on me.* I didn't! But how did it not occur to me that *she* would? And now I'm on my way to tell her about you and about us, to undo what she believes she knows from the airport. I feel a wash of shame that I can't separate from yours, from the fact that you ran, that you had good reason to.

Isn't this what I want, though? Not you in a fancy suit at a fancy dinner, not you paying for loafers or opening doors, not you shaking my father's hand and saying your name outright. No, what I want is the roughness of your voice, your tongue, your hands, how you handle my body like it's yours, how when you root into me, I catch a glimpse of your rose tattoo on your right arm, or your left arm from your perspective—I puzzle over which is the correct word for its location, and this is precisely the dizzying oscillation of it: me seeing you, seeing you see me, we are worth wanting each other, aren't we, Wayne?

The walk up 18th is a graduated ascent, which is exactly as I remembered it from visits to Grandma Rose before she died: shops selling penis biscuits, video stores selling vintage porn, a rainbow of rainbow flags—brandnew to dusty—arcing and wriggling over everything. As I near the intersection with Castro, I check my phone. I'm still early but I'm suddenly starving and even though it'll mean I'm not hungry when we meet at the bakery, I go into Walgreens to buy a packaged ice-cream cone—a petty rebellion—then turn left to keep climbing, looking for a place in the sun to sit and eat.

Past the hardware store with old-school window fronts is the Castro Theatre, which is advertising a double Hitchcock feature. I absently note the times as I admire the iconic posters—the red spiral in one and the shirtless movie star in the other, her bra-slung breast in exquisite profile. I see a sunny plaza where Castro, Market, and 17th converge but a tanned naked white man in a camping chair is holding court with a group of eager tourists, so I skirt it and head up a smaller street, Noe. I notice glass in the doors and realize there's a hidden nest of labs up here, with names that all include the words *Corp* or *Quest* or *Test*. Of course, this makes a kind of sense in the Castro.

I find another, smaller plaza and sit on a bench. I peel away the waxy blue-and-red paper and nibble at my ice cream. Two men sit on a bench nearby, one in jeans with his legs stretched out, the other with a leather beret, his legs crossed at the thigh. I notice them because all the other people in this neighborhood are white. These men are beautiful. They could be thirty-seven or fifty-two. I keep my head down and eavesdrop, trying to catch intimations on the wind. They're friends, not lovers, or maybe former lovers, or maybe still lovers but mostly friends. It has been a long time since I had a friend. They relax side by side, they confide, they laugh, they speculate about the weather and chide the woman looking at her phone as she crosses a busy street. Did they ever feel the rapture? Does it matter? They smile at me, and I think of my father, and as always, I feel at ease and forever excluded.

≈

I'm running late by the time I've finished my sickly sweet ice cream and made my way to the bakery where my mother suggested we meet. It's the epitome of San Francisco chic, BONJOUR spelled in the retro-mosaic floor at the entrance, vintage-rough furniture offset by the chrome fittings and the patterned tile of the counter. She's seated in a corner, a lightly disturbed cappuccino in front of her. A blue dress peeks out from under a gray cardigan, which is loosely belted in a way that reminds me of her old bathrobe. She looks regal and wounded, grand and tender. But she wears a crown of entitlement—new wealth has placed it on her head. I suppose I do, too. We've climbed up a couple of rungs on the class ladder, Charlotte and I, propped on Wayne's ghostly back.

But maybe she was always this way, I consider as I walk over to her. Maybe marrying my father, painting all those stoic, statuesque black mothers, was an innocent kind of slumming. And now with Vigil, she has reverted to the presumption of money from her childhood—*real gold on her fingers and in her ears,* my father had said—the presumption that made her think to collect dues on grief in the first place.

"Cassie," she says, "honeybaby."

I pull out the other chair at her table and sit. She reaches her hand across the table to lay it over mine. I smile, but I'm having trouble meeting her eyes.

"Have you spoken to your father?" she asks. "How is he?"

I pull my hand away, pick at my cuticles. "He's fine, given the circumstances."

"Yes. This is a difficult time of the year for all of us."

I blink. Then I remember. Wayne's birthday. It used to sneak up on me, the knowledge that up ahead would be a whole day rendered blank and stupid by Wayne's loss. When I was younger, I had tried to get her to celebrate his birthday instead of mourning it. But from the start, she had deemed the day he was born rather than the day he disappeared the occasion to gather in grief. Camcorder tapes, the smell of ice—these things still conjure those dread memorials in the den.

"I meant Grandma Lu's funeral," I say. "Dad's good, given *those* circumstances."

"Oh, of course," she says, flustered. "I'm so sorry. I didn't think your father would want me to come, and anyway, with the gala coming up . . ."

"I have some of Grandma Lu's ashes," I say, to press upon her embarrassment.

"You do?" She frowns with surprise. "She wanted you to have them?"

"Well, Dad gave me his portion."

"Ah. I would have been surprised. Lu always did dislike you so." My mother chuckles automatically, then covers her mouth, scandalized. We look at each other, suspended in this frank admission: new news about old news. Then we're both rocking with laughter, on and on, we can't stop, we're on the verge of hysteria, the laughter like keening. It nearly drowns out the Etta James playing over the speakers. Other customers begin to stare.

"Oh, you poor thing," she says. Another kick of laughter. "She really did hate you."

"Yup." I try to stifle it with nonchalance, but I can hear the soreness in my voice.

"Ah, well. I suppose your other grandmother more than made up for it." She touches my hand again, and it feels as if her hand is dust, air, dead leaves sewn into a purse of skin, and she's still talking about Rose: ". . . if she hadn't provided the seed money for Vigil, I don't know what we'd have done. The endowment is our only hope now that the state is in another goddamn fiscal crisis . . ." She's picking through the heaps of civic jargon that junk up the elegant mansion of Vigil. Even as the waiter comes, takes my order, and leaves, she doesn't stop talking. The volume of her voice just rises like displaced water.

"We need to talk about Wayne," I say finally, interrupting her.

That name, so rarely spoken between us, sends the tension in the air leaping up quick as an arpeggio. We can talk about family or about the foundation, but we cannot speak of the absence at the center of both. My mother takes her hand off mine and flicks it at the air.

"Is this about the man at the airport? I don't know what you've gotten yourself mixed up in, Cassie, but that man, that *man*—"

"I told you! He wasn't trying to impersonate Wayne. He was *looking* for him."

"Oh . . ." The sound she makes is of doubt, protest, exasperation. She plunges her hand into her purse and pulls out a pillbox, a white swan encased in lapis lazuli on its lid. She opens it and fumbles a pill into her mouth, takes a sip of cappuccino to swallow it. Too late. Tears splash onto the apples of her cheeks, which, like real apples, have grown spotted and puckered with age. "Why?" she demands. "Why would he be looking for our Wayne?"

I can't tell her everything that you've just confessed to me, so I say what's important. "He thought he'd met him before, as a young man. He thought Wayne was still alive. Because that's what Vigil says, that's what *we* say, on the website and pamphlets, we say that Wayne went missing, that he's *still* missing, when we both know—"

"Yes." She turns to me. Her gray eyes look silver. "We both know that he's dead."

This game has gone on so long—me insisting Wayne is

dead, my mother denying it—that my immediate impulse is to contradict her. But she's flipped the script. For the first time since he died, my mother has given me what I want: confirmation. I feel dizzy. Tinselly jazz twinkles around us. *She knew she knew she knew,* it throbs through me, but she chose the lie again and again. Even after it sent my father away, she used it to rope me closer, to bind me to her Vigil. Her eyes are still as wet and slippery as mercury when she reaches her hand out to me again. This time, I take it. I turn it over and grip it, hard. There is only one question.

"Why?"

She looks at me with pity. "I'm so sorry, Cassie," she whispers. "I just had to."

That's when I believe her. That's when I know that this wasn't some slip, some concession to me, but the truth. And now death is here—not the death of my brother, not the death of my love for my mother, but the death of her doubt. And now whatever hope that doubt has kept lodged inside me for all these years, lurking, down in the silt, emerges, breaks through, hits the surface, and vanishes. I never even knew it was there. When I look again, my mother's eyes have gone dry. The lapidary coolness of them, the matter-of-factness of her ownership over Wayne, over the story she's chosen to tell the world about him for most of my life—it all makes me feel insignificant, blessedly insignificant.

It's like the floating-arms trick, I'm thinking, as I let go of her hand and reach into my wallet for a twenty to leave on the table to pay for the lemonade that hasn't even arrived yet. It's like when Wayne would make me stand in the threshold and I would firmly press the backs of my hands against the door frame while he counted down from sixty to zero with Mississippis between the seconds to slow them, and when a minute had passed, I would step forward, and all on their own, my arms would rise like a levitation. Now I'm floating with this feeling—nothing is as it seems, nothing really matters—and I'm surprised to learn that this is in fact a consolation.

I stand up, carefully tuck my chair under the table, and walk away from my mother, away from Vigil, push through that pretty bakery door, and step into *life life life*. I don't matter, you don't matter, we're all just matter, codes, scrambles of signs and symbols, the language the world mumbles to itself, or maybe its consciousness, our eyes and ears and mouths sprouting from it like polyps, here to watch and hear and sense it, to record its events and ruptures, its growing and its rotting, its dismal spin.

≈

Out on the sidewalk, I make to check my watch, then realize you still have it—or that chipper nurse does, I should remember to get it from her when I pick you up tomorrow. I check the time on my phone instead. If I rush, I can make it to the second Hitchcock screening. A message from my mother blooms on the screen, covering the clock. I ignore it and turn the phone off. I race back up the hill to the Castro Theatre, darting around other pedestrians, and I'm panting when I buy the serrated paper ticket from the booth outside. The thick doors with their porthole windows swing closed behind me, their edges knocking softly.

The theater is massive but nearly empty. The walls are ersatz frescoes. Black square speakers make a mockery of the golden pipes of the grand organ. On either side of the screen, concealing most of it, hang curtains the color of blood, with deep and heavy-looking folds. The E X I T sign glows red, too. I find a seat alone in the middle of the theater and look up at the art deco ceiling, where the jagged chandelier forms a giant iris.

I face ahead again as the menstrual curtains part. The lights go down and the darkness rises, as if they're trading places. But when the film comes on, the light and the darkness are both there and they tangle, conjuring that familiar movie-theater atmosphere: gloom spritzed with brightness, somehow both illicit and friendly. I hunker down in my seat and let the banter and screams enfold me.

Palace

≈≈≈

We hop off the 22 on a whim. Through the bus windows, we see the FOR SALE sign, the balloon straining above it. I look at you and you answer aloud, *Why not?* You pull the yellow cord and we get off the bus. The houses here are small and contiguous, undivided by lawn or yard, set in long multi-colored rows on either side of an empty street. We walk between the pastel facades and precise windows, the decent clutter of Spanish tile on the roofs. They're so prim, these houses. They stare at one another from behind their veils—the curtains in their bay windows—like well-dressed guests who've arrived too early to a formal. It's the kind of neighborhood you've only ever heard of, the kind I've almost lived in. Is it better to be not quite or to have never come close?

The realtor, harried and beneficent, assumes we're married. He refers to you as my *partner* during the false lively chat in the kitchen. We join the other couples already performing the stilted haunting of the Open House: heads craning, eyes seeking, footsteps echoing over barely furnished rooms, water gushing from faucets at random intervals, windows creaking open and shut, checking, just checking.

Finally we're alone together in a shadowy bedroom at the

back of the house, door closed. We crawl under an abandoned bedframe and look up at the ceiling through the gaps between the wooden slats. We clutch our bellies, laughing at the idea of it. You and me, real estate. You and me, partners. Listening to the voices haggling beyond the door, we share a pear I bought at the farmers' market this morning. When its crisp quiet juice turns sugary and warm, when it's spent and sticky on our mouths, we lock our lips with sweet kisses. We drop the core and scramble out from under the bed, releasing giggles in bubbly spurts as we sneak past the desperate couples trying to win over the realtor, those wealthy, choosy beggars.

We're making our way back to the bus stop when you see it: a white quarter circle pieced out of the blue sky, hovering above a horizon of dark foliage in the distance. It's an enormous thing with the heft of a moon and the arc of a skull. Neither of us knows what it is—I'm basically a tourist and this isn't your typical stomping ground—so we turn a corner to see it better, then walk a few blocks until, even more unexpectedly, a pond comes into view. The rotunda we sighted juts beyond it, open air underneath it and a semicircle of columns on either side, lining the water. We walk toward it with unspoken assent.

We stroll along the edge of the pond, which is a calm dark green, furred with rushes. I see a piece of trash on its surface and grumble about litter. You correct me: the drifting wispy thing isn't trash, it's a blossom from a flowering bush on the shore. The pink flower, reflecting itself, looks almost neon. The sun's beginning to set and we've reached that grayish-bronze twilight time of day that sharpens the eyesight, or maybe lets colors be their truest selves. A swan wafts by like a hallucination. The water behind it soothes itself smooth. When nature is wild and rampaging and you're fixed to the ground with awe, it's called the sublime. What do you call it when the soul careens at the sight of nature in stillness?

We walk slowly between the stalwart pillars, which are grouped in clusters of four with a kind of pediment, a large concrete cube, on top. Standing along each of the cube's four vertical edges are identical statues: a woman draped in robes, her back to the world, one knee cocked lazily, her arms resting on the top of the cube with her elbows out and her hands cupping her invisible cheeks. The effect is four women in repose, facing one another, enraptured by something on the top of the cube. What if the stone women were to come alive, turning from their perches to reveal themselves to us? It reminds me of something I read about in that women's studies course, an ancient mud-brick city in the Sahara. Men and children and veiled women were allowed to walk in the streets. But the roofs above were for women alone, the only place where they could walk with their faces bared.

We reach the central rotunda, the inside of the skull we saw from afar, and instinctively look up. The inside of the dome is off-white, like it's only been primed, and divided by rafters into a floral pattern. Birds agitate and swoop up there but seem to have nowhere to land. There's a couple walking ahead of us, talking about caterers and flowers and weather. We cannot escape it today it seems, this joke about marriage. We exchange smiles and make our way around the couple, back to the edge of the pond. You peel away to find a view, an angle for us to see the bay, which you say can't be far off, maybe a mile.

I climb a rock in front of a tree and stand arms akimbo. I survey the water, the small commotion where some ducks have gathered. The birds look cubistic: brown and white and black in distinct blocks of feather, a parallelogram of purple under the wing. They skate the surface with ease and torque their bodies to bite themselves clean. Once in a while, one will tilt over, puckering the pond's surface, then tilt back up and shake its head. *No.*

Two white guys are sitting on the protruding root of a big gnarly tree. One of them is trying to tempt a duck ashore with leftovers from a cardboard container.

"Dude, these ducks are hella tame."

"Well, yeah. Fuckers like us are constantly feeding them."

The sun touches the scalloped clouds, which blush coral. The white guys leave. I linger in the wait. You steal up behind me. You're on the ground and I'm on the rock so we're the same height. I feel your breath on my neck and I know you want me and you know I know, and we're surrounded by desire, a shroud of it rippling over us, and it sends heat through me the way fires grow: a fist stretching its fingers, then one hand, two hands, riot.

You whisper roughly in my ear: "Let's climb it."

I look at you. You dart your eyebrows impishly, directing my gaze up.

"Climb what, the tree?"

You shake your head and tap my chin up to look higher. Stark against the darkening sky, I see that the tree's branches lean close to the cube topping one of the column clusters.

"The columns?"

You say nothing. You put your hand on my hair.

"I'm not wearing the right shoes," I say.

"You never got the right shoes on. Take them off."

There's an ease in how we've been together since you left the hospital. We've softened. We've drifted along the surface, skimmed the skin of the welter.

"Is this how we're gonna get our kicks now?" I ask. "Climbing buildings?"

"Among other things," you say, pulling on a tree limb to test it.

"We could travel," I say. "Where should we go?"

We look at each other. Our knowledge goes back and forth between us, those familiar oscillations accelerating until they blur, until they purr. Because isn't it every unlikelihood that we found each other and survived and are forgiven? Isn't it a miracle that fortune tiptoed in and took our hands in its ghostly ones and joined us? Isn't it a small mercy?

I kick off my shoes. You lock your fingers and bend at the knee. I place my bare foot into your palms, delicate as royalty. You hoist me up and I slide my other foot into a fork of the tree. I feel quick and strong. I grab hold of a branch, then feel a sting, two, three. I slap at my hand. "Ants," I warn you, then pull myself up, and sit astride a limb. I glance around at the canopy of leaves around me. A breeze sends them flipping like a dealer shuffling cards.

I watch you from above as you take off your shoes and socks, as you carefully roll the socks into a ball and put them in the mouth of one shoe, then line the shoes up at the base of the tree. You wrap your hands around a low limb and walk your feet up the trunk, prop a foot in the same fork I used, and throw your leg over another branch. You pull yourself up so you're sitting on a limb across from mine. It gives a little, creaking. I get myself into a squat on my limb, holding it with both hands, and inch toward the columns. My body rolls once but I catch myself. When I'm close enough to the columns, I rise from my squat.

For a teetering moment, I'm standing at the top of the tree, my shirt ballooning, branches scratching up my calves. I leap and a bird beats its wings past and it's the same thing and then I feel the rough texture under my foot and knee and I'm crouched on the top of the cube, the heads of the four women circling me. It's blustery up here.

I dust myself off and look down at you as you follow my path along that same limb, which dips lower with your weight. Your head angles this way and that as you wind your way toward me. I see the open heartshape of your widow's peak and feel a shock of terror and love. When you reach where I stood to jump, you extend your leg instead, putting your bare foot up on an edge of the pediment. I hold your ankle to steady it while you get traction. You lever yourself onto the cube and nearly knock me off. We gasp and laugh. You pull me up so we're flush. I bury my face in your neck, in your smell.

Then you turn me and wrap your arms around me from behind, your wrist against my collarbone. We look out at the water, which is indeed right there, a blue vastness of beaten metal, waves clustering and parting ways beneath that great, swooping, rustcolored bridge. The shadows of its towers and cables are bars of black in the water. The sun is lowering between its legs like a birth. The wind flares around us and the bridge sings its eerie song.

"It's incredible, you have to go all the way around, it's unreasonable, you could slip a groove, we're on the edge of the world, the blooming and dying, it's pointless, you love, it's hard to love, it's endless, love me, keep me. Where have you been? I've never felt this way, don't let go, don't go, I love you, I'm in love with you, I'm madly in love with you, I fought the pinch, I hated his tricks, but there's a kind of hate that has tenderness built into it, I made him stay quiet, I hunted him down, but all this time, I never thought to ask, 'How are you, little man?' I never thought to ask, 'Hey brother, how've you been?' Then shall they begin to say to the mountains, fall on us, and to the hills, cover us, I don't want to die alone, I love you to death, I will love you till the end of time, but how will we know if it's the end? What if it happens when we're not paying attention? What will we do if this is it? God! Incredible, isn't it? Magnificent, and just think, the bridge is swaying all the time."

And then it is swaying—visibly. The suspension cables shift boldly against the sky and the headlights of the cars driving across scatter like bits of glass. It all happens so fast, we can barely hear the screaming brakes and hooting horns and crushing crashes and now there's thunder, even though the sunset clouds—the color of violets and roses and daffodils—are placid in their ornate heap, and that's because the thunder isn't in the sky, it's in the ground.

The column beneath us shudders. You tighten your arms around me. With a heaving groan, the whole edifice bursts pellmell, mortar and concrete. Hell blares into our ears with a blast of grainy wind. We cower and tuck our heads and see the four stone women at our feet, their stone hands cupping their stone faces but beholding nothing, eyeless, terrible.

The column to our right topples with a bellow. I clutch your arms to my chest with one hand, and with the other, I point for you to *look look look* out at the water, its busyness and tumult, the waves disporting themselves with abandon. What hand has reached in and turned the world over? Beasts gyre to the surface of the sea, their skin slick as oil, their amorphous bulk, leviathans—brows unpierced by reason—that roll and tumble over each other, that mount through the black waters of which they seem made, that plunge about in absurd, shapeless games, as if the universe were battling itself in brute confusion and lust, aimlessly, wantonly.

And now, from the midst of the catastrophe, a thicker darkness rises, a tall shadow that grows steadily until it's as big as a house, then a minaret, a skyscraper. It is water or sand or smoke or death. It is the sealing black behind our eyes. It rises, it bulks, it blots out the sky. A mountain walks, stumbles, then sweeps straight toward us, its ravenous mouth wide open.

Acknowledgments

It's important to thank those who bless our stated designs by granting us the space, time, and funds to pursue them. Thank you to John Freeman for publishing part of the novel as "Take It" in *Freeman's: The California Issue* (Fall 2019); thank you to Yael Goldstein Love for publishing part of the novel as "Will Williams" in *Disorder: Amazon Original Stories* (June 2019). Thank you to the Rona Jaffe Foundation Writers' Award for seeing the potential in this novel when I first started writing it, and to the George A. and Eliza Gardner Howard Foundation Fellowship for encouraging me as I moved toward finishing it.

It's also important to acknowledge that an implicit trust in writers—a sense that it's worth granting us space, time, and funds, regardless of what we actually mean to do with them—is often what allows us write at our own will, at our own pace. There is, in short, such a thing as a snuck book. Thank you to these organizations for looking the other way while I wrote *The Furrows* over the years: the Harvard University Graduate Program in English; the University of California, Berkeley, English Department and the Townsend Center for the Humanities; the Stanford Humanities Center; the Tin House Workshop; the New York Public Library's Dorothy and Lewis B. Cullman

Center; and the New York Public Library's Schomburg Center for Research in Black Culture.

It's important, too, to thank those who have both blessed my designs and trusted my instincts. Thank you to Marya Spence at Janklow & Nesbit for her work on the novel in its early days. Thank you to my publicist Michael Taeckens for taking on the task of selling my strangeness. Thank you to my team at Hogarth: Alexis Washam for seeing the vision, David Ebershoff for making it happen, Parisa Ebrahimi for carrying it forward, and Darryl Oliver for the fine-toothed comb. My special thanks to Poppy Hampson, one of the last true editors, from whom I've learned so much and without whom this novel wouldn't exist. And thanks and love, always and ever, to my agent, PJ Mark, whose steady faith in me and my writing have made us family.

Thank you to Jerrell Gibbs for painting the beautiful portrait series that includes *C Note* (2021), and for granting permission for us to use it for the novel's cover.

Thank you to all those who read and responded to (parts of) *The Furrows* in its many iterations: Christina Svendsen, Case Kerns, Nadia Ellis, Swati Rana, Aaron Bady, Hannah Sullivan, Samuel Bjork, Margaret Miller, Michelle Quint, Shawn Mehrens, Rachel Khong, Karen Leibowitz, Glenda Carpio, Georgina Kleege, Yael Goldstein Love, Patrick Hoffman, Scott Saul, Ali Smith, Allison Amend, Elizabeth Greenwood, Fatima Kola, Fiona McFarlane, and Ismail Muhammad.

Thank you to my family, especially to Namposya Serpell and Zewelanji Serpell for reading the rawest versions, and to Derek and Milly Serpell for letting me write while looking at the sea.

And finally, thank you to Jesse McCarthy for seeing that *The Furrows* is an elegy and for finding me.

ABOUT THE AUTHOR

NAMWALI SERPELL was born in Lusaka and lives in New York. She is a professor of English at Harvard University. She is the author of *The Old Drift, Stranger Faces,* and *Seven Modes of Uncertainty.*

ABOUT THE TYPE

This book was set in Garamond, a typeface originally designed by the Parisian type cutter Claude Garamond (c. 1500–61). This version of Garamond was modeled on a 1592 specimen sheet from the Egenolff-Berner foundry, which was produced from types assumed to have been brought to Frankfurt by the punch cutter Jacques Sabon (c. 1520–80).

Claude Garamond's distinguished romans and italics first appeared in *Opera Ciceronis* in 1543–44. The Garamond types are clear, open, and elegant.